REPLENISHING

the

SEA

of

GALILEE

A Family Saga
across Ethnicity, Place,
and Religion

REPLENISHING

the

SEA

of

GALILEE

A Novel

WAGIH ABU-RISH

GREENLEAF
BOOK GROUP PRESS

Published by Greenleaf Book Group Press
Austin, Texas
www.gbgpress.com

Distributed by Greenleaf Book Group

For ordering information or special discounts for bulk purchases, please contact Greenleaf Book Group at PO Box 91869, Austin, TX 78709, 512.891.6100.

Design and composition by Greenleaf Book Group
Cover design by Greenleaf Book Group
Cover Images: ©iStockphoto/forrest9, ©iStockphoto/Svetlanais, ©iStockphoto/DamienGeso

Poem on page 262–263 from poem by Rabi'a al Adawiyya (717–801), Sufi/Moslem woman from Basra. From *The Wisdom of Islam*. Translation (c) by Abbeville Press. Reproduced courtesy of Abbeville Press.

Publisher's Cataloging-in-Publication data is available.

Print ISBN: 978-1-62634-849-3

eBook ISBN: 978-1-62634-850-9

Part of the Tree Neutral® program, which offsets the number of trees consumed in the production and printing of this book by taking proactive steps, such as planting trees in direct proportion to the number of trees used: www.treeneutral.com

TreeNeutral

Printed in the United States of America on acid-free paper

21 22 23 24 25   10 9 8 7 6 5 4 3 2 1

First Edition

In memory of my father, Abu Said Abu-Rish, 1913–2005
Time *magazine correspondent, 1950–1985*

MAIN CHARACTERS AND PLACES

KAREEM DINAR—first generation

AMINA—Kareem's wife

RASHEED DINAR—second generation, Kareem's son

RASHEEDA DINAR—second generation, Rasheed's twin sister

FATHER FEDERICO—Rasheed's high school teacher

AMERICAN COLONY HOTEL—a hotel in Jerusalem

NATALIA—member of the socialist kibbutz Shivayon

ALBINA AND ADRIANA—Natalia's best friends at the kibbutz

CHEREV—Right-wing kibbutz

DAVID ALEXANDER—British intelligence captain

SEAN O'DOWD—*Daily Mail* bureau chief

ST. GEORGES HOTEL—hotel in Beirut

OMAR—third generation, Rasheed and Natalia's son

GISELLE ABIZAID—correspondent, Agence France-Presse

IBRAHIM ALVAREZ—Spanish tourist to Beirut

CHRISTINA ALVAREZ—Ibrahim's daughter

HANIBAKE—assumed last name for Omar

JANICE YOUNG—Baylor medical student

SAMI SANDOOK—Omar's best friend

DR. KISHKAIN—chief of neurology at Baylor

THE PERVERSION OF RELIGIOUS BELIEFS

If human beings understood the essence of their own religions,
there would have been no wars,
no concentration camps,
no Third Reich,
no Imperial Japan,
and no al-Qaida or ISIS.

PROLOGUE

1920
Beit Azar, Palestine

Kareem was the most eligible bachelor in the village. At thirty-one and owning two successful inns and a food commodity wholesale business, he was envied and respected. He rarely socialized in the village, which was located only a few miles from Jerusalem. Most of his friends were other successful young males working in the tourism industry.

The two businesses took all his time. His favorite pastime involved having a drink or two at the American Colony Hotel. Everyone knew him there, but he mostly kept to himself except to speak to the barmen and occasionally to Anna, the owner of the hotel.

He knew Anna well. She always prodded him to get married. He in turn agreed with her, for the hundredth time. Anna had mentioned to him the names of half a dozen eligible young women. He aspired to marry from Jerusalem rather than from his own village, yet he never applied himself to accomplish that.

One morning, after he kissed the hand of his mother, Sara, Kareem headed downhill to his Aunt Hameeda's house, which was kitty-corner from his and his mother's houses. He noticed a young and most beautiful woman coming downhill behind him, heading in the same direction. He hid behind the front column of his aunt's house to peek at her. The young woman knocked, and his mother opened the door and greeted her warmly.

Kareem headed back to see who that beautiful woman was. He went up the alley to the far window and gazed downward. He could see the woman taking off her scarf, relaxing, and then going into the kitchen, where she fixed Turkish coffee and then served Sara and herself.

Kareem knew then that she was close to his mother, yet he had never seen her. He left to see his aunt, downhill. He described the young woman to her. Hameeda had no trouble guessing who she was.

"She is Amina, the judge's daughter. Forget about her. She has already turned down five contenders; one was a physician and another a bank manager. You will be wasting your time. You know her father. He is a supreme court judge and a sheikh of sheikhs."

When Kareem mentioned that Amina had not been wearing her headdress, Hameeda got mad. She scolded him for peeking at her through the window and told him that he was behaving immaturely.

"I hope nobody has seen you. It would be a scandal. You looked at her, with her scarf off, while visiting your own mother! What will people say? They may say you arranged all of this with your mother's knowledge. No, no, this is not good. I have to speak to Sara."

Kareem left for work. Hameeda waited for Amina to leave and headed toward Sara's, twenty yards away. Hameeda told her the story. After lamenting the unfortunate affair, they decided to create a cover in case someone may have observed Kareem doing the unthinkable—sneaking to watch the one who was nicknamed by the females of the village as the Princess of Beit Azar.

Hameeda and Sara decided to ask for Amina's hand. They explained to Kareem that the whole thing was a ruse since they felt the judge would surely turn them down. They wanted to cover up his indiscretion, just in case he was seen by others sneaking a peak at a young lady without her headdress. Kareem, feeling that he had done something he should have known to be indiscreet, reluctantly accepted.

Hameeda and Sara carried through with the plan. They emphasized to the judge that Kareem had seen Amina one time, and they were there immediately afterward. They told the judge that they appreciated him, as a Beit Azari, being a supreme court judge and one of the top clerics, and that they recognized that the Dinar family was not up to his standards, yet they thought that Kareem was a perfect gentleman and very comfortable financially.

To their surprise the judge told them that he had heard about Kareem from two professors at Hebrew College, where he taught. Both had taught Kareem at the Jesuit school, and they knew Kareem well and spoke very highly of him.

"Kareem is supposed to be a very fine person, I am told," the judge said. "I will have to talk to Amina. As you well know, she was the one who turned down five contenders."

Hameeda and Sara were in shock. They had thought they would be turned down on the spot. In a few days, they were invited to visit the judge again. He told them there would have to be three different hour-long meetings before Amina could make up her mind. The meetings would be attended by Hameeda, Sara, five female cousins of Amina, and another five female cousins of Kareem. There Amina and Kareem could talk to each other and ask questions of each other.

The two were very surprised at the judge's suggestion but decided to accept without questioning anything. The meetings took place, and to everyone's surprise, the chemistry between Amina and Kareem could not have been more in line.

When the judge asked Amina about Kareem, she decided not to express her true feelings. "I will go by what you see fit, father," she told the judge. The judge got the message. Within three weeks, the decision to marry Amina to Kareem was made. The Dinars accepted every condition the judge made, including agreeing to a back dowry five times as hefty as usual. The judge asked for no up-front dowry.

The wedding of Kareem and Amina was a celebrated one. One hundred female cousins and friends accompanied her along the mile-long route from her father's top-of-the-hill mansion to the Dinar house. With their headscarves down, they sang and danced all the way. One after another belly danced in front of the procession while the rest clapped and acted as a chorus. They put the scarves back up as they got close to the Dinars' house.

Although Kareem and Amina had spoken to each other on only the three occasions, they each felt they had found the right partner. They both harbored at the time liberal views and practiced what they preached. Kareem treated Amina with deference and respect. She treated him as her loving and prudent partner.

Kareem resumed going to the American Colony Hotel, but now Amina accompanied him. He drank scotch, and she drank lemonade. Their first time there together, Amina told Kareem that she had noticed him before Sara and Hameeda asked for her hand. She had taken several sneak looks at him without him noticing.

Before long, they were socializing with the elites of Jerusalem. On one occasion, Anna arranged for the couple to be invited to a gathering by the British commissioner general of Palestine. Amina shined among the other ten ladies in attendance.

When she was introduced to the commissioner general, her beauty and grace got him to kiss her hand. Amina never forgot the moment. She described it to Hameeda and Sara, and she repeated it to Kareem quite a few times.

Amina and Kareem were by far the most admired couple in Beit Azar. Many would admire their public but graceful exhibit of their love and care for each other. The young women would also wait to look at Amina's most fashionable Italian dresses. This was the couple's love saga for a glorious two years.

CHAPTER 1

1922
Beit Azar, Palestine

Amina and Kareem Dinar's love story came to an end. They were two people who fancied each other at first sight and then fell passionately in love and became the envy and admiration of the whole village. They crossed boundaries, gracefully adopting some Western habits, and above all, treated each other with equal respect and mutual adoration. Their exchange of emotions and the public manifestations of such exchanges defied all customs, not the least of which—and possibly the most important of which—was the defiance of the full dominance of the male over the female.

Two years after their marriage, Amina brought forth two beautiful and loveable children, a boy and a girl, as she left this world. The girl was five minutes younger than the boy but just as sharp, and she turned out to be more inquisitive. On her deathbed, Amina chose the name Rasheed for a boy and Rasheeda for a girl. She did not consider that she might have twins.

During the fog of the tragedy, Sara, Amina's mother-in-law, and Hameeda, her husband's maternal aunt, had to attend to the affairs of the new additions. Fortunately, thirty young women, all from Beit Azar, volunteered to nurse the two babies. Those volunteers were not only ready, willing, and able but also rather anxious to act in the memory of the town's "princess." Sara and Hameeda were more than willing to accept the generous offers and organized a routine whereby eight wet nurses would volunteer per day.

Judge Rami, Amina's father, visited Sara a week later to tell her that he was willing to pay for the services of ten wet nurses of her choosing. He had not considered what had transpired in the few days since Amina's death. Upon questioning Sara, the judge was beside himself. It turned out that as many as twenty-five women had nursed the two babies without anyone recording who they were.

According to Muslim teachings, this meant that Rasheed and Rasheeda did not know whom they were eligible to marry in town. A wet nurse, according to these teachings, was and still is considered and treated as a biological mother. Her biological children are considered brothers and sisters of the nursed children, and they may not marry each other.

Kareem visited the babies only when the wet nurses were not in the house. Sara did not want to risk having him observe the bare breast of any woman in town. But that was not hard to do; it was arranged that Sara would call Kareem before he came over.

The twins were not identical. Both were beautiful and acted independently of each other. Rasheeda took more after Amina, and Rasheed took some characteristics from each parent. In profile they were nearly identical, with nuances due to gender, but head-on, they looked very different. They both had chestnut-brown hair, large eyes, slightly brownish skin, shapely eyebrows, and relatively small noses.

They were also pampered. Kareem would not spare any expense. He engaged the services of foreign language tutors for the twins as early as age five. From the start, he decided that they needed to learn English and French. He did not care about Russian, and he decided that Italian might be added later. Dr. Schneider, Amina's German-born gynecologist, tried to convince Kareem to send them to the German kindergarten; Kareem resisted and instead sent them to the English kindergarten.

Kareem treated both his children equally. When he bought them their first tricycles, he got one for each. He did the same when he bought them their first bicycles.

At the beginning, the twins behaved similarly, but beyond the age of four, their personalities started to split. Rasheed would take the initiative, and Rasheeda would question his decisions. She often asked him to think about or discuss things before he did them. Sara and Hameeda were very impressed by Rasheeda's poise and confidence.

Kareem bought them a small puppy, which was unusual for villagers. Rasheed wanted to call it Baby. Rasheeda reminded him that it would one day grow up and cease to be a baby. She then suggested calling the puppy Baby Ameer. When he got older, they would just call it Ameer. Rasheed liked the idea. He continued to take note of similar pieces of advice from Rasheeda.

All through elementary school, Rasheed and Rasheeda were happy kids. Their relationship remained strong, and Rasheed started to pick up some of Rasheeda's thoughtful habits. On one occasion when Kareem came to pick them up from school, the two got separated, and Rasheed could not be found for ten minutes. Afterward, Rasheeda advised Rasheed that if they were to get separated in the future, they should meet at the gate, on the inside. Rasheeda exhibited the same wisdom when dealing with her classmates. In sixth grade, Rasheed continued emulating Rasheeda's thoughtful behavior and wise expressions, thus becoming more thoughtful himself.

It was a mixed day when the twins graduated from elementary school. Kareem thought that his children had accomplished a lot. They both spoke fluent English and decent French. It had not dawned on him how close they were. Their sense of joint accomplishment was only diminished by the fact that they were planning to go the following year to two different high schools, both run by Jesuits, one for boys and the other for girls.

———

Sara and Hameeda passed away two months apart. Rasheed and Rasheeda were deeply affected and felt lost for the first few months. Although Sara and Hameeda had slowed down considerably before they passed away, they had made up for Amina's absence, and Rasheed and Rasheeda never lacked for motherly love. Sara and Hameeda cared for them with great devotion and warmth. They made the two children feel whole, such that they did not know what they were missing.

It took the children a while to adjust to their new reality and to overcome the vacuum that the death of their grandmother and great-aunt left behind. Hameeda had prepared them. She had commissioned the preparation of two grave sites, one for her and one for Sara. On two occasions, she showed them the plots. She wanted them to feel sanguine about their inevitable deaths. Those visits helped but only partially.

After their deaths, Kareem moved to live with his children in Sara's house, which he inherited. He also inherited Hameeda's assets, most of which he gave away. He decided to split her dairy business among three needy relatives.

At times, the death of Sara and Hameeda invoked a special feeling of loss in the children, particularly upon visiting the cemetery. Rasheed and Rasheeda routinely went to the cemetery five blocks away and read Koranic verses at their mother's grave, Hameeda's grave, and Sara's grave. They both felt more at ease after their cemetery visits.

The cemetery was also where they would discuss matters they would not have addressed in the presence of their father. In their fourth year of high school, when they were seventeen years old, Rasheeda broached the subject of death and resurrection with her brother. She was surprised to find him rather prepared. He told her that he had decided not to think much about it and to accept Muslim teachings, but at the same time he would not dismiss the beliefs of other people. He had a Druze friend and classmate who told him that the Druze believed in reincarnation. "Just like the Hindus!" Rasheeda exclaimed. Rasheed added—and Rasheeda agreed—that his friend, Naseem, was free to believe in reincarnation because he was born Druze and that they should continue to believe that there is no reincarnation, since they were born Muslims.

Rasheeda said it mattered not only what one believed in general but what one believed specifically. When Rasheed asked her to explain herself, she offered a most unexpected example.

She reminded him that he was circumcised, but she added that Muslims and Jews get circumcised because in the old times people bathed infrequently, once every few weeks, and so this and the lack of circumcision caused diseases under the skin. She explained that since some people now bathed twice a week, they may not need to be circumcised.

Rasheed was shocked and asked Rasheeda to give a different example. She refused. "Why are you afraid of this subject?" she said. "Because I am a woman? Understand this: just because I discuss this subject does not mean I want to have sex."

Rasheed was speechless. Then Rasheeda told him that he should read the Hadith, the recorded teachings of the prophet, and the writings of Muslim philosophers. He would then understand that such subjects were not taboo then as they are now. "Rasheed, your reactions indicate that you believe that they need to remain taboo," she said. She reminded him that the Koran had been very clear that Muslims should not eat pork, but no Christian had died from eating pork lately.

At age eighteen and during their fifth year of high school, Rasheeda brought up the subject of foreplay during sex. Rasheed adamantly refused to discuss the subject and reminded Rasheeda that although she was his sister, she was still a female and that such subjects should not be discussed between them. She tried and tried again, but to her disappointment, Rasheed stuck to his guns.

It took Rasheed some time to accept that his sister had become liberal and inquisitive, but with time he started adopting some of her ideas. Before long he would even bring up controversial subjects himself, but only at the cemetery. Those discussions strengthened their brotherly and friendly relationship further.

The summer between their fifth and sixth years in high school went by very smoothly. Kareem took both children to four Palestinian cities, and on one occasion they slept overnight in Haifa. At that time, Rasheeda was being tutored in French, and Rasheed was being tutored in Arabic literature.

During one of their cemetery meetings Rasheed informed Rasheeda that his Arabic literature tutor had taken another wife. Rasheeda asked him why. Had his first wife become afflicted with a terminal disease? Rasheed's answer was crisp, exhibiting his disgust: "The tutor's first wife was his age, thirty-one, and his second wife was eighteen."

"If men continue to marry more than one wife," Rasheeda said angrily, "women should also be able to have more than one husband."

Rasheed could not believe what he heard. He advised his sister never to repeat such a thing again or else the community—including her own relatives—would deem her crazy. Then she told him that she was joking to make a point: *neither* men nor women should have more than one spouse. "One transgression cannot be made right by another transgression," she said.

She told him that she believed in premarital sex between true lovers, and that the only thing she would not do before marriage was lose her virginity. She thought that a woman's virginity should be preserved for a lifetime lover and the father of one's children: one's husband. Even so, she said she regularly dreamed about having sex with Italian movie stars. Rasheed was at first overwhelmed but then became thoughtful. "Whatever you do, I will have nothing to do with it," he said. "And you'll have to do it very discreetly."

But as usual, Rasheed started adopting many of Rasheeda's

beliefs. As the sixth and last year of high school commenced, Rasheed underwent a major transformation. He could see the wisdom in his sister's ideas, and he even came up with challenging thoughts of his own. He started feeling much more confident about himself. He felt he needed to be more assertive.

What started to bother him most was the inequality between men and women, between boys and girls. He developed the deep suspicion that society followed a double standard, allowing or overlooking men's premarital sexual practices but cruelly and unfairly vilifying those of women.

CHAPTER 2

1941
Jerusalem, Palestine

Rasheed was very handy, and whenever he volunteered to help out at school, Father Najjar, the principal, took him up on it. Father Najjar's elder brother had taught Rasheed's father, Kareem. Early one evening, Rasheed volunteered to fix some of the woodwork in the school kitchen and proceeded there with his tools in hand. In the front of the kitchen, there was a sliding window through which food used to be handed out to be delivered to the staff. As Rasheed opened that window to pass his broom, mop, and tools through, he was shocked at the sight before him.

It was Father Federico, his French teacher, and Aisha, the young Muslim cook. Father Federico had moved two long tables parallel to each other, about ten inches apart. He had managed to slip his head into the space between the two tables while Aisha, naked from the waist down, was lying with her buttocks on one table and her legs stretched to the other. Father Federico was immersed between her spread legs in what looked like intense oral sex. Rasheed was shocked—not necessarily at the sex, but that it was Father Federico. He slowly attempted to close the window but dropped the mop in the process. Father Federico turned his head and recognized Rasheed.

Rasheed did not know what to do. He was upset at having drawn Father Federico's attention. Shocked and confused, he kept his observation to himself for two days, until he met with Rasheeda at the cemetery, which looked down on the village. It was an ideal setting, because the view from below was blocked by olive and pine trees.

When Rasheed expressed his fear about retribution from Father Federico, she tried to ease his concerns. "Father Federico is the one who should be worried. It is true that if he denies this, he would be believed more than you. But think carefully: He may lose his relationship with Aisha just to exonerate himself from the charge. Maybe he won't risk that."

She continued, "I need to let you know that Imm Samer lent me two books about sex. One of them describes how men get obsessed with sex once they try it. I think Father Federico is no exception." Imm Samer was the mother of their friend Samer. Her name reflected the tradition of women and men using the names of their eldest son. Rasheed agreed with his sister's analysis.

Two weeks later, it was Rasheed's turn to enjoy himself. Whenever he could, he would meet with his female partner in the woods of the forty-acre campus. And there, against the carob tree, he had sex with Leila, his most recent partner, without penetrating her. Coincidentally, Father Federico was painting by himself in the very same area. When Federico heard noises, he got closer, and to his surprise, saw Rasheed and Leila, who was still wearing her underwear.

Federico observed with curiosity and intense concentration. Soon he heard Leila saying, "What is this? It barely took you two minutes. This is over. I am not going to see you anymore. I don't like this."

Leila ended by covering herself and leaving in haste. Father Federico saw a golden and ironic opportunity. He approached and gently confronted Rasheed, who was totally surprised, shocked, and embarrassed, thinking that Federico had been following him in order to take revenge.

In short order, Rasheed convinced himself that the encounter was coincidental. It was clear that Father Federico had gotten there ahead of him and that the location was no more and no less than a natural spot for painting, surrounded by beautiful natural scenery and lush foliage. It made sense for Father Federico to have chosen that specific spot to paint.

After easing Rasheed's concerns some, Father Federico put his arm around the young man's shoulder and spoke to him softly but firmly. "I am going to teach you how to make love over the coming six weeks, in the time left before your graduation."

Rasheed did not want to have anything to do with Federico. He did not want to be reminded of what he saw Federico do with Aisha, nor did he want to be reminded of his own sexual ineptness. To ease Rasheed's concerns, Federico explained that he planned to leave the priesthood right after the end of the school year. He added that he had joined because his late, very sinful father thought if he forced his son to join the priesthood, God would forgive the father's many transgressions.

Rasheed tried to convince Father Federico that he could do without being tutored about sex and that each of them possessed the other's secret, and as such they were equal. Neither was a threat to the other. But Father Federico would not take no for an answer.

"I am doing this out of care for you," he told Rasheed. "Somebody like you, a nineteen-year-old, should not go through life being a poor lover. Look at you: tall, very handsome, and the first in your class. It would be a big disappointment not to be an accomplished man in love, like you are in other things."

And so it went. Father Federico spent an hour a week for four weeks teaching Rasheed the theory, physiology, emotions, and nature of lovemaking. He reminded Rasheed that although he was Catholic to the core, he followed Mohammad's teachings when it came to sex.

Rasheed felt insulted that his prophet had anything to do with sex, but Father Federico explained that in the Hadith, the narrative of Mohammad, the prophet had referred to sexual behavior many times. "I know, as I was a professor of Islamic dogma and philosophy at one of the Vatican universities. I am here teaching Italian and French because they caught me in the Vatican with a beautiful cleaning lady. They sent me back to my country and stripped me of the right to teach college as punishment for my so-called sins."

Rasheed's encounters with Federico unsettled him. He became much more aware of the teacher's presence. Anytime he had a glimpse of Federico, he could not help but watch him. He noticed that Federico was not having lunch in the school cafeteria on Fridays, and he decided to find out why. One Friday he followed the father and witnessed his rendezvous with Aisha. Federico had no idea he was being watched. He took his time. He was slow and deliberate. He warmed Aisha slowly and gently. In the end, he proved to Rasheed that he practiced what he preached. He even cleaned Aisha after finishing, which was most surprising to Rasheed.

Although sincere in trying to educate Rasheed about sex, Federico was intent to gain some leverage against Rasheed just in case the boy might unexpectedly decide to squeal on him. Federico set his plans out of desperation and totally against his better nature. He approached Aisha with so much hesitation and dread that he wondered if she might totally bolt out of the relationship. When she'd heard the mop drop, she'd expected that someone may have been watching them. In this case, Federico reversed one sequence; he told her that Rasheed asked to watch one time in exchange for him not telling what he had seen in the kitchen. Aisha objected but then tearfully agreed to his plans. She was a simple cook in love with Federico, and she did not want to lose him, despite the age differ- ence. Federico told her that she should not worry, since she would not be able to see Rasheed during the planned liaison. And anyway, Federico could have easily kept the event to himself, and she would never have known about it.

To Rasheed's utter surprise, Federico suggested that Rasheed watch him make love to Aisha during the fifth week at the same spot where Rasheed had been making love to Leila. Federico advised Rasheed to hide behind a specific tree, remain totally quiet, and observe him step by step. When Rasheed wondered how he could be asking such from him, being a priest, Federico answered in a serious tone.

"I am a priest by name. I never wanted to be a priest, I never liked being a priest, and I never felt like a priest. I was always interested in love and love's pragmatic manifestations. I am grateful to the Jesuits for educating me; without them I would not have learned even ten percent of the knowledge I possess now."

He reminded Rasheed that what he had taught him and what he was planning to demonstrate had nothing to do with Christianity and everything to do with Islam. Federico added that since he was planning to leave the priesthood immediately after the school year, it was all right, as a civilian, for him to indulge in teaching others proper sexual behavior.

"You see, Rasheed, my father died two months ago, and I am free from his demands and his sins," Federico said. "He will end up where he deserves, and it is no longer up to me—it really was never up to me. His final rest cannot be conditioned by any of my own acts.

"What I am telling you comes almost directly from your prophet, Mohammad," he continued. "I will pin his sayings to the tree you will be hiding behind; many are about foreplay, which until recently you knew nothing about. Over the years, I took the liberty of choreographing the advice of the prophet. The prophet was not very detailed in this sense."

Rasheed was in a state of astonishment. He could not wait for his regular meeting with Rasheeda, so he immediately went to share the news with her. Her pleasant surprise bewildered him. She was excited that Father Federico would allow Rasheed to observe him in the act. She did not express the slightest condemnation of Federico's practices.

Instead of condemning or criticizing the arrangement, she told Rasheed that it was a rare opportunity, and that she wanted to observe too. Rasheed at first resisted but then relented, as he believed that equality between the sexes allowed for equal inquisitiveness. He asked her to camouflage herself well, as they could not afford her being discovered by Father Federico.

The day before, they went to the site and rehearsed how to

observe. The pine tree designated by Federico stood on a plateau overlooking the carob tree, about seventy feet down an incline.

When the time came the following day, they arrived fifteen minutes early and found nailed to the pine tree a typewritten one-page list of a few of Mohammad's admonishments about sexual foreplay:

1. When you intend to have sex with your wife, do not rush, because the woman also has needs.

2. When any one of you has sex with his wife, then he should not get to her like birds; instead he should be slow and delaying.

3. None of you should fall upon his wife like an animal but let there first be a messenger between you. The messenger should include kisses and romantic words.

4. When his semen comes out, let him keep his body over her until she comes as well, because she comes late.

Rasheed and Rasheeda read Mohammad's admonishments and looked at each other silently. They were more revealing to Rasheed, since Rasheeda had read a version of the Hadith and knew that such advice existed.

Father Federico and Aisha arrived on time, and Rasheed and Rasheeda stopped talking. Federico leaned against the carob tree and hugged Aisha. He slowly rubbed his hands along her body. He massaged her ears and earlobes repeatedly before he slid his hands down her sides all the way inside her thighs. Slowly he went up her thighs, and just as he passed her crotch, he crossed his hands all the way to her breasts. He then circled his hands on each breast three or four times.

He followed that by unbuttoning her blouse and gently removing one clothing piece after another, all the while massaging her. Within fifteen minutes, Aisha was naked, immersed in her excitement and joy and responding enthusiastically to Federico's careful fondling and caressing.

He sucked her breasts, making sure he went one inch beyond the nipples. As Aisha eased her legs open, Federico's hands went to her genitalia, and with his right hand he massaged her labia and clitoris. Afterward they indulged in oral sex. Aisha reached climax twice. Federico then penetrated her slowly and gently. She went through two more climaxes, as did Federico.

When they finished, an even greater surprise hit Rasheed and Rasheeda. Federico poured water on a towel and cleaned Aisha, which she seemed to expect. She kissed and squeezed Federico as he cleaned her up. He then dressed her piece by piece.

The twins waited for the lovers to leave and then left quietly. They glanced at each other, but they did not talk until it was time to meet at the cemetery. "I liked what Father Federico did except for the penetration," Rasheeda said. "It will not happen to me. I will only allow my husband to do it."

"I liked everything except for the oral sex and him cleaning her up," Rasheed said. "I will not do that."

Having noticed that her brother never commented on her likes and dislikes, Rasheeda told him that they were not that far apart, but they had some minor differences. She could tell he accepted her as equal, free to choose her own way while at the same time bringing his newfound maturity to the fore, taking the lead whenever he could.

———

The following week, Father Federico sought out Rasheed and asked him what he thought about what he had observed.

Rasheed answered, "I hope you don't mind my saying it was a star performance."

Federico said that he had been slower than usual so that Rasheed could observe. He put his arm around Rasheed's shoulders and said, "It is now your turn. You need to pass your final test. Bring Leila back and show me if you have learned your lessons well!"

Rasheed was visibly in shock and resisted, but Federico said that if it was good for Rasheed to observe, it should be good for Rasheed to be observed. After much thought, Rasheed said yes, but only if he could convince Leila, which might be difficult since she was mad at him.

No sooner had he left Federico than Rasheed rushed to talk to his sister. He expressed his deep concerns about convincing Leila to have sex one more time. Rasheeda surprised him. "Go talk to Leila and apologize to her, even if you have to humble yourself. Kiss her hand if you have to."

Rasheed could barely believe his ears.

"Persist if she turns you down, but be gentle and conciliatory. Humble yourself."

———

Rasheed went to the Jesuit girls' school to look for Leila. Initially, she would not talk to him. He told her that he was there to give her a silver cross from his father's inn. She studied the gift. As he dangled the cross, Rasheed said that he needed to see her. "I know things didn't go very well last time we were together, and I am here to apologize to you. I promise you that things will be different in the future."

Leila knew exactly what he meant and what he wanted now. He told her that if their encounter was not satisfying for her, they would never see each other again.

Leila looked him in the eye after sensing his humble demeanor and said that if it wasn't different this time, she would spit in his face.

"If it's not different, you can spit in my face twice," he told her.

Encouraged by Leila's words, Rasheed was about to let her know that a priest would be watching. He thought she might not mind since she and Federico were both Catholic. In the end, he could not bring himself to tell her. He knew that the act of anyone watching would have been totally unorthodox and equally wrong. He instead decided to keep it from her.

While Leila liked Rasheed a lot, it was all about sex for her, as she was Christian and would not think of marrying a Muslim. But she was curious about Rasheed's promises.

They ended up meeting at the carob tree, as they had done before. Leila was apprehensive and somewhat leery, but then she relaxed. Rasheed asked her not to pull her skirt up and said that he would take care of everything. He told her that he had gotten some water and a towel for her to clean herself afterward. "Unless you want *me* to clean you!"

Leila could not believe her ears. "What happened to you? You are even talking differently! You and I are the same age, but suddenly you sound much more mature!" she exclaimed.

Before long, they were at it: slowly, methodically, and gently, all according to the steps outlined by Federico. Within an hour, Leila achieved three climaxes, Rasheed two. After she cleaned herself, she dressed. After a short pause, she grabbed Rasheed's head and kissed it ten different times. She told him how great he had performed and that she was sorry she was leaving after graduation to enroll in a nursing school in Haifa, far away from him.

Her satisfaction with Rasheed's performance did not last long. Federico was holding on to a branch that accidently broke and made a noise. While Leila could not see him, she figured out that someone was watching, and she was convinced it was with Rasheed's full knowledge. She gave him a disgusted look, spit in his face, and left without saying a word.

Father Federico invited Rasheed to his office within days and told him that he had done exceedingly well and deserved an A. He also told Rasheed that he and Aisha were moving to Cyprus. He had an offer to teach and tutor French and Italian. He promised that he would be in touch

Federico then said, "Remember, do not let them undress themselves or wait for you naked. You must do the honor. They will love you for it afterward."

Before he left, Federico looked at Rasheed pensively and said in a quiet voice, "I am sorry I put you through this. I had my own critical but selfish reasons, over and above my desire to teach you how to be an accommodating lover. I will make it up to you and to Aisha. I don't think I will have the opportunity to make it up to Leila."

CHAPTER 3

Rasheed and Rasheeda both graduated with distinction. Rasheed joined his father in managing the two inns, and his father taught him to drive.

Rasheeda took several math courses by correspondence with schools in London. As expected with a straight-A score, she ended up being accepted by the University of London. At the university, she managed to finish six courses over a three-year period, all with top grades.

As high school graduates with fluency in two foreign languages each, the twins felt that they had accomplished more than the average village kid, that their lives were fulfilling, and that the future looked promising. In time, Rasheed started assuming an older brother's role, and Rasheeda started deferring to him much more than the other way around.

Despite his general satisfaction with assuming more responsibilities at the inns and getting to meet tourists of all kinds from all over the world, he felt he could do more. His command of the English language had become very strong and his vocabulary quite good. He engaged in lengthy discussions with some of his guests about current affairs, especially about the war in Europe, and many of his English-speaking hotel guests marveled at his ease of expression and fine diction.

One morning it took Rasheed just minutes to finish his customary small breakfast of yogurt spread, cucumbers, and tomatoes. He held his cup of mint tea in his hand as he went around the ground floor to turn off a couple of the lights in his father's spacious house, which had been enlarged twice over the years and was easily three times as large as a typical house in Beit Azar.

The living room on the ground floor could easily seat sixty people. The ceiling there was a double height. All the five bedrooms except one, that of his late grandmother, were on the second floor. The ground floor had access to the yard on three sides. The upper floor also accessed the yard by two sets of stairs.

He was in a good mood as he walked through the living room. He was holding a handwritten income statement for the inns that he had prepared, and the results were more impressive than he had thought they would be. After he set down his teacup, he went down three steps to warm up his small British-made Morris car, a habit he picked up from his father. Rasheed kept it in tip-top shape, and at six years old it still seemed brand new.

He had barely gone a block from his house when he noticed a light blue flatbed truck parked on the opposite side of the road. It had its front wheels on the pavement, but its back wheels were stranded on the shoulder, a foot from dropping down a ledge into a fig orchard.

He heard gravel ricochet off the flatbed truck. As he looked to his right, he noticed three kids, all around ten years old, throwing pea gravel from a construction site across the road.

The kids ran away when they saw him. He stopped his Morris, got out, and crossed the highway to inspect the truck. At first, he could not see anybody. He went onto the shoulder to look at the back of the truck and saw the legs of a crouching person. Rasheed crouched and made out a good-looking woman in her early twenties hiding underneath. She was motionless, with distinct fear in her eyes, as if she couldn't figure out the cause of the kids' attack on her.

Likewise, Rasheed could tell from her complexion and green eyes that she was European. He motioned for her to stand up and then immediately extended his hand. "My name is Rasheed. What is your name?" he said in flowing English.

"My name is Adriana," she said hesitantly.

"Oh, good, you speak English. Nice to meet you, Adriana. I can see you have a flat tire. I can help. My cousin Hassan lives in this house right here." He pointed to a simple one-story stone house with green window shutters, barely forty feet away. It had an addition added to it, a garage for Hassan's repair business.

Even before Adriana responded, he started hollering in Arabic. Within seconds, Hassan came out in mechanic's overalls, which were similar to what Adriana was wearing but more faded and smudged. Rasheed introduced Hassan, who also spoke English well. He had been an assistant mechanic at the British Army base near Jaffa. Hassan smiled at Adriana and shook her hand, while behaving deferentially to his older cousin.

In a matter of an hour Hassan had fixed the truck tire and excused himself, winking at Rasheed. Adriana took some money out of her pocket. "No, this is on us," Rasheed said. "You had your flat tire in our village, and by tradition we take care of the damage. Don't worry about it."

Adriana shook his hand and thanked him. As she was about to leave, she said, "I cannot go without repaying your kindness in some fashion. I would like to invite you for a drink at the American Colony Hotel with my friends Albina and Natalia. Are you familiar with the American Colony—" She stopped herself. "Excuse me, do you drink in the first place?"

"Yes, I drink scotch, but not Polish vodka," he said, guessing that she was Polish from her accent. "My father used to have his weekly drink there, and my late mother used to have lemonade. I also deal with the American Colony on a daily basis," he added. "We are in the same business. My father owns two inns, and we refer guests to each other on a regular basis, whenever we're full. Where are you from? Poland, I would guess."

Adriana said that she was part of a Polish Jewish kibbutz between Jerusalem and Nablus. She hastily added, "We are not like many of the Jewish kibbutzim—we are socialists and believe in equality for Arabs and Jews. We seek to create a socialist state in Palestine." It sounded as though she wanted to assure him that she and her fellow kibbutzniks were not there to take over Arab land. "Although I have to admit, you are the first Arab man I have met."

Rasheed caught her looking at him. "I am surprised I am the first, since you are trying to bring Palestinians and Jews together. I have met foreign Jews of all kinds and from dozens of countries— Germany, Poland, England, and Ukraine. They stay at our inns all the time. Anyway, thank you for the invitation. I will try to make it to your gathering with your friends if I can get away. What did you say their names were, Albina and Natalia?"

Adriana looked at him and smiled. "You have a sharp memory, and you have no difficulty recalling Western names," she said. "The

Arab women who help at the kibbutz can barely recall any of our names."

As Adriana got back in the truck, she waved goodbye. Rasheed waved back and winked at her.

She was cute despite wearing overalls one size too big for her. On the other hand, he cautioned himself, he had to keep his distance. European women could be trouble.

Rasheed had met many foreign women staying at his father's inns. He had been propositioned, but they were usually too old. On one occasion, he was approached by a young Swedish beauty. When he responded to her obvious interest by saying, "I will see you tomorrow," she replied that she was leaving for Beirut the following morning. That was the closest he came to having that kind of fun.

All week, he thought about seeing Adriana again and meeting her two friends. For the last three years, he'd thought of trying to meet women but never got around to it. Now that the invitation had come, he would not let the opportunity pass. He decided to make it, no matter what. He worked hard to change his schedule and to make himself available the following Thursday.

————

Rasheed entered the English garden of the two-story American Colony Hotel and looked around to greet anyone he might know. He briskly hopped up the three steps fronting the ground floor, as he had enjoyed doing over the years. He looked back into the immaculately manicured English garden to savor the surroundings. Roses of all colors and fragrances sprang up through the greenery.

The stonework and figurines in the garden were subdued by the lush bushes but noticeable. Many of the figurines acted as small fountains. They seemed to belong more to an understated country estate than a hotel. He went into the lobby to admire the layout of the furniture. He fancied the prints and stripes of the upholstery, an elegant combination of Italian and Middle Eastern motifs.

As he approached the secluded bar to the right of the lobby, he paused and took his hands out of his pockets. He cleaned off a couple of spots on his navy-blue jacket and his taupe gabardine slacks. Then he stood up straight and entered the bar. As he did so, he saw Adriana. She was wearing maroon trousers, a beige blouse, and a tailored black jacket. Her hair was loose but pulled over her right ear, revealing her bright, made-up face. She looked very attractive, far better than she had in those dusty overalls.

Adriana recognized him immediately and seemed pleased to see him. She moved one stool over and said, "Come and join us. Sit between me and Albina."

She introduced her two friends. When Rasheed focused on Natalia, he noticed her glowing complexion and could feel his pulse quicken. She had a small Polish nose, glittering blue eyes, and a soft smile. She wore a short-sleeved light gray blouse and a dark blue skirt. Her blondish hair was pulled back behind her neck. He was struck by more than just her good looks. Her eyes had a soft, sympathetic look that drew him closer. He immediately wanted to find out more about her.

Natalia looked at Rasheed without saying anything. It was the way she barely smiled and lowered her right eyelid that added to Rasheed's curious fascination. He responded by making a slight nod, long enough to be observed but short enough to be denied.

Within a few minutes, after the two exchanged several looks to make sure they were on the same wavelength, Adriana and Albina excused themselves. Rasheed felt confident, but he also felt that he wanted to open up to her, as if some kind of perimeter had been lifted.

"I graduated from an English Jesuit school," he told her.

"Me too. I graduated from a Jesuit school, in Warsaw, and continued for two years trying to become a teacher. I quit college when my father died." She added that her mother had been a teacher all her life.

This sounded a little familiar to Rasheed. "My mother wanted to become a math teacher but had not finished her college courses when she passed away."

When he told her that his mother was deceased, and Natalia paused to hear more, Rasheed hesitated; he did not want to talk about it. Neither of them went into any details. Rasheed then mentioned that he came from a village nearby, where he had met Adriana, but he did not mention its name.

Natalia spilled some water on the counter as she was gazing into Rasheed's eyes. He immediately got a towel and wiped the counter dry. "Did you get any on your clothes?" he asked. When she pointed out several spots on her blouse, he wiped them off. A third spot was over her right breast. He gave the towel to Natalia. "You go ahead and do the rest," he said, trying not to blush. She took the towel with a laugh, as if to say, "What is the big deal?"

"Thank you for being such a gentleman," she said as she continued to smile.

The rest of their time together went likewise, with Rasheed intentionally pausing in the give-and-take, leaning back to give her space to react. Above all, he did not dominate the conversation. Whenever he finished talking about himself, he would wait for Natalia to tell him something about herself.

A week later Rasheed was there before the three arrived. Albina and Adriana took a friendly posture, just watching the interaction between Rasheed and Natalia. They had seen the smile on Natalia's face when she first met Rasheed that afternoon.

Rasheed insisted that all three women have two drinks each. They sensed what Rasheed was doing, though: covering up his attraction to Natalia.

He took Natalia's hand and asked, "Would you like me to tell your fortune, Middle East style?"

"I thought you used a Turkish coffee cup to tell one's fortune," Natalia answered in a whimsical tone.

"No, that tells your immediate fortune. The palm tells your long-term fortune."

"Yes, please do," Natalia said, smiling.

"You are destined to meet someone you had not planned to meet. Meeting him will change the course of your life in a way you had not anticipated."

"Can you describe this person to me?" Natalia said.

"No, it is now your turn to describe him and add details of what will happen in the future," Rasheed said.

Natalia laughed. "This is all a trick on your part, and you are good at it."

"No, no, you have to continue," Rasheed said.

"Is it possible that I have already met him, and he is, as they say, tall, dark, and handsome? That is what you wanted me to say!" she cried as her eyes stayed fixed on him.

"He is tall, and he is dark, but I don't know if he is as handsome as you are beautiful," he responded.

She smiled broadly. She put her hand on his and then grasped his arm with both hands. He kissed her gently on the lips as she slid her hands softly down his arm.

"It is time to go," she said. "I will see you next week." She waved goodbye, smiling at him.

CHAPTER 4

Rasheed again met with Rasheeda at the cemetery. "There's an opening for a head barman at the American Colony," he told her, "and I plan to apply. I have already talked to Anna, who suggested that I do so. Besides, that is where I met Natalia."

He was about to describe Natalia when his sister interrupted him. "Are you serious? A barman? What about the inns?"

"I've thought about the inns, and I have a plan. Hold your comments until you hear the details."

Rasheed wanted Rasheeda to share in his excitement about his relationship with Natalia and how his plans would make it easy for them to meet openly. He had always known that Rasheeda wanted him to find someone to his liking and fall in love. But she could only concentrate on the idea of his being a barman. "Are you sure of what you are doing? You'd be accepting a job so much lower than what you are doing at the inns, and one that would pay so much less. You are practically boss at the inns. I don't understand!"

"Rasheeda, you haven't let me finish. It is time that you became Dad's assistant. You deserve it, and you can do it."

Even liberal Rasheeda cringed at the suggestion, but then she asked curiously, "You mean you want me to take over your place?"

"You're just as smart and just as hardworking, if not more. What's the big deal? Running hotels is not half as demanding as owning twelve dairy cows and running a dairy business, with all its distribution requirements. That's what Aunt Hameeda did all her life—and she finished school only up to second secondary. Furthermore, just like Dad helped me at first, I'll help you out the first six months."

Rasheeda paused for a long while, then said, "I'll do it. I'd love to do it, actually, but I don't want to propose this arrangement to Dad. You have to do it yourself."

"Why are you so negative, Rasheeda? Father was happy to have Mother continue her correspondence courses at the University of London. He is more liberal than you give him credit for."

"If you are so insistent, you approach Dad, but don't even mention that you've discussed this subject with me," she said. "It has to come from you."

"I'll take care of it, and I will keep you up on everything," he said. "I am going to tell Dad how I feel, that I want to further buttress my languages, not only English but also French and Italian. What does a barman do most, after all? He spends more time talking than preparing drinks! I also want to write. You know the Jesuits did not encourage writing about current events. I feel that writing and languages are in my future."

Rasheed visited with his father three times before he felt he could broach the subject. The fourth time he did not hesitate. "I think it's time for me to go out on my own," he said. "Anna offered me the position of the head barman at the American Colony. Rasheeda is more than qualified and able to replace me."

Kareem had not anticipated this development. His surprise was apparent. "What are you talking about?" he said. "No, no, I am not going to discuss this terrible idea with you. Think about it some more, and you will abandon it on your own."

"I don't need to think about it more," Rasheed said. "I wouldn't have mentioned it in the first place had I not thought about it at length. I've been thinking about it for the last three weeks. Don't you think I need to prove myself in the open market? I don't want people to suspect that what I accomplished is only due to having been born into wealth."

Kareem looked at Rasheed with great surprise. "This is the way I became successful and how so many other people become successful: they inherit property or a business, and they improve on what they inherit. This is life."

Rasheed had expected such resistance. He held Natalia's image in his mind before and during his discussions with his father.

"Dad, if you think I am going to abandon the inns for good, you are mistaken. All I am doing is broadening my experience," he said. "Imagine if in the future we decide to expand: my experience at the American Colony will give me more insight into how other hotels are run and how to appraise such hotels, don't you think? Furthermore, I really like to practice speaking foreign languages, talking to customers in their own language, and I want to write about what I see and what I experience.

"I respect your opinion a lot, but you're forgetting something: that you encouraged Mother to pursue her studies and, even more, admired your aunt for having been the first woman in the village to own her own business. I want you to think of Rasheeda as if she is part Mother and part Aunt Hameeda. She is educated like Mother

was and as diligent as Aunt Hameeda. Just because she is not a wife
or an aunt should not lessen her chances to prove herself!"

Kareem could tell that Rasheed was not only prepared for
the occasion but adamant. Rasheed had touched a nerve in his
father by bringing the memory and the experiences of his mother
and aunt into the picture. He was also reassured that Rasheed
was thinking of the future of the inns. He was silent, short on
arguments and intent not to create any friction with the son he
admired. He paced awhile, then said, "I will try Rasheeda for six
months, but if she does not take charge, she will be fired, just like
any other employee."

"I am sure she will do well," Rasheed said, "but I don't expect
you to keep her if she does not perform. You would have done the
same to me had I not performed."

Later when Kareem approached Rasheeda, she acted as if it were
unexpected. "Who came up with this crazy idea?" she asked, pretending she was not sure about the whole thing. "Dad, if you think
I am qualified, I'll take the job on a trial basis."

Kareem did not know that it was all planned to please him, so he
nodded agreeably. Rasheeda, to show her appreciation, did something she had abandoned a long time ago: she kissed her father's
hand and placed it on her forehead.

––––––––

At first, Rasheed accompanied his sister to the inns part time. She
was inquisitive and wanted to learn everything quickly. He was
eager to feed her the information she needed.

After three months she told Rasheed that he needed to make

himself available only when she needed him. She excelled; she was well aware of what the consequences of failure would be, both psychologically and professionally. She did not take anything for granted and aspired to prove that she could do things as well as Rasheed did. She learned bookkeeping in no time and kept very organized records, just as Rasheed had.

Rasheed welcomed his sister's independence and was confident that the results would not only ratify his plans but also please his father. They *did* please his father, who was surprised by his daughter.

Meanwhile, Rasheed trained at the American Colony bar. He first had to get accustomed to maneuvering between the immediate area behind the counter and the two supply rooms, which were accessed through separate doors, one on each side of the bar. The rooms were full of alcoholic drinks, above all, hundred-year-old liqueurs, brandy, port, and sherry. The rooms also contained more than two hundred bottles of forty- and fifty-year blended and single malt scotch whiskey. The shelves behind the bar contained more than four hundred bottles of different liquors and liqueurs.

He didn't mind being a trainee, since now he could face Natalia across the counter. The three Polish ladies visited every Thursday. Each would have two drinks, and then Albina and Adriana would leave Natalia with Rasheed.

One Thursday Rasheed was waiting for the three to show up when he got a call. It was Natalia. "We are not going to be able to make it this afternoon," she said. "As you probably know, the taxi drivers are on strike, something to do with a new British tax."

"This is nonsense," he said. "You are less than half an hour away. I'll pick you up at the kibbutz, and I'll drive you back when it's time."

"You don't have to do that," Natalia said.

"I want to. I don't want to wait until the strike is over to see you."

"That's great! Stop your car a hundred meters from the gate of the kibbutz. We should be by the gate, waiting for you," Natalia said. "You know, we're not supposed to let anyone in unless they have been screened in advance. It is all because of the right-wing fascists. They are extremely dangerous. I know them well. We have some just five hundred meters from us, Kibbutz Cherev. I don't even consider them Jewish." Natalia explained that her kibbutz was called Shivayon, meaning "equality" in Hebrew: equality between the Arabs and the Jews in Palestine.

"You know, we are not all the same," she continued. "We like David Ben-Gurion. He is kind of in the middle. He is a labor organizer and believes in a democracy for the Arabs and Jews. Yet sometimes we have our doubts about him. He does not carry out what he promotes, and he is the interlocutor with the British authorities."

After telling Natalia that he would see her in less than half an hour, Rasheed hopped into his Morris and headed out. When he got there, he stopped a good hundred meters from the gate but could not see any of the three women.

He looked around, somewhat disappointed. He thought he would find landscaped surroundings. Instead, a dirt road led to the gate of the kibbutz, which was around twelve feet high. The road was full of rocks, and some were big enough to pose a challenge to his small car if he were to go farther. He could not see what was behind the high wall of the kibbutz. He now understood why a

Thursday visit to the American Colony Hotel was so important for the girls. He imagined that the kibbutz was like an army camp. It was too basic and too constrained.

He waited in the car for a couple of minutes and then got out, planning to walk down the road, toward the gate. Before he had taken his third step, two men began walking briskly toward him, one of them brandishing a revolver. "Get back into your car," said one. "Not into the driver's seat—into the passenger's seat."

Rasheed almost froze before he could do anything. The two were shorter and smaller than he was. They looked haggard, and their clothes were smothered in mud. They smelled of a mixture of sweat and dirt, as if they had been working in a field. They would have been much less of a threat had it not been for the revolver. At first, Rasheed thought they were holding him up for money. When they started speaking in Yiddish, he picked up a couple of words and surmised they were from a kibbutz.

The three girls came out and saw what was happening. Natalia grabbed her head in disbelief for a few seconds and then hollered as loud as she could: "Rasheeeed, don't get in the car!" Then she slipped off her shoes and ran down the dirt road toward him as fast as she could, followed by the other women. Suddenly, as if she recognized the man brandishing the gun, she called out between gasps for air, "David, you fascist bastard, leave him alone, or I will kill you with my bare hands! Leave him alone!"

Albina picked up a few rocks and threw them, and Adriana followed suit. Just then ten young men exited the Shivayon kibbutz, one holding a shotgun, and began running toward the car. When the two right-wingers could not get Rasheed into the car, they fled on foot the same way they had come.

Rasheed was in shock, though he felt relief at being spared. He had evaded the grasp of potential killers, but he felt confused and challenged about what to do.

Natalia jumped into Rasheed's arms and hung on to him, her feet hanging in the air. She kissed him all over his face, exhibiting her feelings for him in public for the first time. "I thought I was going to lose you! I wouldn't be able to live with myself if anything had happened to you. Those two are vicious and could have killed you. They killed a thirteen-year-old Arab boy two weeks ago."

Rasheed did not know what to do under the circumstances, considering the ten men still coming toward him from the kibbutz. He grabbed Natalia's head, kissed her on both cheeks and on her forehead, and then gave her a short kiss on the lips. Reacting to Rasheed's tepid show of affection, Natalia said, "You don't have to be bashful. These are my friends, and they will be yours when you get to know them. They encourage us to mix with the local population because this is going to be our future together. They all know about you and how much I love you."

Rasheed whispered in her ear, "And I love you beyond your wildest dreams. I wasn't scared of them as much as I was scared never to see you again."

Albina and Adriana hugged Natalia and Rasheed as the ten kibbutzniks reached them. They shook hands with Rasheed; a couple of them hugged him. He looked at Yitzhak, the one with the shotgun, and thanked him profusely. "I don't think they would have let me go if they had not seen your shotgun."

They all invited Rasheed into the kibbutz. One of them, named Ariel, asked him if he would mind having his picture and fingerprints taken. "Sure, no problem. I have nothing to hide. I can give you all the rundown on my background," he said, "as long as I do not have to strip down."

"Oh no, not for this purpose," Ariel replied with a smile, looking at Natalia.

Natalia teasingly pinched Ariel on the arm. "Mind your manners," she said, "or else I'll use this shotgun on you."

Rasheed proceeded to the kibbutz and had his picture and fingerprints taken. He gave Adelajda, one of the kibbutz security personnel, his address and answered a few questions.

Afterward he took Natalia to the side and gave her a very juicy, lengthy kiss on the lips. "I like your friends. I think they are very nice. I may become a socialist one day, if you don't confiscate my father's inns. Then we would have to meet in the open air." He winked at her.

———

After the hair-raising kibbutz experience and Natalia's exchange of affectionate expressions with Rasheed, she expected their closeness and the prospects for intimacy to have gotten more intense. She could not help but recall how she felt when she thought she might lose him. She also could recall his response.

In a way, as much as she hated what had happened, she thought that such a life-threatening experience might have eliminated all barriers between the two of them. She was looking forward to him taking the initiative to arrange a romantic get-together, but he did not.

Rasheed continued his daily routine for three months without making the additional effort. He intentionally wanted to come across as a gentleman. He did not want Natalia to think that he thought she was easy. Likewise, he did not want her to think that he was taking advantage of the kibbutz episode for ulterior motives. His approach to her was careful and measured.

Nevertheless, he mostly made the right moves. He wanted to be reserved, and he was. There were moments when a kiss on the lips would have been natural, but instead Rasheed would rub his cheek against her cheek. He would sometimes grab Natalia by her waist and spin her around, stop her in his arms, and then follow it with a kiss on the forehead.

Within a short period of time, he developed a high degree of attraction for her, though without much action. One afternoon, she asked if the two of them could sit at a small table in the bar. She was hoping with the new seating he would show more intimacy.

Rasheed hadn't been with anyone since Leila. He still was not sure about romancing a European girl. He decided to be careful, fearing that he would make the wrong move and be sorry afterward.

Before being tutored by Father Federico, his supposed sex education had come to him casually and haphazardly, through talking to his macho friends in high school and circumspect cousins in the village. Much of it was either exaggerated or outright wrong. And almost all of it did not take the interest of the female partner into consideration. He fully understood that he should not depend on such contrived advice, especially when it mostly consisted of self-serving statements and braggadocio.

The next Thursday Natalia sat at the bar by herself while Rasheed finished working. Anna had proclaimed his training over and that he should take the afternoon off. He looked at Natalia cheerfully and said, "Let's go to the Khan and celebrate."

At the Khan, the larger of his family's two inns, he opened the car door, held Natalia's hand, and eased her out of the automobile with a large smile on his face. They barely made it to the lobby when one of the employees approached him with a plumbing problem. As Rasheed shook his head in disappointment, he gave Natalia the key to the suite. "I will be up there in ten minutes," he said.

She proceeded to the suite, clearly disappointed but not wanting to show it. Almost an hour later, after he spearheaded the repair of the plumbing, Rasheed hurried to join Natalia. He entered the suite, looked at the miniature bottles, and realized she had already had three vodka drinks. She was lying in bed, a white sheet pulled up over her head. The contour of her naked body was clearly visible through the fabric.

As she pulled the sheet off her face, Rasheed winked at her. "What do we have here?" he said, grinning. "Oh my, somebody was having fun while I was gone. You are all flushed in the face."

Natalia said nothing. She covered her head with the sheet again. After sitting at the edge of the bed, Rasheed pulled the sheet off her face and gave her a kiss on the cheek. He then softly slid his hands all the way from her neck to her waist.

"Do that again, on the other side. I think I'm waking up," she said. "Before you touched me, I was feeling numb all over."

Recalling Father Federico's advice and realizing that her unclothed body was too clear an invitation to ignore, he whispered in her ear. "Natalia, I am going to ask you to do something different, but please be patient."

She nodded. He took a short breath, waited for a few seconds, and then said, "Please get out of bed and get dressed. Don't jump to any conclusions; it is going to be all right."

He could see that she was mad. She rested her cheek on the pillow, turned her back to him, and stared at the wall.

"Just trust me," he said.

She snapped the sheet off herself, got up, and turned around and faced him with her exposed crotch. She looked down on him, with an oblique look full of anger and mild disdain.

"Didn't I tell you not to jump to any conclusions?" Rasheed said. "And here you are doing just that. I can see it in your eyes. Very shortly you will see what I mean."

Natalia got dressed slowly, taking her time as she seethed. Rasheed took her by the hand and opened the door.

"Please go out and knock on the door," he asked her. She exited the suite and took her time trying to overcome her bewilderment and the effects of her drinking. After a while, Rasheed was beginning to think that she had left. Suddenly, he heard a faint knock on the door.

He opened the door, and when he saw her, he gave a smile of joy and confident resignation, as if to say he was happy to have the opportunity to prove his point. He walked toward her, kissed her on the forehead, and then gave her a short but juicy kiss on her lips. "I am *walhan*," he said.

"What does that mean?" she asked in a subdued voice.

"It means I am so much in love, I can barely see straight!

"Are you *walhana*?" he asked her as he looked into her eyes.

"Sure I am, if it means a female lover that cannot see straight."

"That is exactly what it means, *walhana*," Rasheed said.

He held her right hand with his and slowly pulled her toward him, walking her forward and wrapping his arms around her. He rested his back against the front wall of the suite. For the first time, he murmured, "My love," and then he kissed her on the neck and proceeded to follow the teachings and instructions of Father Federico, just as he'd done with Leila three years earlier, in the woods of his Jesuit high school.

Gently he undressed Natalia, piece by piece, as stressed by Federico. At the same time, he was slowly undressing himself. Before he got her naked and now revived body into bed, Rasheed managed to help her reach one climax without removing her panties. He then removed her panties while massaging her genitalia, and he helped her to another climax.

When they finished, to the full satisfaction of both, and while they had their arms around each other and their bodies squeezed against each other, Natalia caught Rasheed laughing to himself.

"Share your thoughts. What are you laughing about, love?" she inquired.

"I am thinking about Federico; I had a great time, but he performed better than I did."

"You mean you watched him, and he and his partner had more fun?" Natalia said.

"No, it is just that he performed oral sex and he was happy to clean Aisha up. It keeps popping up into my head. It is all so intriguing coming from an Arab, even an uncommitted priest," he said. "Like I said, I am afraid you are going to do the cleaning yourself."

Natalia jokingly said, "I insist that you follow Federico to the letter." She kissed Rasheed on his cheek. "This was worth the three-month wait. Thanks to Father Federico, but I don't think I want him to conduct mass at my church."

"Don't worry, he would not want to either. He just wants to love and make love to Aisha."

They lay in bed, Natalia resting in his arms, pretending to be asleep. He kissed her and caressed her, and on several occasions whispered, "My love."

She suddenly perked up from her rest, mischievously giving Rasheed a pointed look. "Would you like to test Federico's guidelines for one more round?"

"Sure, that is a good idea," he said. "Let us test them without leaving the bed!"

Natalia nodded repeatedly and approvingly.

CHAPTER 5

1944
Beit Azar, Palestine

After he made love to Natalia for the first time, he felt he owed it to Rasheeda to tell her that he had fallen in love. It was their chosen cemetery day. Before they exchanged their liberal thoughts about a myriad of subjects—top among them was love and sex—they read Koranic verses of mercy for their mother, their grandmother Sara, and their great-aunt, Hameeda.

They sat opposite each other inches apart, each at the foot of an opposing grave site on top of elevated granite slabs. The cemetery was slightly manicured with local greenery. There were varieties of shrubberies in the shade of a dozen eucalyptus trees. What stood out were the jasmine and the white rose shrubs; the color white represented the Muslims' submission to the will of God. Their views were mostly sheltered by the headstone behind each of them.

Rasheed took the initiative by asking Rasheeda to be quiet, to give him time to talk, and for her to listen to him without interruption. "I think I have fallen in love," he said. "No, I *know* that I have fallen in love!"

She looked surprised. "This happened so fast, all in one week! Is she foreign, and how many times have you slept with her?"

Rasheed did not hesitate: "One time, yesterday. And I met her four months ago."

"I am afraid you have to make up for your indiscretion," she said teasingly. "You need to find me a boyfriend, either from outside the village or a foreigner."

She reminded Rasheed that he had the luxury of working in Jerusalem, where he would meet all kinds of people. "I cannot do at the inns what you do at the American Colony," she said. "If I were to find a boyfriend there and somebody caught me, they would accuse me of becoming a whore. You see my dilemma."

He told her that he understood both situations very well, and that she should make sure to be as circumspect as possible. "I know how to do all of this—don't worry. I am even more careful than you are."

————

Slowly Adriana and Albina stopped accompanying Natalia to the American Colony. Every Thursday Natalia would hop into the same taxi and travel from the kibbutz to the American Colony in half an hour. Then the two would go someplace, eat, drink, kiss, and hug. Neither Rasheed nor Natalia pushed having sex on a regular basis. They both were falling deeply in love and could not think intently of anything other than their love for each other.

One afternoon as they approached his great-uncle's sprawling orchard, they stopped to locate a choice spot. They could see the tops of hundreds of the olive trees that cascaded down the terraces, which were buttressed by stone-studded retention walls, built as far back as the Roman times. Rasheed spotted a dense tree formation to protect them from passersby.

He took Natalia's hand and ran toward the spot. He spread a sheet between the olive trees, and they lay down facing each other. He drew her attention to the trees. "When you look at the trunks, you can feel they are as old as Christianity. My uncle did a good job of preserving such a graceful and wise tree, the olive tree, as if it were a record of the events that went by them."

That gave Natalia the opportunity to ask about Rasheed's great-uncle and the rest of his family. "I would like to meet your family. Other than what you told me minutes ago, I know nothing about them, and they are only four kilometers from the American Colony."

Rasheed told her that it was not a good idea to socialize with the family members due to the way the villagers think. "They don't look favorably on their boys associating with foreign girls for fear that their behavior will get corrupted. But, if you like, I will be happy to arrange you getting together with Rasheeda. I think she would like meeting you."

"Yes, yes, you had mentioned having a sister, but you never mentioned her name. Rasheeda is your female namesake, like Christian and Christina?"

Within two weeks Rasheed managed to set up a meeting between Natalia and Rasheeda at a small upscale restaurant in Jerusalem. He knew the owners of the restaurant well. Muslim Khalil and Christian Mary did all the cooking themselves. They fell in love in high school. They were childless by design as they both decided to defy their families by not having children, in preference to choosing one religion or another for the children. The restaurant seated twenty-six, with one table sheltered and isolated, like a cave. That was the one Rasheed reserved.

When Natalia saw Rasheeda for the first time, beaming and cheerfully getting out of a taxi, she could tell that she was Rasheed's twin sister. Rasheeda was dressed in a turquoise silk dress that went down eight inches below her knees. She wore a headdress, with a fashionable hat over it. Natalia kept looking at Rasheed as if to question him about why he had not shared with her this beautiful and well-composed, graceful creature.

"This is your sister!" she said with implied criticism.

"This is my sister."

Natalia gave Rasheeda a big, warm hug, and they kissed each other on both cheeks. "It is all Rasheed's fault," Natalia said. "We should have met much, much earlier."

Rasheeda was no less elated at meeting her new friend. She put her arm into Natalia's and gave Rasheed a sideways glance. "Walk behind us," Rasheeda said to her brother. "Make sure we are not being followed, especially by somebody from Beit Azar."

Rasheeda told Natalia that she had been looking forward to meeting her. "You are tall and more beautiful than Rasheed described you. I also blame Rasheed for us not having met earlier. I have so much to talk with you about, not the least of which is the subject of men. I am sure you can teach me a thing or two."

"Well, smart women figure men out in short order," Natalia said. "Naïve women suffer from not knowing them well, ever."

"Are you kidding me? They don't think about us," Rasheeda said. "We are an afterthought to them. They think they are entitled to pleasures that women are not entitled to—the same pleasures that are automatically denied to women, especially in marriage."

The conversation was a complete surprise and a shock to Natalia, not because of its content but because of who was expressing it. Natalia agreed with Rasheeda completely, but added, "Rasheed is one of the most considerate men I have ever encountered, of any age."

"I know that, Natalia. That is why he promised to help me find the man of my dreams."

"You want to get married!" Natalia said.

"No, I want to fall in love first, just like you and Rasheed."

They continued walking on the cobblestone sidewalk without paying much attention to the vendors selling freshly roasted mixed nuts, fresh juices, sweets of all kinds, and Turkish coffee along both sides of the sun-sheltered, narrow alleyway. What they couldn't escape were the aromas of the merchandise all around them.

Rasheeda's subjects and opinions overwhelmed Natalia, discriminating as they were. She had her own thoughts about men, yet her thoughts were unprejudiced enough to separate "more egalitarian" men from the majority.

After pausing briefly, Natalia said, "I am going to do everything in my power to help you out, but only if I happen to know the person well. You should not in the least be in a desperate situation. All that you need is exposure—you are just so beautiful."

Rasheeda suddenly felt more assured about her physical looks because of Natalia's compliments. She had heard similar comments within Beit Azar but had given them no importance, given that her village never developed into a venue of love or romance due to the wet nurse fiasco. She heard similar compliments at the two inns, but never reacted to them as she was intent not to give her father cause to dismiss her.

"Now that we have met, let's see each other more often," Rasheeda said. "God, it takes only ten minutes to drive to the American Colony."

"Let's meet once a month," Natalia said.

"Consider it done. I will propose a date and let Rasheed know, and he will let you know."

Rasheed was very happy with the arrangement. He was particularly happy that Natalia and Rasheeda bonded right away. He was trying to figure out what his role would be, but in the end, he decided that he would relay messages between the two and let them figure out how to relate to each other. He trusted Rasheeda's judgment and was getting to trust Natalia's more and more.

A month later Natalia surprised Rasheed by telling him she once knew a British intelligence officer named David Alexander. "He was interested in me, but I had no interest in him whatsoever. He was a fine gentleman and a handsome young man, but he was not my type. I never even considered it, but I think he may be a match for Rasheeda."

In a playful mood Rasheed said, "What was it that did not interest you?"

"Well, let's say he was tall and handsome but not dark and not as charming as you are."

"Obviously, he is English and Christian, but as far as I am concerned this does not matter. I am going to leave it up to your discretion—just be careful. Be more than circumspect; be almost secretive. Do you know what I mean?"

"Believe it or not, he is a member of the Unitarian church. I understand that you can be a Muslim or Christian and be a Unitarian at the same time," Natalia said.

"I am not familiar with this church. What is it all about?" Rasheed asked.

"It is an umbrella religion. Like the Muslims, they believe in the single manifestation of God. Not like us Catholics. We believe in the three manifestations: the Father, the Son, and the Holy Spirit."

"I thought you were Jewish," Rasheed said.

"I still go to the Catholic church, but I feel I am Jewish," Natalia replied—to Rasheed's surprise.

CHAPTER 6

The following week Natalia made a conspiratorial face and said, "Hey, Rasheed, I made contact with David Alexander, and we are supposed to meet next Wednesday, this time with Rasheeda, of course. What do you say about such quick work on my part?"

Rasheed noticed that Natalia was pleased with herself. He told her that he would talk to his sister and then arrange for the three of them to have lunch.

In no time, the arrangement with the restaurant was made. It was an even smaller restaurant than the one Rasheed used to patronize with Natalia. It was in a secluded area that did not front a street. After taking about twenty steps from the street, patrons would climb an eight-step staircase. It had a large water fountain in the middle that was adorned with very old Arab mosaics. Each table abutted only one other table. Rasheed had asked the owner if he would keep the other table unoccupied so that the women could talk in privacy.

Rasheeda and Natalia met. They ordered appetizers and wine

for Natalia and beer for Rasheeda. Rasheeda told Natalia that her
limit was three sips. Natalia kept talking about the different Arab
appetizers, hesitant to bring up David Alexander. She talked so
much about how much she liked hummus. Rasheeda told her that
before the next time they met, she would prepare enough hummus
for twenty people for Natalia to share with comrades at the kibbutz.

Natalia suddenly looked Rasheeda in the eye and said, "Why am
I spending so much time talking about food? You don't strike me as
a prude. I am here to talk about David. I think you will like him."

"So all this talk about hummus was small talk?" Rasheeda snickered. "You want to tell me about David; well, go ahead. I want to
hear all the details about him. Where is he from? What does he do?
What does he look like? Go ahead, don't hesitate."

Natalia was relieved to hear that Rasheeda was open to the
potential introduction. Natalia emphasized that while he was not
her type, he was a young twenty-seven-year-old captain in British
intelligence. She described him as handsome, blondish, tall, and on
the slim side—a gentleman through and through.

"He likes to wear short-sleeve shirts, but he avoids wearing
shorts as he does not want to be mistaken for an Australian," she
added. "I would not have guessed he was English until he started
speaking in a perfect upper-class manner. He likes to show off the
hair on his chest, as he knows most European men have little hair
on their chest and arms. No doubt, he is handsome. Just come with
me and see for yourself. It surely will not be my decision."

CHAPTER 7

Natalia went to the Khan the following Friday to arrange for David and Rasheeda to get together. She planned to share what transpired between her and Rasheeda with Rasheed, for him to coordinate the rest. To her surprise, Rasheed was not there. When she asked the receptionist if her partner had arrived, he said, "Oh no, he is not able to make it. He called this morning and left you a message."

"What kind of message?" she said anxiously. The concierge handed her Rasheed's dictated message:

> *Sorry, love, something most pressing happened. It is nothing to worry about. It will be over, and I will see you a week from tomorrow, same time same place. Please do not worry. Love, Rasheed.*

Rasheed's message was partially comforting but rather vexing as the two had not been apart for more than a few days since the relationship started. She headed back to the kibbutz and went right away to see Albina and Adriana. They tried to ease her concerns. Albina told her, "If it was anything serious, he would not have been so sure to see you in eight days. It could be anything; most probably it is nothing important."

———————

Rasheed was busy all week carrying out his duty as the elder son and could barely mourn the death of his father. Rasheeda was equally busy, since she had to take care of the arrangements entrusted to the women of the family. As sad as she was, she refused to wail as was the tradition among the female mourners. She would go off to the side and shed tears as she attended to her duties. She did follow the Palestinian-Arab custom of refraining from serving anything with sugar for weeks after a death, and in doing so, she received and served black sugarless Turkish coffee.

It was a huge funeral. Mourners came from all the surrounding villages and from Jerusalem. There were also a dozen Jesuit priests from Kareem's, Rasheed's, and Rasheeda's high schools. The tourism industry was heavily represented, including many foreign tour agents and operators.

———————

Natalia could not wait eight days to see Rasheed. She took a cab to the Khan every couple of days and checked on him. The receptionists there felt for her but told her Rasheed would not be arriving until Saturday.

The Saturday he was expected to return, she showed up an hour early. Noticing her anxiety, the receptionist told her, "Don't worry, he will be here within an hour, I am sure."

Twenty minutes after Natalia arrived, Rasheed showed up. He ran to her, hugged her very tightly, swept her off her feet, and carried her behind the reception area. They both started kissing each other passionately. It took a whole two minutes before Rasheed said something. "If it was not urgent, I would not have missed seeing you for anything. My father passed away."

Natalia looked at Rasheed, held his head, and pressed it against her shoulder while tearing up. "Oh, Rasheed, you should have told me. I am so sorry. I want to share with you the good times and the bad times. I want you to share your grief, and I want you to share mine. You should have told me. I was so worried, and I needed you. I needed you so badly. I am so sorry."

Natalia's soothing and emotional words meant a lot to Rasheed. He could not agree with her more. Rasheed felt, and he thought Natalia felt this way as well, that they needed to be in each other's lives on a daily basis.

Rasheed looked Natalia in the eye. "I hope we will not have to be apart in the future. This was totally unexpected. It was hectic all week. I did not have a chance to grieve or even to cry. Let us head off to Mount Calvary to replenish the Sea of Galilee."

"Replenish the Sea of Galilee? What do you mean?"

"I am sorry," he said. "This refers to a poet who lost his lover. He cried so much for her, which made him somewhat delusional. He wrote a poem about it, about how he would cry and replenish the Sea of Galilee with his tears during a major drought in Palestine. Now, when people familiar with the poem want to cry for their dead, they say, 'Let us replenish the Sea of Galilee.'"

"Sure, let us both try to replenish the Sea of Galilee," Natalia said. "We need it." They hopped into the car and headed to Mount Calvary, where Christ is supposed to have been crucified, and where the Dinar family owned property.

"We can look down on all the holy places," Rasheed said. "I love it there. You get a sense for what Jerusalem is all about. If you believe what the scriptures say, Jesus resurrected, and we will shed tears and relieve ourselves of our burdens."

When they arrived, Rasheed took Natalia by the hand and had her climb up a well-contoured rock, opposite him.

"I want to start first," Natalia said.

"Start first? How? I want to read Koranic verses. How can you do that?" Rasheed asked.

"You will understand shortly." She made the sign of the cross first. Rasheed was surprised as he also thought she was Jewish.

When Natalia noticed his surprised look, she said, "I am ethnically and politically Jewish, but I am still Catholic."

Rasheed could not understand what she was talking about. He just accepted it as being inconsequential, but murmured to himself, "I thought I was confused about my own religion!"

Natalia pulled Rasheed's head and placed his forehead on hers:

> *Mama, this is Natalia, your daughter in Palestine.*
> *Why, why, Mama, did you refuse to come to Palestine?*
> *You refused to join me here.*
> *I told you they were evil.*
> *They killed my father because he was Jewish.*
> *They killed you because you married a Jew.*

It is so strange; you died the same day Rasheed's
father died.

At that point, Rasheed pulled his head away, looked at Natalia
wistfully, his eyes watering. Tears slid down his cheeks as he looked
at Natalia with total astonishment. At the same time, he tried to
wipe off her tears, but they were pouring off her face.

Natalia then continued:

Mama, you would not believe me.
    You thought because you were Christian they
would spare your life.
    Guess what, Mama? The commandant who
ordered your death was Catholic, just like you and
I were.
    He had massacred Catholic priests, both in
Poland and in Germany.
    Would you have come over if I remained
Catholic?
    I would have gone back to be Catholic, for you,
anytime, anywhere!
    You make me sad, so sad. I am replenishing the
Sea of Galilee with Rasheed, my love.
    Had you come over, you would have met him
and loved him.
    He is my love; he is my life, and without him I
would not have survived having lost you.
    I love you. Rest in peace. We will meet again.

Natalia again made the sign of the cross.

It was even more confusing to Rasheed, who just heard her telling her deceased mother that she was Jewish. Again, he chose initially to ignore the contradictions.

"Natalia, you are confusing me. You go back and forth from Catholic to Jewish."

"It is just my mother did not believe you could be ethnically Jewish and religion-wise Catholic," she said.

Natalia continued sobbing and seemed to be about to faint. Rasheed pulled her up and hugged her tightly. It took her minutes to stop crying and gasping. As she recovered her composure, he kissed her all over her face, wiping her tears in the process.

"I am sorry, so sorry, not having told you about my father. I was selfish and inconsiderate. Please forgive me," he told her.

She looked at him and snickered. "I will forgive you, but I cannot be seen with you. Look at your lap. It is wet with my tears. Anybody who sees you will think that you peed on yourself."

As Rasheed was trying to dry up his wet crotch, Natalia looked at him and said, "You know, you have not read to me the poem about the Sea of Galilee."

"Well, it so happens I know it by heart. I had to translate it for our civics class. It is all allegorical, you know."

"I'd like to hear it."

"It is called 'Tears in the Sea of Galilee,'" Rasheed said and began reciting a translation of the poem.

You spoke to me from beyond the sea
To soothe my soul
That you are where you want to be
Before you left, you set your plans in motion
Where your lover held back no tears
To create a limitless and vast ocean

So that our people can revive
After the Sea of Galilee is replenished,
to keep us, in your honor, all alive.

Natalia held his head in her hands and kissed him on the lips. "This is so good, so tender," she said. "I am glad we replenished the Sea of Galilee together. I love you so much."

The two of them went silent for a few seconds until Natalia said, "We keep talking about ourselves. It is time to prepare for Rasheeda's getting together with David. Let's go. We have work to do."

CHAPTER 8

Before the three got together, Rasheed visited the restaurant and prepaid the owner to use the best ingredients and to have him follow his mother's recipes in preparing four different dishes. Two of the dishes were Rasheed's favorites: rice and minced meat stuffed in maroon carrots and cooked in tamarind sauce, and artichoke bottoms and chicken cooked in sun-dried goat cheese.

They were the same dishes his mother, Amina, taught Sara and Hameeda to prepare. Amina came from a line of celebrated home cooks. Her mother and grandmother used to send their cooking as presents to the different tribal and town chiefs in Palestine.

Between Rasheed's attempts to soothe Rasheeda's feelings of anxiety on one hand and his explicit encouragement on the other, she could not help but feel nervous. She could tell that her proposed rendezvous with David was the real thing. The thought of David being a Christian and a foreigner was eating at her though. She wondered whether her mother would have done the same.

Her thoughts went back and forth. She admonished herself

not to be afraid but to be resolute. She reminded herself that she always believed in equality between men and women, and that if going out with a Christian and a foreigner was good enough for Rasheed, it was good enough for her.

She decided that if David satisfied her fancy, she would go for it. She rationalized that she was a generation younger than her mother and that what would have prevented her mother from acting should not block her, twenty years later.

When David met Natalia, he was surprised that she had a companion. He took a pointed but very brief look at Rasheeda. Her eyes sparkled as she looked at him intently out of the corner of her eye. He liked what he saw of her, but he did not know how the gorgeous-looking young woman fit into the picture.

They sat down at the table. Rasheeda and David shook hands and introduced themselves to each other. David and Natalia talked casually while Rasheeda listened. Natalia did not mention Rasheed. David told Natalia that he was busy with added security for some of the bridges because two had been recently blown up by either the Palestinian or Jewish underground.

Rasheeda asked David about the bridges that had been blown up, and she began telling him about the engineering of the bridges of Palestine. She shared that she was taking engineering courses by correspondence through the University of London.

Impressed, David inquired further and found out that Rasheeda had just finished a research paper about Palestinian bridges for her first structural-engineering course. He asked her to share her paper with him.

Rasheeda responded playfully, "It all depends." At that point Natalia excused herself and moved to the next table, having noticed the spark between her friends. "You two work out the bridge problems," she said. "You don't need my help. You have half an hour before we go back. I have to meet my fiancé."

David got the message, and his attention shifted to Rasheeda. As David turned back to her, Rasheeda took the initiative despite her nervousness. "Relax. You look fidgety. Would you like to talk some more about the few bridges there are in Palestine?" she asked.

David looked her in the eye. "I would love to—that and other subjects, if you like."

"Sure, it all depends on the subject," Rasheeda answered with greater confidence.

"Any subject you like, as long as it does not have anything to do with my line of work."

"I can think of so many subjects, but today Natalia is short of time. Why don't we do it some other time?"

Having overheard the conversation, Natalia looked at Rasheeda and pointed to her watch to indicate there was still plenty of time. But Rasheeda did not want to show her open attraction for David on the spot, and she pretended that she was not anxious to prolong the meeting.

"Either of us can talk to Natalia," he said, not sure of the proper follow-up to this successful rendezvous, "here in Palestine!"

"You talk to her, and I will talk to her," Rasheeda said with clear confidence, as if to say, *It's okay with me if it's okay with you*, as she stood up and shook hands with David to say goodbye.

Natalia came over from her table, shook hands with David, and said, "We hope to have another cup of coffee *soon*."

As the two hopped into a taxi, Natalia grinned at Rasheeda. She gave Natalia a knowing look and nodded agreeably with a wink.

———————

It took only two days for David to call the kibbutz to get in touch with Natalia. The British intelligence service had a file with full contact information about each kibbutz in Palestine. He asked her if she could arrange for him to see Rasheeda again.

Acting coy, she said, "I have to check with her. You know the Arabs are much stricter than us Europeans." Her answer was only a pretense; she immediately contacted Rasheed and asked to see Rasheeda, which she did the following day.

When Rasheeda got out of the taxi, Natalia was there to meet her. Before Rasheeda could greet her, she said, "David called. He wants to see you."

Rasheeda nodded and winked.

"Don't try to be coy with me," Natalia said. "We are beyond the nod and the wink. I need to know your likes and dislikes in detail before this develops further."

Rasheeda took Natalia's arm as they entered the restaurant. She leaned over and whispered into her friend's ear: "I am beside myself. I hope I am not going to be disappointed, but I feel very good about David. I have a feeling that he is to me as you were to Rasheed when you first met. I am so excited. I will keep you up on everything. I will be more explicit with you, but I will play it cool with David. I am not going to let him know how I feel. Not yet."

They agreed to meet again on Friday, which Rasheeda considered the most convenient day to meet. When he was alive, her father had always gone to mosque on Fridays, and during those hours she had felt a sense of freedom, free from his watchful eye. The feeling of liberation remained into adulthood, and she continued to reserve Fridays for plans her father wouldn't have approved of. It would have been a disaster if her father had discovered that she was in a relationship with someone who was a Christian as well as a foreigner. Her shame would have been doubled. The only thing worse would be becoming pregnant by such a man.

The meetings went on for three weeks: same people, same time, same place, same tables. On the third date, as David sat down, he whispered, "Listen, Rasheeda, how about meeting in the woods, next to my barracks? It is a restricted area, ten minutes away from here, and only those with special permits can enter it. As far as I know, only British subjects carry such permits."

"Are you kidding me?" Rasheeda said. "For sure!"

"Fantastic. I'll have my Land Rover in front of the restaurant, and as soon as you and Natalia get out of the taxi, you both jump inside. Have Natalia sit next to me, and you sit in the back seat. It will all look legitimate."

Rasheeda nodded approvingly several times, and David grasped her hand. "Let's go," she said to Natalia, who was surprised at the brevity of the rendezvous but went along. Rasheeda explained the new setup to Natalia. Natalia was pleased.

The following week, David took them to the wooded area next to the barracks. The British military headquarters stood on the other side of the building. As a captain in military intelligence, David had permanent and easy access to the area. As they walked into the woods, Natalia veered to the right and sat down and began reading an English newspaper, while David and Rasheeda walked on.

David did not know how to behave while alone with Rasheeda,

his first liaison with a local girl. They looked into each other's eyes. He slowly tilted his head to the side and gave her a kiss on her cheek.

"Listen, David, I don't mind this kind of kiss. I know well enough that you are much looser in the West. You even have premarital sex. This is not going to happen here. I hope you appreciate what I am talking about. Do you?"

"I do understand what you mean," David said, surprised. "I wasn't thinking about sex. I would not have thought of it had you not mentioned it."

"I am happy that you understand this. You can hold my hand, if you care to, and we can walk together, farther away from Natalia, to get to know each other better."

David held Rasheeda's hand and started to talk about his country life in England.

"Is it as pretty as this here, with olive, carob, and eucalyptus trees all around you?" Rasheeda asked.

"Just as pretty, but greener and with different kinds of trees. I think you would love my country. The greenery is so lush, and the breeze is so cool, all year round."

"I would love to see it. I would love to visit England and France and speak to the locals in their language. You know, I know English fluently and French almost fluently. Don't you think so?"

"You speak English so well and so gracefully, but I didn't know that you also speak French. So do I."

After an hour of talking, gazing at each other, and sometimes laughing and giggling, they went to fetch Natalia. David drove them back to the restaurant, and before Rasheeda stepped out of the car, he kissed her hand.

Natalia looked at the two grinning at each other and noticed the unexpected hand kiss. She wondered how Rasheeda felt with David and whether her swift attraction to him felt strange to her, having never dated before. She was pleasantly amused at the progress between the two.

"I understand that my mother enjoyed Westerners kissing her hand," Rasheeda said, "including the commissioner general."

David looked at her admiringly, having heard that her mother had her hand kissed, and by no less than the commissioner general. "I did not know that your parents knew the commissioner general!"

"It was more than twenty years ago, before my mother died giving birth to me and Rasheed," she said wistfully.

David asked her if his kissing her hand was as important to her as the commissioner general kissing her mother's hand.

"Yours is more important," she said. She looked David in the eye. "Much more important."

David smiled and kissed her hand again. Rasheeda pulled her hand slowly out of his soft grasp but kept looking at him with a faint smile. She and Natalia then proceeded to the taxi queue.

CHAPTER 9

Rasheeda returned home anxious to speak to Rasheed about that day's rendezvous with David. She was dying to tell him that David kissed her hand. Speaking to him would be difficult, since Rasheed usually visited with one of their cousins after work.

It so happened that Rasheeda had one of her female cousins visiting her. The cousin was trying to convince Rasheeda to accompany her to extend their condolences for the death of an important village patriarch. Rasheeda did not want to have anything detour her from sharing the news of her satisfaction with getting together with David, especially his kissing her hand. She was floating on air. After her cousin left, Rasheeda called Rasheed to the large living room and shared with him the news that David had kissed her hand twice.

Rasheed said in a playfully chagrined tone, "He actually wanted to kiss you on the lips, but since he could not, he decided to kiss your hand. Or has he kissed you on your lips?"

"Don't be silly. Of course he has not," Rasheeda said. "I guess you have not kissed Natalia's hand since she does not mind being kissed on the lips. No, I think you should kiss Natalia's hand. It shows respect more than love. At least this is the way it feels to me. I think if you respect Natalia, you should kiss her hand!"

"I don't mind kissing Natalia's hand. It does not at all mean I am not masculine if I kiss her hand. I don't care what they think in Beit Azar. It does not mean I am inferior to her either."

He thought for a moment. "Well, I have news for you, too," he said. "An Australian journalist read my writings in the old high school newspaper. You know the ones that were hanging on the news board next to the chapel? He liked my articles a lot, and he encouraged me to pursue writing. I think I will try to do that somehow."

"I am happy for you, Rasheed! For a while I thought you talked about writing to cover up the fact you really just wanted to work at the American Colony and meet Natalia openly!"

"I talk about all three—Natalia, languages, and writing. How come you have forgotten? I think your mind is on David," he whispered.

Rasheeda slowly nodded, confirming that her mind was on David.

"I will be honest with you," she said. "I can't wait until I see him, and once a week is not often enough. But what can I do? I can't afford to neglect the inns. I am on my own."

The following Thursday, Rasheeda met with Natalia and David next to his camp, and then Rasheeda and David walked toward a more wooded area and sat against an olive tree.

"I want to thank you," Rasheeda said.

"For what?"

"For kissing my hand last week."

"I wish I could kiss you somewhere else," he said.

Remembering her brother's words, Rasheeda said, "Like on my lips!" When David nodded yes, Rasheeda said, "You men think alike. That's exactly what Rasheed said."

"Who is Rasheed?" David said calmly.

"He is my brother. He works as head barman at the American Colony. That is where he met Natalia. He wants to be a writer and may one day become a journalist."

"So that's who Natalia is engaged to, your brother!"

"They're not really engaged. Natalia just mentioned having a fiancé to give you a hint that it was *me* who was interested in meeting you, not her. They love each other so much."

She went silent for a moment and then said, "How about if I give you a peck on your lips, since you have been a good boy?"

David gave her a peck on the lips.

"It is interesting that your brother wants to be a journalist. My favorite uncle is an opinion writer at *The Times* of London. He knows all about Palestine, and some of his friends are generals, serving here in Palestine and in the Trucial States. He served in India for twenty years. I will talk to him about Rasheed. He may have an idea or two."

"Sure, why not?" Rasheeda said. "Let me know what your uncle says."

After a while Rasheeda began to stand up to leave. David gently pulled her back toward him.

"I know what you are doing," she said. "You want another kiss—go ahead. It is okay."

"Are you sure?"

"I am sure you are hoping for one, so go ahead."

As David moved his head toward hers, she reciprocated by moving her head toward his and closed her eyes. David gave her a moderate kiss on the lips. Then they walked hand in hand toward Natalia.

CHAPTER 10

David called Natalia and suggested the four of them meet up. Natalia was intrigued by the idea. "Why not? It will look so natural, if anyone sees us together," she said, thinking that people would assume she was with David and Rasheeda was with her brother.

When they met the following Thursday, Rasheed introduced himself, and then he and David walked slowly away from the two girls. They sized each other up as they walked. It was their first meeting, and the circumstances were difficult, coming two weeks after Kareem's death.

Rasheed was more curious as he gauged David for the benefit of his sister. David was handsome. He looked fit and athletic, around two inches shorter than Rasheed's six foot three inches.

"I can see now why your mother chose the same name for the two of you," David said. "You look so much alike, and I presume the girls are after you as much as the men are after Rasheeda. What struck me most is how mature and wise she is, for her age. She loves you, and she spoke so emotionally and glowingly about you."

"Rasheeda is all the family I have. I am blessed I have two women who are great but different, whom I love unconditionally, and I presume they love me as much. I think and believe that Rasheeda is very lucky she has you."

"I consider myself the lucky one for her being in my life. You can't imagine how much better Palestine feels to me now that I have met her. Please let her know that, when you speak to her later today."

"God, you made my day, knowing how you feel about my sister."

David looked Rasheed in the eye and said, "I need to let you know why I wanted to see you right away. I must confess it was not about Rasheeda. It is about an opportunity you may be interested in. You see, my uncle is a retired field marshal, and he has just informed me that the British government in Palestine is planning to recruit eight Palestinians to train as officers and war correspondents. You may want to consider becoming a war correspondent through this program. Rasheeda told me that you want to be a writer."

"David, be reasonable," Rasheed said. "I am not thrilled about the British in Palestine. You were supposed to give us our independence, as part of Syria, after the Ottomans, and now see where we are. I am not sure accepting such an offer would not be a betrayal of what I believe in. I believe in a free Palestine or a Palestine that is part of free Syria!"

"You would go through only three weeks of military training, and the rest would be all journalism, English language, and conversation," David said. "It should be no challenge to you. You speak perfect English. Talk to Natalia and Rasheeda about it before you make a decision."

David asked Rasheed to consider it seriously. His uncle had told him that the British did the same in India, on a larger scale, and that most of the Indian war correspondents ended up becoming some of the most prominent Indian journalists in India.

"Thanks, David, although I am dubious about the whole proposal, I will give it serious consideration," Rasheed said. "I will probably see more of you in the future. You see, I hate to say this, but now that my father is dead, I don't care what anybody else says. I can spend more time with Natalia, and you and Rasheeda can spend more time together. Rasheeda and I have already talked. She is going to hire one of our cousins to help out at the inns. At any rate, I will let you know about your proposal shortly."

David suggested they all go to a more densely wooded area, in the same area of the camp.

Rasheed liked David. David's friendly attitude influenced him to go along into the woods in the first place and listen to his new friend's idea. It was the same attitude that nudged Rasheed to lean more toward applying to become a war correspondent. He was yearning to find an opening or opportunity to train in writing. In his mind, he tried to reconcile the possibility that such training would come through a program designed by the British colonial authority, an authority and a presence that Rasheed thought was illegal.

In the woods, Natalia and Rasheed went to one side, and Rasheeda and David went to the opposite side. Rasheed told Natalia about David's offer to test her reaction.

She was not happy about it. "You want to be an officer under the British flag? It makes no sense to me," she said. "You have described them as your oppressors. It is true you are not officially a socialist, but your thoughts and attitudes are similar to mine. We both know Britain is squarely against socialism!"

"This is really not a military assignment; it is a journalistic assignment. After I learn the trade, I will leave them in no time."

"How about us? What will happen to us?"

"Natalia, listen, nothing will happen to us. I will not let anything interfere with my love for you, you understand? This goes without saying, and the other important person in my life, Rasheeda, knows it. The two of you are all that matters."

Natalia said nothing but was still not totally convinced.

Having noticed her continued concern, Rasheed said, "Let us both think about it and talk again."

Half an hour later, the four regrouped. David and Rasheeda looked happy and relaxed. But that was not the case with Rasheed and Natalia.

Natalia asked Rasheeda if she could speak to her, and they went walking by themselves. "Did you hear what Rasheed wants to do? Did David tell you?"

"Yes, he did. I think it is a great idea. Don't you think so?"

"Working for the British is a great idea?" Natalia asked. "I don't think so."

"In the case of Rasheed I think it is a great idea. You see, the British use you by making you financially dependent on them. They cannot do this to Rasheed. You know that we make ten times as much as they would offer him. Furthermore, once he is trained, he can use the same training against the British. Do you really want to see him as a glorified barman, a head barman, for the rest of his life? Or do you want to see him as an established journalist, doing what he loves to do most? I think he will not do it if you are against it. So think about it!"

At first Natalia argued with Rasheeda, making a strong argument against the British rule in Palestine, but Rasheeda would not budge. She kept repeating to Natalia how much different Rasheed was from other recruits of the British colonial authority in Palestine.

Finally, Rasheeda raised her voice. "If I were to accept your argument, Rasheed and others should not even serve drinks to the British. But as you see, Rasheed's bar clientele is more than fifty percent British civil servants and officers. I think if you trust Rasheed and his judgment, you will not hesitate a second to recommend to Rasheed that he join the war correspondents' training program."

Rasheeda's arguments got to Natalia. "I have to confess I never considered your two arguments, especially the one about how Rasheed and you are too comfortable to be compromised by the British. I think you have a point."

She scratched her head and then held her arm and said, "Let's go!" Natalia dragged Rasheeda along and went back to join Rasheed and David. Within minutes Natalia took Rasheed to the side. "If you give me a kiss, I have something to share with you," she said.

"Only one kiss? You are inexpensive. What is it?"

"I don't want you to be jealous, but you have a very wise sister. She really makes lots of sense. She is very logical. She convinced me that you can become a great journalist."

"I sure hope so. How exactly did you resolve this issue?" he asked.

"I think you should apply to become a damned British officer. The matter was resolved because it is all for a good cause, and you are not the kind who could easily be compromised. I know you can become a good journalist, eventually independent of British rule. It is not to show off your British uniform." Natalia smiled.

"This is great, I guess. How about ten kisses?"

Natalia went toward Rasheeda and hugged her. She told her then that Rasheed was going to apply to become a war correspondent.

"Natalia, you are so great and understanding; let me go and share this with David. He is totally convinced that this is the best and easiest way to become a journalist. His uncle saw it happen in India."

Rasheeda told David. He was elated. He told Rasheeda that he would coach Rasheed on how to approach the snobbish interviewers, a British colonel and two captains.

The four got together, this time all smiling. Natalia held David's arm and thanked him. Rasheed looked at David and said, "It is a go." He gave Natalia a kiss on her cheek.

CHAPTER 11

As David and Rasheed huddled in David's barracks, they had one thing in mind: for Rasheed to be prepared for his interview. Rasheed was very familiar with British social customs, but he was not familiar with military protocol or typical attitudes of British officers.

David did a thorough job preparing Rasheed for his interview. Not only did he brief Rasheed on procedures, he also gave him a thorough idea of the different personalities of the officers interviewing him. In one case, he told him about a captain who used to go silent when he wanted a deeper answer. "In that case, Rasheed, you need to explain the point further, without having to wait for a follow-up question."

The panel of officers were very impressed with Rasheed's answers and his command of the English language. They *did* wonder as to why this refined and financially well-off young man was applying for officer training. They took the opportunity to ask him about his sophisticated vocabulary and how certain words applied to him. His answers explaining the different meanings of the words and how each specifically applied to his case prompted the panel to dismiss their objections and accept him into the program.

————————

The day Rasheed finished his basic training, Natalia was there to meet him. She ran toward him and hugged him. She took the sides of the keffiyeh in her hands and folded them over each other on top of his head before kissing him with great passion.

"You look so handsome, so spiffy in your uniform. One day, I hope you will wear the uniform of the socialist state of Palestine."

Rasheed and Natalia went to the Khan, the larger of the two inns. There they found Rasheeda and David. It was Rasheeda's turn to hug Rasheed and kiss him on his forehead. She was beaming with pride and asked him to stand still for her to size him up and down.

"You make me so proud. Natalia is so proud of you also. David tells me the rest should be much more to your liking: learning and writing for the next eight months."

They went up to one of the suites and shared a bottle of champagne. Not much of a drinker, Rasheeda only had one glass, but David, Natalia, and Rasheed chugged the rest.

David left, and Rasheeda went to the smaller inn to give Rasheed and Natalia some space. Rasheed was so anxious to describe to Natalia his experiences at the camp. He told her as he paced in the suite, "Natalia, can you believe it? For the first three days we were exercising in our underwear, and during the last three weeks I have had only three baths altogether."

Natalia walked to Rasheed and said, "I recall my cousin complaining about the same thing to his trainer. The trainer told him that if he did not like it, he could do his push-ups naked."

She then gave him a beguiling and teasing look. "Consider yourself fortunate you were not made to exercise in the buff. Well, you can make up for it now. Stay still."

She got closer to him and commenced untying his tie, taking off his shoes, and unbuttoning his shirt.

"What are you doing, Natalia?"

"I am undressing you to give you the best bath you have ever had."

"You must be kidding. I am not going to be naked in your presence. I feel like most Arabs. We don't undress in the open. It is all under our blankets."

"Sure you are. You were naked when you made love to me. You can get naked now, without making love. What is the difference?"

"You are serious!" Rasheed said.

"I am dead serious, and it is going to be the best bath you've ever had, with massage and care you've never experienced."

Rasheed relented, but not before he asked Natalia to close the drapes all the way. She then soaked his body in steaming water.

"This feels so good. It was worth getting naked for," he told her as she rubbed his body and cleaned his hair. "I feel I am in a trance."

As he closed his eyes, Natalia quietly took her clothes off and slowly slipped into the bathtub with him. At first, he did not react, but as she kissed him, he woke up to reciprocate her passion.

CHAPTER 12

1947
Jerusalem, Palestine

Not long after Rasheed finished his training in journalism, the British government suspended the Palestinian correspondent program. Rasheed now had the training to be a journalist, but no place to practice his craft. He called David and asked if they could meet. David said yes. He then called Rasheeda. She was surprised by his news, but she saw the bright side when he told her that David was going to be there at two that afternoon.

The twins were pleased to see David arrive, accompanied by Sean O'Dowd, the bureau chief of a leading London paper, the *Daily Mail.* Sean was known to them both, especially Rasheed, since he used to patronize the American Colony bar on a regular basis. It didn't take Rasheeda long to isolate David and take him behind the bar and kiss him passionately on the lips.

David and Rasheeda returned to Sean and Rasheed. David was the first to explain the situation. "It's the beginning of the end. I don't think we will be here a year from now. I know you are on paid leave. It is not only you. Many other civil servants have also been put on leave. His Majesty's government is preparing for the final exit. Lately, it has been too expensive in the lives of British soldiers."

"I agree with David's assessment, and I have been aware of it for a week," Sean added. "This is the beginning of the end, but I have what I hope you will consider to be good news. London gave me permission to hire you as a junior correspondent for the *Daily Mail*. I can only hire you on a temporary basis, since you are still an officer in the army. I can hire you on a permanent basis once you are released from your commission. In either case, I have to secure permission from Brigadier Anderson."

Rasheed looked at Rasheeda. She winked at him to go for it. He nodded repeatedly at her, signaling that he had already decided to accept Sean's offer. "Go ahead, Mr. O'Dowd, ask Brigadier Anderson," he said. "This sounds great."

"From now on, you can call me Sean, since we are going to be colleagues."

————

When Sean approached Anderson, the brigadier was more than happy to allow Rasheed to work for the *Daily Mail*. "I am sorry to be losing Rasheed Dinar; he is a first-class journalist, and I believe he will serve the *Daily Mail* well," Anderson said. "He and the others will be decommissioned within the coming three months."

Sean drove to Beit Azar the following day to give Rasheed the good news. Rasheeda fixed Sean a Turkish coffee and excused herself to go to the inns without waiting to hear the details.

"Anderson was pleased to hear that you will be working for us,"

Sean said. "He considers this to be a natural progression for you and the others to eventually become mainstream correspondents."

Rasheed smiled. "And you like it because the British Army is paying my salary while you are getting the benefits."

"What are you talking about, Rasheed? You should be most grateful, as you will be paid by both of us at the same time; do you want to know how much we will be paying you? More than the army, for sure."

"I don't want to know, and I don't care," Rasheed said. "I am pleased this is developing the way I had hoped, and I'm looking forward to working with you."

Sean told Rasheed that he needed his help badly. He advised him not to be directly critical of the British presence in Palestine, since he was still a British officer. He asked him to continue writing about social affairs in general and about the expulsion and exodus of the Palestinian refugees toward Lebanon and Syria in particular. Rasheed was eager to start to learn from Sean, as he knew that working for a newspaper or magazine was going to be his best bet in the long run.

Despite the fact that Rasheed's inquiries to Sean were extensive, he never planned to talk about pay because he didn't want it to keep him from getting hired. Initially, he was not sure whether he was going to be paid, as he was mostly under the erroneous impression that he could not be paid by the British Army and the *Daily Mail* at the same time. He was glad this was not the case.

On his first assignment, Rasheed got to set an appointment with Hajj Amin Al-Husseini, the head of the Arab Higher Committee, a Palestinian government in exile that was popularly accepted to be the adversarial shadow government. It was this entity that was opposing the presence and plans of the British colonial power, particularly the idea of the division of Palestine between the Arab population and the Jewish population.

Rasheed knew that was not exactly what Sean had wanted from him, which was to cover the exodus of the uprooted Palestinians, but he thought it was an opportunity not to be wasted. With Sean's approval, it required a trip to Cairo, which Rasheed took by land over a two-day period. The interview took place in Al-Husseini's office in the Helmeyat AZ Zaytoun district.

The committee was headed by seven Muslim clerics and jurists, though the full membership was made up of a wide social and religious spectrum of Palestinian society.

Rasheed was most respectful and deferential toward Al-Husseini, who claimed lineage to Islam's prophet, Mohammad. On the other hand, he thought that Al-Husseini was too classical and not as progressive as Rasheed had hoped he'd be. In Rasheed's eyes, Al-Husseini was staid and respectful but did not exude a strong presence.

Although the planned article was supposed to be written under Sean's byline, Rasheed, due to his active military commission, was careful not to elicit direct or harsh criticism of the British authorities in Palestine. He didn't mind securing strong criticism of the same, provided it was polite. Rasheed asked Amin Al-Husseini, "What do you think about the decision of the British to withdraw from Palestine?"

Al-Husseini looked surprised and demurred, changing the subject. Rasheed decided not to press him for any details.

Rasheed then got to interview Menachem Begin in Tel Aviv, the head of the Irgun, an extremist underground Jewish group. He was the first Arab journalist to interview Begin.

After passing messages to Begin through a Jewish tailor in Jerusalem, Rasheed met two men at a designated restaurant. He followed the two to their car after they identified themselves. He was blindfolded and placed facedown in the back seat of the car, driven for fifteen minutes, and ended up sitting opposite Begin, who sat behind a very old desk. The desk was covered with political and historical pamphlets about the suffering of the Jews and about Palestine, mostly in Hebrew but some in English, Arabic, and Polish. The room was barely seven feet wide, and the walls were stained by rain that had seeped in. Typewriters in the corner drew Rasheed's attention: one was English, another Arabic, and a third Hebrew.

When Rasheed asked Begin if the pamphlets were his or somebody else's, Begin did not answer. "I know what you are doing," Rasheed said. "You are faking pamphlets and ascribing them to your enemies, the Arabs and the British." Still Begin would not comment.

Begin seemed more intrigued with Rasheed than the other way around, which seemed odd. Begin had been designated as a terrorist by the British and considered an outright mass criminal by the Palestinians, the result of the Irgun's very violent activities.

Begin interrupted Rasheed's interview frequently to ask questions. Rasheed had to stop him several times to get to what he thought was the main question: "What do you think about the planned British withdrawal from Palestine?"

Begin changed the subject. "How come the other Arabs are not as professional and polite as you are?"

While Rasheed was not expected to respond in any serious manner, he told Begin, "It is because I have not lost my family's

land to your people, and I am so far not threatened to lose it anytime soon."

Begin then went back to Rasheed's question about the British
withdrawal. Rasheed noticed that Begin pretended he knew all
about it while trying to pry more details from him. "Did they spec-
ify an exact date?" Begin said. "My answer depends on when they
plan to leave, and the sooner the better."

Rasheed sensed that Begin was also not aware of the British
decision. Rasheed realized that he may again have revealed something he was not supposed to reveal. Yet he felt that as a journalist
he needed to ask the same questions to be fair to the subject of
British withdrawal.

Rasheed knew he had stumbled again, forced to it by his first
stumble with Al-Husseini. After all, those two interviews were his
first with high opposition officials. He chose to change the subject
and proceeded with the rest of the interview. As much as he disliked
Begin's gruffness, he admired him for being assertive—far more so
than Al-Husseini was.

Sean, in writing the article, failed to notice any potential unin-
tended revelation on the part of Rasheed, and Rasheed had not
shared with Sean his concern about potential damage in asking
about a matter that may not have been confirmed outside the
British circles in London and Palestine.

Sean's article was published three days later, in the *Daily
Mail*. Unexpected by Rasheed, in the article Sean acknowledged
Rasheed's work and gave him credit for interviewing Al-Husseini
and Begin.

Rasheed was initially very pleased to have been credited so
soon and so publicly. But upon further contemplation, he asked

Sean if his questions, to both Al-Husseini and Begin, about the planned British withdrawal from Palestine, had been a breach of military conduct.

Sean realized what he had overlooked. "Don't worry about it," he said. "We will handle it if they say anything about the matter."

CHAPTER 13

The British wanted to know intricate details from both interviews, the one with Hajj Amin Al-Husseini and the other with Menachem Begin, the leader of the Irgun.

Brigadier Anderson summoned Rasheed to his quarters. "Rasheed, you know it is your duty as a British officer to share with us any crucial information," Anderson said. "It doesn't matter that you are on leave. What did Husseini and Begin tell you?"

"I understand, sir. It is just that no crucial information was shared with me. They were both more interested in what I knew than in sharing any of their views or plans with me."

In order to make sure, the British intelligence office intentionally spread a rumor that they had convicted Rasheed, as a British officer, and supposedly sentenced him to death in absentia, for treason, ostensibly for sharing the news of their planned withdrawal from Palestine with others. It was a ruse to pressure Rasheed into sharing his conversations with the intelligence service.

Brigadier Stewart heard about it and thought it was absurd and ridiculous. Stewart knew that such news was more widespread than the British wanted to admit. He managed to hide Rasheed with another unit and pretended that Rasheed was a leftover from one of the Australian regiments that had already left Palestine.

Having failed to induce Rasheed to share information with them, the British Army in Palestine clarified their position, dismissed the rumors they had instigated, and declared Rasheed's innocence.

When the Stern Gang, a Jewish underground terrorist group, heard about the pardon, they construed it as the British siding with the Palestinians. Yitzhak Shamir, the titular head of the Stern Gang, decided to pass the death penalty on Rasheed and his family, without any charges or trial.

David Alexander, who was the third man in the intelligence office, conveyed the intercepted decision of the Stern Gang to Rasheed and Natalia. But David was angry that the Stern Gang's conviction, unlike the British fake conviction, also included the immediate Dinar family—Rasheeda. David could not share with anyone outside the British ruling establishment that the intelligence office had a plant in the Stern Gang, who passed information to the British whenever he could.

Natalia, on her own, dug deeper into it at the kibbutz and found out that the Stern Gang had already chosen three members to carry out the death sentence. The three were to wait for further instructions about when and where to carry out the order. Natalia's source was part of the Kibbutz Cherev, the same kibbutz that almost kidnapped Rasheed. The kibbutz was loosely associated with the Stern Gang and had provided the gang half a dozen fighters over the years.

Her information came specifically from a Cherev member who

fancied her. He had proposed to unofficially marry Natalia as some ultra-right kibbutzim used to do, with the intent that the marriage would become formal once the Jewish state became a reality.

Natalia immediately went to meet with Rasheed. Before she could tell him anything, she hugged him with tears in her eyes and said with a raspy voice, "I want to keep hugging you. Don't let me stop. I have some disturbing news. The Stern Gang has decided to kill you and Rasheeda."

Rasheed looked at her with amazement. "Why? I have not done anything to them. Is it that they are jealous of the Irgun and my interviewing Begin?"

"No, it has nothing to do with the Irgun. They just think that the British forgave you despite their belief that you passed important information to Husseini. They believe that the British plan to use you in the future to pass more information to Al-Husseini."

She told Rasheed that the Stern Gang were not sure when the order would be carried out. Rasheed kissed Natalia on the lips and told her not to worry, that he had always managed to find solutions.

Rasheed's words soothed Natalia's worries for a while. But a few days later, she went to see Rasheed in Beit Azar to tell him that the three assassins had already been dispatched, and that they would act whenever they found a suitable opportunity, against him or Rasheeda. That additional news came to her from the same source.

Expressing genuine concern for Rasheed's safety, Natalia hugged him and placed her head on his chest and said, "I think it is time for you and Rasheeda to leave town. Don't worry about me. I will find you. In the meantime, communicate with my sister in Warsaw. I will secure your whereabouts from her."

"You are being too paranoid and taking this much more seriously than it deserves. You may not know it, but I have always managed to get out of one predicament after another," Rasheed said.

"They are killers of the first order, and I am not being paranoid. Since they have already dispatched the assassins, they will carry it out even if they lose one in the process. I know them, and I know what I am talking about."

Rasheed looked at Natalia wistfully and in disbelief. He could not imagine leaving her behind. When he said that he would not leave without her, Natalia pleaded with him. She told him she could not leave that easily, that her passport was hidden outside the kibbutz, and that it had expired. She promised Rasheed to join him once her passport situation got cleared up.

Rasheed argued vehemently with Natalia. He tried to tell her that he could not stand leaving her behind to face potential danger on her own. He insisted that she accompany him wherever he went, valid passport or not. "I am going to be worried about you all the time. Life will never be the same knowing you're by yourself. You have to come along, and I will fix things one way or another."

Natalia said she had the support of the kibbutzim and that staying in Palestine was the easiest of all choices. "I will know where you are at all times," she said. "I just cannot risk being stuck or put in prison at the border. I will be protected by my socialist brethren. Do not worry. They are some of the best friends and colleagues one can ever ask for. They know you, and they know of our love for each other. They will find a way to get us back together."

Almost in a daze, Rasheed took Natalia's face in his hands. He looked her in the eyes, kissed her with resigned confidence, and then smiled slightly. "I will be waiting for you in Beirut. Lebanon is the easiest place to move to, and I know lots of people at the border and in Beirut itself." Above all he knew several families from his reporting at the border between Palestine and Lebanon. There in Lebanon, he told her, he could continue working for the *Daily Mail*. "I will make sure that they know my name at the St. Georges Hotel, just like they knew it here, at the King David Hotel in Jerusalem."

Natalia nodded.

"If you get stuck trying to secure your passport from the communist regime in Poland, don't despair. If need be, I can send a couple of guys to smuggle you into Lebanon." He kissed her.

He asked her to stay overnight in Beit Azar and dispatched a message to David Alexander asking him to inform the kibbutz that Natalia would not be back till the following day. He also relayed to David that he and Rasheeda were leaving at sunset, first to Haifa and then to Lebanon.

At around midnight David knocked on Rasheed's door. He told Rasheed that he got his messages, and he asked for Rasheeda.

Rasheed went to his sister's room and woke her up. "Your man is downstairs. He is here to see you."

Rasheeda got up and smiled broadly. "Do you mind if he comes up here?" she asked.

Rasheed gave her a surprised look and then said, "Sure, why not?" He showed David to his sister's room. She was waiting for him at the door in her nightdress. They hugged and kissed all the way to her bed.

Rasheeda, as usual, took command. She hugged David, and he hugged her. "I am so glad you are here," she said. "Things are moving so fast, and I don't know when I will see you next. I know

I hesitated in the past, but I want you to make love to me. Just don't penetrate."

David told her he would see her the following day no matter what, and that he had not come over for sex. He had come to see her.

"But I want to, David, unless you do not want to."

"I want you to be safe and to wait for me tomorrow."

At that point Rasheeda took off her nightgown and bra, but she kept her panties on. They made love as best they could.

"Can you stay till the morning, David, just like Natalia is staying with Rasheed overnight?" she asked.

David told her no, but that he would be at a certain intersection, one kilometer east of Haifa, by ten in the morning. He kissed her passionately and asked her to look for him at that intersection.

He then knocked on Rasheed's door and told him the same about the rendezvous. The plan was welcomed by Rasheed, who went back to make love to Natalia for the third time. They did not go to sleep till three, and they woke up at five thirty in the morning.

Their farewell was long and emotional. Natalia cried her heart out. Rasheed looked so wistful. He kissed her right hand and kept it placed on his lips, as if he was wondering whether or not he would see her again. He kept looking at her and she at him, until he got into the car. He drove off looking into the rearview mirror.

It was less emotional for Rasheeda, for she was still expected to meet David in Haifa. She could see the sad emotions between Rasheed and Natalia. She lowered her head and said nothing, not knowing what to say under the circumstances. Rasheed took out his handkerchief and blew his nose in an effort to cover up the fact that he had teary eyes. Neither spoke. Rasheeda leaned toward Rasheed and kissed him on the forehead.

CHAPTER 14

1947
Beit Azar, Palestine

Rasheed felt light-headed. His emotions were suddenly aggregating inside his head. He could not think straight. He had a blank look on his face. His fears overwhelmed him, and his thoughts confused his decision-making. Rasheeda looked at him with great concern. It was not sadness or lamentations she saw on his face; it was utter confusion, all in a matter of seconds.

"Rasheed, look at me. It will be all right. You will be with Natalia before too long. I love her too. She is the sister I always dreamed of having, and she is the love you found, whom you esteem and adore. Let us go. We will all be together before long."

His left eye dropped a tear, which he wiped from his cheek without trying to conceal it. Before he drove off, he looked at Natalia for the last time. Tears poured down her cheeks, and she was sniffling and breathing heavily. With his arms on the steering wheel, he nodded to her and flickered his eyes. She raised her right hand and waved goodbye repeatedly and firmly.

Rasheed looked ahead, and at 6:15 a.m. they were on their way. As they passed through Jerusalem, Rasheeda noticed they were being followed. It was a chase after that. Fortunately for the twins, the three designated assassins were driving a small flatbed truck while Rasheed was driving a Chrysler sedan.

With the flatbed following them all the way, the trip seemed to take forever, and yet all at an astonishingly fast speed. Rasheed tried continually to keep the flatbed in the rearview mirror. His preoccupation with the truck almost caused him to go off the road and potentially have a major accident. He managed to put some distance between them by using alleys he was familiar with, but somehow the truck managed to almost catch up to them. They were driving much more aggressively than Rasheed was. They also had a couple of near accidents, and spare parts kept flying off the back of the truck.

Two hours later, as they approached the city of Haifa, Rasheed located an intersection. "Is this the one?" he asked nervously.

"No, no, he said it was the third intersection," Rasheeda said.

Rasheed got somewhat disoriented, and it took him longer than he'd expected to locate the intersection designated by David. The flatbed made some headway and was closing in on Rasheed and Rasheeda as they approached the appointed intersection. The assassins started shooting at them, and a bullet scraped Rasheeda's arm. Rasheed noticed blood dripping from her arm. He could barely get out his handkerchief to give it to her due to the speed and wobbly car. "It's minor. Just apply the handkerchief and press on it until we see David." Surprised, Rasheeda wanted to yell. But Rasheed stopped her. "It's minor. Don't worry about it for the time being," he told her.

As the assassins rushed to catch them, the sniper, who'd been lying on his belly on the flatbed, lost his footing and rolled off the back of the truck, still clutching his rifle. The truck screeched to a stop and reversed to pick him up. From Rasheed's rearview mirror, it was clear the man was unconscious.

By the time the sniper had revived and was given first aid, Rasheed was long gone and had located the right intersection.

Within seconds they saw David's Land Rover.

Having heard that Rasheeda was hit, David ran toward her and she toward him. He did not hesitate to kiss her passionately in the open before he and his aide attended to her wound. Using the contents of their first aid kits, they cleaned the wound, applied ointment and antibiotics, and bandaged her arm.

David took Rasheeda behind the rocks to hug and kiss her, and she responded with equal passion. "Don't worry. I will stay in touch, and before long we will be together," David told her. "Regardless of where you end up, I'll find you. I have three more months to go, and I will be out of the army. Remember, you have my mother's address and my uncle's address. My uncle is more understanding, since he served in India. I am always in touch with him. Reach out to him first."

To Rasheed David said, "You have my love traveling with you. Take care of her. I know that you will without my asking, but this time take care of her for you and for me."

"You took the words out of my mouth," Rasheed answered. "I am leaving my love behind, and I want you to take care of her, as much as you can. I am so worried about all the potential complications. Try to help her join me in Lebanon. I don't think I can live without her."

David grabbed Rasheed's right forearm. He looked him straight in the eye and shook his hand. "I will protect her as if she were Rasheeda, rest assured. Safe trip, my friend."

David helped Rasheeda into the car, smoothly sliding his palm down her bandaged arm. He gave Rasheeda a fingertip kiss on her cheek.

She and Rasheed proceeded to drive another fifty-five kilometers before stopping, as advised by David. They were two kilometers into Lebanon, and they easily found an inn that housed them for the night for two Palestinian pounds. The border crossing had not been a challenge. The immigration officer quickly stamped their passports—after they paid a hefty five Palestinian pounds each, five times the official visa fee.

The following day they were in Beirut, at the St. Georges Hotel. They stayed there for one night and then moved to another upscale but lesser known hotel, the Normandy. They figured the St. Georges Hotel was too well known and much more exposed than the Normandy.

They followed a strict schedule of walking through little-known alleys, if they could, in order not to be detected. Those alleys were challenging to maneuver, as they sometimes ended up where they started, and sometimes they ended up wandering into one cemetery or another.

"Let us not take the alleys. I don't want to end up attending anybody's funerals—above all, our own," Rasheeda told her brother.

Their concerns were unfounded, however, as the Jewish underground had no presence in Lebanon.

Within days, Rasheed met with Sean O'Dowd, the Middle East bureau chief for the *Daily Mail*. Sean hugged Rasheed and said,

"What can I do? You seem to have a job offer wherever we meet." He hired Rasheed as a stringer and offered to hire Rasheeda as a secretary and bookkeeper.

CHAPTER 15

Natalia was driven to the kibbutz by Rasheed's cousin, Saleh. She barely spoke to him as tears slid off her cheeks, slowly but continually. Saleh tried to start a conversation with her but to no avail. As he was about to drop her off, he looked into her red and wet eyes and said, "After every predicament, there is resolution. That is what the Koran says. I have a feeling the resolution is going to be that you and Rasheed will be in each other's arms, hopefully before long."

Natalia, trying to be polite, nodded silently. She wiped the tears from her cheeks, touched his right shoulder with her hand, and said, "Being in Rasheed's arms will be my resurrection, as I don't know if I can live without him."

At that point Saleh stopped. "We all have our destiny waiting for us," he said. "Nothing will please me more than for this love to blossom and to produce the most beautiful children."

Natalia got out of the car after she shook hands with Saleh. "You know where to find me if you hear from Rasheed or hear anything about him. Just come over right away. I live at Kibbutz Shivayon."

"For sure."

As Natalia entered the kibbutz, she was so disoriented she could barely tell where her room was. The layout was not dissimilar to a fort. The front was a solid concrete wall with a guarded gate in the center. The wall surrounded the living quarters and common areas on four sides. Behind the wall was a U-shaped structure that faced the front. Each side comprised eight rooms. Each room housed two to three kibbutzniks.

As she went through the gate, she stopped to collect herself. Her room was kitty-corner to the right, but she headed for a room on the left. As she approached that room, her roommate Albina saw her through a small window overlooking the court. She observed Natalia looking to her left and right as if she were lost. Albina woke up their other roommate, Adriana, who was napping.

They both ran toward Natalia. As they addressed her, Natalia gave them a blank look, barely recognizing either one. "Natalia, this is Albina. Look at me. What is wrong?" Albina said. Natalia did not answer. Suddenly she felt she was about to drop to the ground. Albina and Adriana managed to hold her up. Two male kibbutzniks came to their help. The four carried Natalia to her room.

They put her to bed. It was a torturous sleep. Natalia was going through one nightmare after another. On a couple occasions, she would attempt to talk to Rasheed: "Hold Junior for a minute. Let me get the door," she was heard blurting in her sleep.

Albina and Adriana wondered if Natalia was pregnant. They could not tell. When they summoned the kibbutz physician, he told them not to misconstrue things and that such nightmares were sometimes related to one's reality and sometimes they were totally unrelated to reality.

Four hours later, Natalia woke up feeling much better. Albina and Adriana insisted on giving her a bath. They borrowed the large aluminum bathtub from the supply room and bathed her for forty minutes.

She rested until her hair dried, and then she told her roommates that she felt better, totally revived, and she wanted to take a walk outside the kibbutz.

"I feel like fresh air, all in the open," she told them. Adriana suggested she and Albina go along.

"No, I just want to clear my head. Don't worry," Natalia said.

She walked toward Kibbutz Cherev. In twenty minutes, she was halfway between the two kibbutzim.

Out of nowhere, she saw someone heading toward her. She turned around to go back to her kibbutz and then heard the person calling her by name. She stopped and looked back. At first, she could not tell who it was, but as he got closer, she realized it was Israel, the one who had a crush on her and wanted to informally marry her until he could marry her formally once the state of Israel was created.

Israel would have been of no attraction to Natalia even if Rasheed had not been in the picture. He was just five feet six inches tall, three inches shorter than she was. He was dressed in a pair of black slacks and a long-sleeved white shirt, rolled up at the arms. His stubby beard was sparse and messy, like his unkempt hair.

"It is me, Israel. How come you did not recognize me?" he asked her.

"Hi, Israel. Nice to see you," she said. "I am not feeling well. I just want to be alone."

"What is wrong?" he asked. "Let me try to help. I'd like to spend some time with you. You know I still would like to marry you."

"No, Israel. Nobody is going to marry me. I just lost my boyfriend. He is gone. He left Palestine this morning," she told him as she opened up to him for the first time without any thought of the consequences and without any consideration that he was from Kibbutz Cherev, the right-wing kibbutz.

As he collected himself and pretended it was of no consequence, he said, "You have a boyfriend! Did he go back to Poland?"

"To Poland! No, he went to Lebanon, no thanks to the Stern Gang," she answered.

Taken aback by the revelation, Israel acted disappointed but at the same time tried to elicit more information. "I have never met a Lebanese Jew," he said.

Still without much thought, she looked at him with some disgust. "A Jew? He is a Palestinian Arab."

Israel looked at her with total surprise and almost revulsion. "A Palestinian! I guess I will leave you by yourself."

Natalia recalled that Israel's father had been a communist who fought with the Russian advancing armies and later joined the foreign ministry of the communist Polish government. As Israel was leaving, she said, "Maybe your father can help me! I need my passport renewed."

Israel ignored Natalia's inquiry and hurriedly headed toward his kibbutz. She did the same but toward her own kibbutz. She was not her normal self and totally disregarded the implications of her exchange with Israel. He was the only one who was considerate toward her and her friends, but his treatment of her was based solely on his own private hopes.

Natalia spent the first two days after Rasheed left in a daze, going into tears at times or napping or just wallowing while gazing at the wall. On the third day, she took another walk, the same walk she had taken the prior two days, but this time she didn't return to the kibbutz.

After two hours, Albina and Adriana went looking for her. They were careful not to approach Kibbutz Cherev and were accompanied by five male kibbutzniks, two of them carrying handguns. They were unsuccessful.

Adriana and Albina then suggested to the council of the kibbutz to contact the council at Kibbutz Cherev. Twelve kibbutzniks headed to Kibbutz Cherev. They were expected and were let in. Upon inquiring about Natalia, they were told that her whereabouts were unknown to them.

Albina then shared with the group the name of Israel and the fact that he had proposed marriage to Natalia. The group from Shivayon invited Natalia's roommates to meet with him. Adriana took the lead. "Israel, have you seen Natalia lately?" she asked. "We know that you proposed marriage to her several times and that you fancied her."

"No, I have not seen her in a long time," Israel said.

Adriana glanced at Albina, and both realized something was wrong.

"You know and I know that you are lying," Adriana said. "You saw Natalia three days ago, and she told us what you two talked about. You didn't like the fact that she was in love with an Arab. Isn't this the case?"

When he heard that Adriana and her friends knew about his encounter with Natalia, he changed his tune. "Yes, I saw her, and I talked to her, but I did not have anything to do with this disappearance," Israel said. "I think she was kidnapped by three people. I think they belonged to the Stern Group."

Everyone noticed that Israel referred to the Stern as a "group," while just about all the kibbutz communities in Palestine referred to them as a "gang." They did not know what to make of his choice of words. They decided to go back to their kibbutz and regroup. They told Israel and the Kibbutz Cherev council that they would like to come back to see them the following day.

They then scoured the area. They located an Arab sheepherder. One of the male Shivayon kibbutzniks who spoke Arabic asked the shepherd if he had seen Natalia. They described her height and looks to him. Luckily, he had. He said he saw her arguing with three men.

"Did you see the men?" Adriana asked through her Arabic-speaking friend. The shepherd answered in the affirmative. She added, "Listen, if I buy one of your sheep, could you come with us to see if you could recognize the men?" He readily accepted their bargain.

Two days later—and after the council at Kibbutz Shivayon told the council of Kibbutz Cherev that they had a witness—it was arranged that the shepherd would first look at Israel and then they would have the shepherd look at all the men in the kibbutz. To their surprise, the Cherev council accepted.

The shepherd studied Israel and said he had never seen him before and that all three men were heavier set and taller than Israel. It took a whole three hours for him to try to identify any familiar faces at Cherev. In the end, he could not find one familiar face, and he claimed he was sure none of the three men he'd seen Natalia with were there at Cherev.

Yet, the Shivayon group were suspicious of Israel. Albina proposed that they interview Israel again. She thought he was hiding something. It was arranged for him to be interrogated again. The Shivayon group wanted to know about his encounter with Natalia in full detail. They wanted to know where the two met, what they said to each other, and how long they spent with each other.

In the interrogation, Israel gave two opposing answers to the same question. He first said that Natalia meant nothing to him, and then he said that he wanted to marry her.

Adriana asked in a loud, threatening voice, "Did you have anything to do with Natalia's kidnapping? Although you may not have done anything to her yourself, did you have others do something to her?"

Israel's face reddened and then slowly became pale. He ran out of the room without saying a word.

The Shivayon group then met with the Cherev council. They told them what had happened. Although the Cherev council was sincere in trying to find out what had happened to Natalia, Israel refused to talk.

Early one morning, Israel was nowhere to be found. After thorough investigation, the Cherev council told the Shivayon council that they found out that Israel had gone back to Poland, where his family still lived and where his communist father was working in the foreign ministry.

The efforts to find Natalia continued on a daily basis, yet nothing new was unearthed. Both the Cherev and the Shivayon councils concluded that Israel knew what had happened and may have been involved, but they were unable to reach him or his family to inquire further. Other than the Jews aligned with the communist regime, most Jews were not looked upon as loyal to the new pro-Russian government.

Albina and Adriana became very distraught and guilt-ridden over Natalia's disappearance. On the other hand, they promised themselves and each other never to stop looking for her. They were afraid that she had been killed, or that she had been kidnapped to prevent her from possibly marrying an Arab.

CHAPTER 16

For more than three weeks, Rasheed and Rasheeda did not hear from Natalia. Alicia, Natalia's sister, told them that she had not heard a thing from Natalia either. They checked with Kibbutz Shivayon but learned nothing. Later Adriana sent Rasheed a note through the Jesuits:

> *I am heartbroken to inform you that Natalia is not at the kibbutz. It has been almost three weeks since she disappeared. We think she was kidnapped by the Stern Gang. I am so sorry about all of this, but I and Albina and my other comrades will not stop until we find her. We hope and believe she is still alive. The Stern Gang has killed other Jews but only on rare occasions. I will keep you informed of any developments. Stay with me. I am still optimistic. Be strong and wait for Natalia.*
>
> *Your sister,*
> *Adriana*

Rasheed was beside himself and could not sleep for days. Rasheeda was stunned at the news. She felt like she had lost her only sister. She tried not to show her emotions openly for fear she would cause Rasheed more pain.

One evening Rasheeda went into her brother's room and tried to soothe his shattered emotions. She found him half-asleep in bed and nudged him to wake up.

"I think she is paying the price for what I am accused of," he said, blinking as his eyes adjusted to the light. "I think the Stern Gang will execute her, if they have not done so already, to take revenge and make my life miserable. I should have acted like a man and insisted on bringing her along, passport or no passport. I am to blame." He set his head on the pillow, which was wrapped in his right arm, and slowly went to sleep.

His behavior became frantic, and sometimes Rasheeda did not know what to do. She tried to avoid being in the same room with him. He kept murmuring to himself that he was to blame.

He contacted the British, American, and Polish ambassadors, but none were able to help him. It was only the Jesuits who kept him up on the general local news of Palestine.

In the end, Rasheed could not tell if it was the Stern Gang or one of its splinter groups that kidnapped Natalia. He made it known that he was willing to pay a ransom of five thousand pounds for Natalia, but after four weeks there were no takers. The ordeal was devastating to him. Rasheeda kept him from going crazy, despite her own sense of deep loss.

She was deeply worried about Natalia but chose not to show it in order not to exacerbate Rasheed's deteriorating state of mind. The pressures on Rasheeda were mounting as she was juggling so many emotions, some of which were positive, yet everything was overwhelmed by the news of Natalia's disappearance. While not feeling truly confident about the situation, she consoled herself and even exhibited confidence through her inner thoughts that David would be in her life, in some form. She was waiting for him to assure her of that.

Coupled with her feelings for David, she gathered strength by recognizing the new freedoms that Beirut provided her. It was easy for her to notice the many Muslim women without headscarves. She observed them moving around town, unaccompanied by a male, shopping and going to the university. The social freedoms for women were visible, and the potential for her own personal growth was clearly apparent.

In her mind, she had several things she was hoping to accomplish by taking advantage of the new open social setup she was in. Yet Natalia's situation created a fog, which prevented Rasheeda from crystalizing her thoughts and her hopes.

Their life in Beirut became multifaceted. Good news trickled in, along with greater and more varied challenges. The first touch of good news was meeting Sean O'Dowd, who was very impressed with Rasheeda.

Initially when Rasheed relayed Sean's offer of employment to Rasheeda, she was apprehensive. She thought she was being offered a job she was not trained for.

Rasheed went to see Mr. O'Dowd. "Sean, I think you know that both Rasheeda and I are going through a tough time," he said. "Rasheeda is concerned that your generous offer may end up doing more harm than good. If she fails at this new assignment, it would just add a new failure to an even bigger failure, that of keeping

Natalia safe. Any additional failures would be disastrous, especially for Rasheeda."

Sean asked Rasheed to give him the room to talk to Rasheeda. He told Rasheed that he realized that they both were ultra-sensitive due to their recent traumatic experiences, but at the same time neither of them recognized how talented Rasheeda was. "I know what I am talking about," he said. "I know about the talent that is available here and what is available in London, and I know that Rasheeda is two grades above the best of them."

When he met with her, Sean said, "Listen, Rasheeda, I am going to repeat to you what I told Rasheed," he said. "You are better than the best of them. I believe I know you. Leave it in my hands. I will train you, and you will be proud of yourself. How about it? Trust me."

"I am happy to try it out," she said, "but let me know if I don't do as expected."

"I will train you," he said.

It was the statement Rasheeda was waiting to hear. Sean managed to calm her concerns.

Sean O'Dowd told Rasheed that Rasheeda, by helping her late father run the two inns and being fluent in English and French, had more knowledge than she knew she had. He reminded his friend that Rasheeda typed English and French very well.

Rasheed took Sean's words to heart and decided to encourage Rasheeda to accept the offer. Rasheed's strong encouragement changed her mind about accepting Sean's offer.

"You will do well," Rasheed said. "Do you recall when you were apprehensive about managing the two inns, and how well you did? This is the same; you will see."

Rasheeda started thinking very positively about her acceptance of Sean's offer. In short order, she switched from being apprehensive to feeling that it was an opportunity to realize her dreams by becoming a well-rounded and sophisticated woman.

She wore a headdress for the first three days at work, but she discarded it on the fourth day. It was easy for her to see other Muslim women who were not wearing scarves working at other news organizations. She expected Rasheed to say something about it, but he didn't. Rasheed wanted Rasheeda to start feeling good about her own decisions, without the necessity of his approval or lack thereof. Rasheeda stood out for her beauty and fine clothing, but in general she seemed to fit right in.

Rasheed wanted to show his appreciation to Sean, since he initially was worried about Rasheeda being unprepared to take on the responsibilities assigned to her.

"I think I was wrong, and you were right. With your guidance, she seems to have blossomed in her job."

"Listen, Rasheed, when I observe Rasheeda interacting with the other girls around this business neighborhood," Sean said, "I see a beautiful and very graceful rose among lesser roses."

"I am glad you feel this way. I hate to say it about my own sister, but I agree with you, and I don't know what I would have done without her. She has always been there for me, before and after Natalia's disappearance."

Little by little, with the brotherly, caring help from Sean O'Dowd, Rasheeda more than got the hang of being a secretary and office manager. She was intrigued by so many things in Beirut, big and small, including when Sean asked her to prepare and serve coffee to his visitors. She had no idea that coffee was served in offices. She was used to being ladylike and offering and serving drinks at home. In Jerusalem, most neighborhoods had their own small coffee shops. A waiter used to make the rounds every twenty minutes and take orders. In Beirut, it was the duty of the exclusively female secretaries to prepare coffee and tea.

———————

Since leaving Palestine, Rasheeda had been getting messages from David's uncle in London. David was still in the army, busy first with leaving Palestine and later getting settled in temporary quarters in England. The messages were short and general. They all said, in one way or another, that David was well and sending his love. When she received a fourth message that said, "David misses you and sends you his best," she started to worry that David and his uncle were avoiding relaying bad news and letting time ease her out of David's life.

Such thoughts gave her impetus to fill her time to the brink, to try to take her mind off David. She first sat for four exams to qualify her correspondence courses for acceptance by the American University of Beirut. From passing the tests with high grades, she earned full credits for the whole first year of engineering school. Then she enrolled at the American University of Beirut, taking two additional engineering courses.

She loved taking breaks from her work to enjoy a cup of tea with her friends from the other news services. She marveled at how things were much more organized than they were in Beit Azar.

Villagers there used to visit each other without notice, just about any time after sunrise and before sunset. At the *Daily Mail* office, most everything was done by appointment.

Rasheeda was still hopeful about David but slightly disheartened. Then out of the blue one day as she was typing one of Sean's articles on the Telex machine, David entered the *Daily Mail*'s offices. Without looking up, she said, "I will be with you in just a moment," one of the routine statements Sean had taught her. Upon finishing the article, she looked up to see David watching her, beaming.

She was stunned for a few seconds and then ran toward him. He hugged her and squeezed her warmly and passionately. "I missed you so much!" he said. "They let me go early and decommissioned my unit."

As her eyes teared up again, she said, "And I missed *you* so much. I was getting worried after receiving the polite messages from your uncle."

"Those Telex messages were being read by four or five different people, at any time," David told her. "That's why we kept them nondescript. When I got to read them later, I was afraid that you may have gotten the wrong impression, and that is why I got here as fast as I could."

She went into Sean's office, smiling and bright-eyed and holding David's hand. "Look who I have here," she said as she approached his desk.

After greeting David warmly, Sean told Rasheeda, "What are you waiting for? Go! Go and surprise Rasheed at the St. Georges Hotel."

Rasheeda and David walked together the two blocks. Since they were in public, they did not hold hands, but they looked and smiled at each other, enamored by the moment.

David could not wait. He was anxious to calm Rasheeda's anxiety before meeting Rasheed. "Will you be my wife?" he asked her without much fanfare or introduction.

"Yes, yes. Who else could I marry! It is you and only you, yes!" she said after she got over her pleasant surprise.

Rasheed was no less warm in greeting David than Sean was. He felt some relief that his sister was no longer in a forlorn state, as he was. "Thank God you are here, David," he said. "You can't imagine how great it is to see you."

CHAPTER 17

1948
Beirut, Lebanon

Rasheed's state of mind improved, especially with the news about Rasheeda and David getting engaged. Rasheed was so happy that David had proposed to his sister. As he was the male and nearest to being a father figure in her life, he felt that her planned wedding was the fulfillment of a duty that had passed to him after their father died.

But as much as he tried, he could not bring himself to sustain such feelings of satisfaction on an even keel, not with Natalia gone. Rasheeda's good news was an intermittent respite but not a permanent relief.

The following morning, Rasheed entered the St. Georges Hotel lobby at eleven. Before turning right toward the bar as he went through the rotating door on the north side, he looked to his left into the depth of a very long and elegant reception area. There he saw an Irish hat resting on a coffee table on the left side, one that seemed familiar.

Rasheed did not want to look straight at the owner of the hat, who was looking southward. Instead, he waved to the chief concierge who was standing behind the concierge desk on the right, with a commanding view of the reception area. Rasheed pointed to the owner of the hat, asking if the concierge knew him. The concierge shook his head no.

Rasheed proceeded to the desk to peek from an advantageous angle. To his utter surprise, he found Father Federico waiting for him. It was Federico's hat after all, as Rasheed had suspected. After they hugged and kissed, they sat down to have orange juice and coffee.

"I know your mind is on Natalia all the time, so I have held on to this news for two weeks," Federico said, "hoping that she would be with you before we got together. But I could not wait any longer. The Vatican wants an answer right away. They want to buy your Mount Calvary property very badly. They have had this in mind for some time. I managed to squeeze from them four million pounds for that land. Is that acceptable?"

Rasheed, completely astonished, said, "Are you kidding me? Of course, it is more than acceptable. Are you sure it is four million pounds?"

"I am one-hundred-percent sure. I have the offer in writing."

After lunch, Federico left to go back to Cyprus to process the sale. Before Federico left, he admonished Rasheed not to count his chickens before they hatched. Federico knew well that the Vatican was also very political.

Despite that good news, Rasheed began drinking more, but not heavily enough to impede his journalistic duties or to prevent him from acting prudently. He got somewhat confused. He was drinking to celebrate the unbelievable sale of the Calvary land but also continued to be overwhelmed by Natalia's disappearance. Natalia's case got the best of the situation, and his celebration was a mere excuse, under the circumstances.

Rasheeda noticed the increase in her brother's alcohol consumption, and one afternoon she said to David, "You know how much I care about Rasheed. Now that we are planning to get married, we—I mean, you and I—in a concerted effort, should use the time between now and our wedding to soothe his feelings. I know it is difficult, but let us think of ways. I have been unable to find a way, but maybe you will."

David answered that he hoped that their wedding would change things for Rasheed.

"We both know how much your happiness means to him. It may trigger a revival in him," David said.

Rasheeda asked him to visit with her brother on his own and try to help, to try to find an opening.

David met with Rasheed at the St. Georges Hotel bar at eleven in the morning, just as Rasheed commenced his daily drinking. He went around and around but could not get to the subject. David always considered Rasheed to be the wiser one, as Rasheed always managed to come out with philosophical proverbs that froze David's arguments. As they were drinking, David noticed another elegant gentleman sitting at the bar with a rather sad look. David thought bringing that gentleman into the conversation somehow might give David a potentially indirect way into the subject of Rasheed's state of mind.

David introduced himself. "I am here to visit my fiancée," he said to the man. "Whom do I have the pleasure of meeting?" The other man introduced himself as Ibrahim Alvarez. David introduced Rasheed to Ibrahim. "He is my future brother-in-law."

David then asked Ibrahim if he always started drinking at eleven in the morning. "That is what many do in my hometown, London," David said.

"Not really," Ibrahim said. "I am used to drinking wine in the evening only, but I am now drinking scotch this early because my troubles have gotten more serious. I am on my way to Jerusalem, waiting for my visa to come through, seeking help from the Virgin Mary at the Church of the Holy Sepulchre!"

"I don't think your troubles could be half as serious as mine," Rasheed said, "at least I hope they are not."

Anxious to share his troubles with someone, Ibrahim took the opportunity to unload on Rasheed, telling him that he was about to lose his business, made up of four wineries and worth over three million pounds sterling, solely because he was short sixty-five thousand pounds sterling.

"Well, you have not lost them yet," Rasheed said. "I have already lost my one and only love. Some group decided to kidnap her, and we don't know who exactly this group is," Rasheed said, having already consumed two stiff drinks.

Ibrahim, in a very sophisticated way, lamented Rasheed's misfortune. He then added, "I wish I could help you, but how can a Spaniard help this situation here in the Middle East? If it were in Spain or somewhere in Europe, I might be able to help."

"What are you looking sad about? Is it anything other than sixty-five thousand pounds sterling?" Rasheed asked.

David, having lost control of the conversation, excused himself and quietly left to see Rasheeda.

As the two were talking, a very beautiful young lady sat where David had been sitting, blocking their vision of each other. Rasheed did not want to be presumptuous. He did not know whether Ibrahim and the lady knew each other. Within minutes another beautiful lady stopped next to the first one, and the two started talking to each other. Rasheed suspected then that the two did not know Ibrahim. His alcohol had slowed him down, and he did nothing.

It took the two ladies less than ten minutes to leave together. Rasheed and Ibrahim resumed their conversation.

Rasheed then invited Ibrahim for lunch. "I will accept your invitation if you allow me to take care of the drinks!" Ibrahim said, and he proceeded to attempt to take his wallet from the inside pocket of his jacket.

"Holy Mary, my wallet is gone," Ibrahim said. That statement sobered Rasheed up a bit. Ibrahim looked all around him and in every pocket in his slacks and coat. He was at a loss to figure out where his wallet was.

Rasheed asked how much money he had in the wallet. "The money is not the major issue; the major issue is my passport, which was in the wallet."

Rasheed gazed into Ibrahim's eyes, went pensive for a split second, and then tapped him on the shoulder and said, "Wait for me here; I will be right back."

He hurried out into the lobby and headed to the reception desk. There he asked to be connected to the deputy chief of police, Colonel Baraka. Baraka was one of the many officials Rasheed dealt with on a regular basis, and they had become friends in the process.

"Colonel, I have a guest, and I believe he has been had by the same pickpocket gang you told me about the other day. They fit your description all the way—beautiful, sophisticated, and work in twos or threes. One of the two was carrying a box of sweets from Tripoli, where you told me they are supposed to have their headquarters."

Baraka was quick to arrive, and after a few questions to each, he was also convinced that it was the same gang. "In a strange way you are in luck. We are giving this gang our top priority as they pulled the same on two members of parliament—one of whom is the speaker of the house. If you are willing to cooperate with us, we may be able to catch them red-handed," Baraka told Ibrahim.

Ibrahim agreed to cooperate but mentioned that all his money and his passport had been taken.

"Don't panic," Rasheed said. "Between me and the colonel, I think we can help you out."

Rasheed led Ibrahim to the front desk and spoke to the receptionist. "Listen, Joseph. I am guaranteeing Ibrahim Alvarez's room charges to date and charges for another week's stay."

"Consider it done," Joseph answered.

Ibrahim was relieved and felt assured that he was not going to be out on the street.

"I cannot believe it. We have just met a couple of hours ago, and you are going out of your way to help out," he said. "I am most grateful and very impressed. I just hope I am going to have the opportunity to reciprocate this generous treatment."

Rasheed took Ibrahim to his office, only two blocks from the St. Georges Hotel. He invited him to use one of the four offices, on the twelfth floor of an office high-rise, to make as many calls as he needed to Madrid.

Ibrahim then called his aides in Madrid to have them transfer money, in care of Rasheed. The following day, the Spanish bank Telexed Ibrahim informing him that the transfer had already taken place and it was only a matter of time before he would receive the sum.

"Ibrahim, you can keep me company in the meantime until your money arrives," Rasheed said.

Ibrahim's sorry episode was a relief of sorts for Rasheed; it helped him take his mind off Natalia's disappearance. At the same time, he was enjoying Ibrahim's company, especially his openness about his problems and his level of sophistication.

To distract Ibrahim from worrying about the loss of his wallet, Rasheed made small talk; he asked him why he was given his first name. "Ibrahim is a popular Arab first name!" Rasheed exclaimed.

"My name was given to me in recognition of my Arab roots," Ibrahim said. "My great-great-great-grandfather, generations ago, fought with the Muslim forces invading Spain. He was an Orthodox Christian. They helped the Muslims in the invasion, as they did against Byzantium, on the basis of all being Arabs." He told Rasheed that his original family name was Al-Faris, which was changed to Alvarez as the family converted to Catholicism, after the Spanish Inquisition.

He shared with Rasheed that he inherited two wineries from his father and bought two more on his own. His father made mainly white Malvar wine, and Ibrahim wanted to get into producing Garnacha red wine.

Unfortunately for Ibrahim, the wine market got hit badly just after he bought the two wineries, which led to his financial problems. While he was able to service his loans to the bank and had been doing so diligently for five years, the bank, as a result of the decline in the price of wine, decided to call the loan. Ibrahim found himself short sixty-five thousand pounds.

Ibrahim was twenty-seven years old, one year Rasheed's senior, and handsome with a serene face. He was engaged to a school-teacher from Barcelona. They had not set a date for their wedding out of fear his financial situation would deteriorate further.

His worries were visible on his face, and whenever he exhibited a pensive look, he looked years older. He wore well-tailored suits all the time, complemented with streamlined and well-matched ties. Rasheed, who did not like to wear ties, wanted to make Ibrahim feel good about himself, so he also started wearing exquisite-looking ties.

Eventually, the police discovered the thieves and raided their house. Ibrahim's items were recovered, and he was taken to Rasheed's house. Ibrahim was effusive in thanking the police for their quick action. As he was handed his money and passport back, he looked at Rasheed and said, "I will be forever indebted to you. I really did not think I would be getting my things back. I can't imagine what I would have done if I were on my own!"

CHAPTER 18

More good news came Rasheed's way. Federico, this time accompanied by Aisha, showed up again, totally unexpectedly. Federico's presence always cheered up Rasheed. Federico wanted to talk to him, but Rasheed was still busy with Ibrahim's case, trying to wrap it up with the police. While they had apprehended the two pickpocket ladies, they were keen to get to the leader of the gang. Rasheed wanted to use all the good news, including Federico's presence, to divert his attention from thinking of Natalia.

That evening, Rasheeda was cooking as Rasheed welcomed David, Ibrahim, Federico, and Aisha to his place. Federico was getting antsy, as he had not had a chance to tell Rasheed any part of his good news.

When he finally got the opportunity, he asked to see Rasheed on the side. There he told Rasheed that he had concluded the four-million-pound deal for the Mount Calvary land. Rasheed could not believe his ears: the deal had almost gone through.

By the time Federico repeated the news, Rasheed had gone into the living room to tell Ibrahim. "Finally, I have good news for you. I think your loan will come through within days."

That evening everyone was drinking and having fun. Rasheeda, sitting warmly next to David, directed the attention toward Aisha. "I am so impressed that you speak English and French so fluently," she said. "You are so natural and smart. Congratulations." Federico was waiting to hear something of the sort. He was more pleased with the praise than Aisha was.

In the morning, everyone but Aisha went to the Italian embassy. Rasheed and Rasheeda signed off on the documents of sale, and the other three acted as witnesses. Also joining them was the representative of Barclays bank.

The bank arranged a loan of sixty-five thousand dollars to Ibrahim, with Ibrahim providing a collateral to cover half of the loan. Rasheed guaranteed the other half. Ibrahim could not believe that a man he had met only three weeks earlier would save him from bankruptcy. He told Rasheed, "I am indebted to you for the rest of my life, and I hope I will have the opportunity to reciprocate your unusual generosity."

Rasheed sarcastically replied, "My arranging the loan was not enough to make up for my delinquency in protecting you from our local thieves. I became your host and forgot to alert you to some of the dangers around here." He called Rasheeda and David to the side and asked his sister if she minded sharing a hundred thousand pounds with Federico, for his help in the sale of the land.

"Why are you asking me?" she said. "It's your land."

"No, Rasheeda, everything that father left will be evenly divided between the two of us."

Rasheeda was most pleasantly surprised, as under the best

of circumstances she was entitled to half of Rasheed's share, per Islamic sharia. David told Rasheed that he and Rasheeda did not need the money, and that on top of his many real estate holdings, he alone owned seven separate companies, with a total of twenty-one hundred employees.

"Rasheeda deserves the money. She can do with the proceeds anything she sees fit; it is no longer my role to tell her how to spend it," Rasheed said.

Federico tried in vain to turn down the gift, but both Rasheed and Rasheeda wouldn't take no for an answer.

CHAPTER 19

Having talked to Rasheeda and secured her approval, David got rather drunk, having consumed four stiff scotch drinks. He decided to ask for Rasheeda's hand one more time. "With your approval, Rasheed, I am hoping that as of four months from now, Rasheeda and I will become known as Earl and Lady Alexander."

Rasheed went silent for a long while, but as he composed himself, he said, pretending it was a new announcement on the part of David, "Whatever pleases Rasheeda pleases me, and I just want to hear her say that she is in agreement with your wishes."

Rasheeda played along, not minding restating her approval: "He is my love, and what pleases him pleases me. I want to be his wife, with or without title; it just does not matter."

Sean O'Dowd, the *Daily Mail* bureau chief, gave another toast. Ibrahim's visa never came through, but he had secured his loan. He was enormously grateful to Rasheed. He drank a lot that evening, feeling overwhelmed by Rasheed's generosity. He, like David, lost track of what he had said and once again told Rasheed that he would do anything for him, when and where he could, and for Rasheed not to hesitate to ask for his help for as long as they both lived.

A few months later the state of Israel was created, and the news about Natalia died altogether. None of the ambassadors could find anything about her. Despite many attempts by many news organizations, Natalia was nowhere to be found or to be heard from.

It took Rasheed ten months to realize that he was physically and mentally wasting away as a result of his excessive drinking. What triggered that realization was a significant piece of news, relayed through the good offices of the Polish ambassador in Lebanon, that he, Rasheed, and Natalia had a baby boy called Omar, who was being cared for by Alicia, Natalia's sister in Warsaw. The ambassador also relayed that the baby was smuggled out of prison by her friend, Albina, and then flown to Warsaw. The ambassador could not give Alicia many details, as Palestine was in chaos and large homes were being converted into prisons by one group after another.

Upon hearing the news and the details, Rasheed could barely contain himself. He could not compute what had happened. He was confused and angry but also elated—confused because he couldn't understand why Natalia had hidden her pregnancy from him and angry that she had done so, and elated because he was a father, even if it was unexpected. He was also particularly confused because the ambassador could not tell him anything about Natalia's whereabouts, though the embassy must have questioned Albina and asked which prison she smuggled the baby out of.

A few days later the ambassador contacted him again to inform him that Natalia was still missing, and Alicia wanted to deliver Omar to him, if he wanted to raise the baby. When he asked about how the baby had been saved but Natalia was still missing, the ambassador told him that Natalia's kibbutz knew that the baby had been separated from Natalia and that they took an enormous risk to save the baby. They did not know where Natalia was—then or now—and they did not know whether she was dead or alive.

Rasheed told the ambassador that he had budgeted the money to finance anything needed for his son, including delivering him into his care. The ambassador, hoping to nurture a close relationship with a prominent journalist, refused to accept any money and promised Rasheed that the Polish government would take care of the expenses in delivering Omar to him in short order. Rasheeda immediately became a loving surrogate mother to Omar. She cherished the opportunity and hoped that Omar's surfacing would ease Rasheed's never-ending pain. That gave her a second excuse to resign from her job at the *Daily Mail*. She concentrated on Omar's care and her two courses at the university. She took pictures with Omar and mailed them to David on a weekly basis.

Per Rasheed's request, a Catholic convent sent him a nanny named Maria. With each day, Rasheed could see Natalia's likeness more and more in Omar, and he increasingly doted on his son. Omar's appearance began Rasheed's very slow and trying recovery, from a sense of total loss to a sense of some compensation, which was incomplete at best.

Shortly after Omar's arrival, *Newsweek* ended Rasheed's occasional journalistic contributions to the magazine. They thought his views were slanted toward the Palestinians. That separation came to the attention of Henry Luce, the editor-in-chief of *Time* magazine, who had read Rasheed's articles in the *Daily Mail*. Knowing that Rasheed was no longer working for his competitor, Henry Luce, on his way to interview the Shah of Iran, stopped in Beirut to offer Rasheed a staff correspondent job. Rasheed accepted the offer with much appreciation and great expectations.

As Luce and Rasheed talked, dined, and toured Lebanon, mutual affection and friendship started between the two. Luce was impressed by Rasheed's contacts with Middle East officials and politicians and especially contacts with many of the shadow characters, whether rebels or kingmakers, who hesitated to make public appearances. Rasheed allowed their positions and opinions to be known without a hint of their persona or their whereabouts. Luce liked Rasheed's approach and promised to back him to keep his sources concealed.

No sooner had Rasheed concluded his very successful meetings with Luce than Rasheeda left for London. Within a couple of weeks of her departure, Maria began calling Rasheed several times a day to seek his guidance. He realized that Rasheeda had performed like a caring mother to Omar, obscuring the failings of Maria, who wasn't exactly up to the job.

"I don't know what to say, but the nanny is failing to attend to Omar's needs," he told his sister in a phone conversation. "He has gotten sick too many times since your departure. I am terribly sorry; I won't be able to make it to the wedding. I need to stay here. I haven't had any success finding a trustworthy replacement. I have no choice but to take care of Omar myself, under the circumstances. He has not been feeling well lately. He just recovered from pneumonia, and his pediatrician is concerned his immune system has suffered and he may catch pneumonia again or some other infection."

Sensing Rasheeda's disappointment, he added, "I have already talked to Ibrahim and Sean, and they are eager to escort you through the ceremony."

———————

Three days a week during the weeks leading up to the wedding, Rasheeda and David toured London and the surrounding countryside for Rasheeda to get acquainted and develop a feel for her surroundings. During this time, she was also getting ready for the wedding. Even though David had all kinds of helpers, professionals, friends, and family members willing to do whatever was necessary, Rasheeda, like her mother, wanted to choreograph the ceremony.

She chose to wear a specially designed Palestinian white thoab with buttons in the back and Beit Azar's embroidered signature design. She wore her hair at its usual length, with a two-inch-wide slice braided from the front of her head, going back to her shoulders.

She wore the thoab in the Unitarian church, escorted by Sean and Ibrahim, as the minister and the guests heard her and David give their vows. The guests—many of Rasheed's friends and colleagues living in England, some from other European countries, and some from as far as Lebanon and Palestine—were excited to watch this modern-looking Muslim female accept their church and its simple rituals.

Rasheeda asked and was given permission by the Unitarian church to have Koranic verses recited at the ceremony. They were verses of blessings of the marriage tradition. While they were from the Koran, they were applicable universally and were appreciated by all the guests.

You shall encourage those of you who are single to get married.
They may marry the righteous among your male and female servants.
If they are poor, God will enrich them from his grace.
God is bounteous and all knowing.

After church, they went to David's late grandfather's palatial house, which was used by the different family members for special occasions. There she continued to be escorted by Sean O'Dowd and Ibrahim Alvarez. She walked into the center of a very long hall while the guests cheered and clapped. As the guests stood up, she and her escorts stopped. Two young ladies unbuttoned the thoab and removed it. From beneath it, a shining aqua-blue—her mother's favorite color—Syrian brocade wedding dress appeared, gloriously and gracefully embroidered in Damascus. The change of dresses seemed to signal a transformation from her own village to her new surroundings in London. The guests were amazed and taken aback by her beauty and poise.

Sean and Ibrahim gave her to David, and David and Rasheeda walked arm in arm and made a full circle, going back to the center of the room and sitting at the middle point of one of the two-hundred-foot long tables. It was a glorious and joyous wedding, attended by most of the royal family members, short of the Queen and her husband.

None was happier at the occasion than David's uncle, James, who had known Muslims and Hindus in India and maintained friendships with them through the years. James gave them a huge house in Nice, France, as a wedding gift. They also received half a dozen considerable gifts, including two Arabian horses from David's mother, one for him and one for her.

After dinner, the dancing began. Without telling David, Rasheeda had taken three weeks of intensive dance lessons. She was almost a natural. One thing she had not been told was that she would be expected to dance with many at the ceremony. She was under the impression that she would dance with David only. David's uncle was the first to ask her to dance. More importantly, he was the one to let her know that she would be dancing with possibly half a dozen men, and that she should be gracious and welcoming for being asked.

James also told her to engage in conversations with her partners—nothing serious, just a few exchanges to kill the time. The celebrations lasted till two in the morning. Rasheeda and David were beside themselves at how well the evening went.

By the time they went to bed, they were floating on air. At first, they reminisced about all the steps they had to go through to get to that point, starting in Palestine. In short order, they switched to talking about their plans. They hugged and kissed with great passion and pleasure.

Rasheeda went to the next room and changed into a nightgown she had specifically chosen. Unlike her mother's, it was a see-through nightdress with nothing underneath. She crouched over David and helped him undress. "This time I fully surrender and give you myself," she told him.

"I give you myself now, and as long as we live," he answered.

They resumed their romantic play—slowly, passionately, and with deliberate deference for each other.

Per Federico's guidance, Rasheeda, who was more in control, knew how to reach her desires before David did. She climaxed twice before she lost her virginity and twice after. It was all music to David's ears. He did not need to micromanage the fully immersed connection, and he felt that Rasheeda did a super job, for herself and for him. Rasheeda had never mentioned Federico's program to David and had no plans to mention it in the future.

––––––––––

Rasheeda settled into her upper-class duties and, like her mother, behaved compassionately and humbly. She became known for helping the needy, both those in need of material items and those in need of emotional help. Like her mother, she was observed on many occasions helping the invalid and the infirm. Her good name spread beyond the Unitarian church to other churches and institutions.

David was impressed by his wife's dedication and energy. She had already acquainted herself with some of her husband's businesses during her four-year engineering program. Upon graduation she became the second in charge of engineering for the family's many businesses.

Shortly after she finished her university studies, Rasheeda got pregnant. It was a joyful piece of news for the whole Alexander family, who had thought that all that wealth would go outside the family for lack of potential family heirs.

She gave birth to a girl whom she named Summer, a name used in many countries, including England and Palestine. David and Rasheeda were thought of as the perfect couple, for they did not engage in the local or royal family gossip. It was a dream marriage, built on both partners' contentment with what is important in life. Above all, they were contented with each other's gift to one another.

Rasheed made sure he was present when Rasheeda gave birth. Although he had visited Rasheeda several times before, he usually stayed for only three nights. This time he intended to visit for ten days, accompanied by Omar. He wanted to make up for not being able to be there for her at her wedding, six years ago. He found his sister to be very happy and found David feeling that he was very lucky. Rasheeda seemed like the answer for most, if not all, of David's needs. Rasheeda's joy with her daughter was easily doubled by Rasheed and Omar being there for her.

Rasheeda made sure that Omar recognized that he had an aunt and now a cousin. She could finally see definite signs that Rasheed was on his way to overcoming the loss of Natalia. She wanted him to go forward and to quit torturing himself about the loss of a lover, albeit a very special lover.

Rasheed and Omar spent ten days with Rasheeda, David, and Summer. Omar in the end warmed up to and became attached to Rasheeda, and he was elated when she promised him that all three of them would visit him in Beirut.

CHAPTER 20

1954
Beirut, Lebanon

Rasheed lived and breathed to nurture two entities: Omar and journalism. *Time* magazine was a perfect match for him. He liked its style; correspondents wrote their articles with full details, which were later summarized by a contributing editor.

In short order, after listening to Rasheed, Luce ordered that he be allowed five thousand dollars a month for an unquestioned expense account. This came about when Luce was last in town. Rasheed arranged that the two of them interview Mullah Mustapha Al-Barzani, the tribal head of a very nascent Kurdish insurrection in Iraq. He then told Luce that he had been paying, out of his own pocket, expenses related to dining, entertaining, and interviewing certain people, such as Barzani, whom he could not name or identify, even to his own employer.

One day, as Omar and Rasheed were about to climb the stairs of the Foreign Press Club, Rasheed saw that the gathering was not social but was for a presentation by the correspondent of *Der*

Spiegel, a German publication. That meant it would not be a family affair. Rasheed reversed course and started heading down the stairs. A very good-looking young woman said hello, and then asked, "Who is this handsome boy?"

When Rasheed introduced himself and told her about his mistake—thinking it was a different kind of meeting—she introduced herself as Giselle Abizaid. She volunteered to spend time with Omar and skip the meeting. With her French accent, she told Rasheed that she did not care much for Hans, the *Der Spiegel* correspondent, and that he was too long-winded for her. She was one of the correspondents of Agence France-Presse. Although they had never met, Rasheed recognized her name.

She was smartly dressed in flats, a dark skirt, and a pink safari blouse. Her large dark eyes were her most striking quality, followed by her puffed and contoured pitch-black hair, which was semi-rounded to complement her round face. Mainly on the thin side, she partially revealed her ample chest when she leaned down to talk to Omar. Above all, Rasheed noticed her grace and softness when she interacted with his son.

He was fascinated by Giselle.

"I think *you* should introduce Hans, in English," she said. "Rather than the president of the club, who is the French-speaking correspondent for *Le Figaro*."

Giselle was persistent about taking care of Omar, despite Rasheed's attempts to the contrary. He ended up accepting her offer with gratitude. Two hours later, after Giselle had lunch with Omar, Rasheed met them downstairs in the Foreign Press Club. She suggested that the three of them go for ice cream. Rasheed could hardly turn her down, especially since Omar favored the idea.

As they sat at the ice cream parlor, they got to know more about each other. It turned out that Giselle was only twenty-three, younger than she looked and nine years younger than Rasheed. After they said goodbye, she asked if she could see Omar in the future. She may have had her own ulterior motives regarding his father, but Omar *was* cute.

Omar kissed Giselle goodbye. He then slipped her a piece of paper with his home number. "You don't have to call my father first," he said. "You can call me at home."

A week later, as she expected to see Rasheed at a government press conference, she called Omar. He answered, and she said, "You took too long. I have been waiting for you to call for a whole week. I thought you would call me the following day." She then promised Omar that she would have lunch with him within a few days. "If your dad approves," she added.

She called Rasheed and asked if she could take Omar to lunch. He agreed, and then he asked if he could come along. "No, this is between me and Omar. But you and I can have lunch together the week after. How about it?"

"That sounds good, provided *Time* pays for lunch."

"If *Time*'s paying, then it better be good."

Over the friendly, warm lunch, Rasheed told Giselle the story of Natalia. He wanted to get it out in the open, as his feelings were still mildly raw, and Natalia's memory was not all gone.

Giselle was under the impression that Rasheed was divorced. After listening to Natalia's story in detail, she was surprised that Rasheed still had a slim hope of finding his former lover. She could see it in his eyes, and his expressed feelings were deeper than she would have thought.

The situation did not sit well with her, although she respected Rasheed for being honest about his feelings. Despite her attraction to him and her attachment to Omar, she did not want to be an emotional second fiddle to another woman's memory, no matter how sincere those emotions were.

She tried not to show her disappointment, but Rasheed sensed it. As she was about to leave, he brought up her faith. "I do not need to guess. I am sure half of the eligible young Maronite men in Lebanon would give their right arm to court you," he said. "I am sorry if I disappointed you."

"Above all you are a gentleman, and that is a breath of fresh air nowadays," she replied.

"I want to say something that's on my mind," she continued, "an observation that I feel is highly important, and I hope you won't feel I am being too forward. You have a jewel in Omar, but at the same time you are still deep into the tragedy of his mother. I feel that as much as you love Omar and care for him, more than anything else in your life, your emotions are split between the present—Omar— and the past, his mother. I think you need to show him more of your emotions. He is craving this, and he needs it badly. But you are kind of sharing it with Natalia, thinking such feelings would help in keeping her memory alive. It is noble on your part but may not be as nurturing to Omar."

Giselle knew there and then that it would be the last time she caressed his hands. From then on, she intentionally managed to avoid the Foreign Press Club meetings, except one, when she knew that Rasheed was in Kuwait for an interview. She also never called Omar back.

Omar asked about her repeatedly, and most of the time Rasheed told him she was working in France. For a while, Rasheed thought of calling her, only because Omar was continually mentioning her name. But in the end, he decided against it. On a couple of occasions, he envisaged her next to him and fantasized about her elegance, poise, youth, and warmth. He equally managed not to allow such thoughts to germinate.

————

Giselle's insight into his relationship with Omar struck a nerve with Rasheed. In response to her advice, he decided to direct much more attention and emotions toward his son. His guilty feelings for leaving her behind drove him to obsess about Natalia's memory. He may have thought that leaving her behind was bad enough; he did not want to let go of her memory. Giselle's advice prompted him to dwell on his emotions. After all, Omar was Natalia's son, and he rationalized that Natalia would have wanted him to concentrate on Omar's affairs and emotions.

He spent more time with Omar and made it a point to get acquainted with colleagues with children of a similar age in an attempt to expand Omar's universe. Omar seemed to respond to his father's efforts. He was happier at school and started talking about his school friends more often. Four years of elementary school had gone by, and Omar excelled academically, ranking first, second, or third in his class each year.

————

Five years later, in 1959, when Omar was eleven, Rasheed thirty-seven, and Giselle twenty-eight, she very unexpectedly called Rasheed. It was almost eleven years since the disappearance of Natalia. Rasheed was at the time totally convinced that the Jewish underground had killed Natalia, and that the perpetrators had belonged to the main body or to a splinter group of the Stern Gang. He initially thought that Giselle's call was to check on his affairs, but she had a genuine excuse; she had been offered a job with the Associated Press. She was concerned about her ability to write in English.

After indirectly blaming each other for their lack of contact, she asked Rasheed if he would mind assisting her when she needed help. "You are one of two Arab journalists who write English perfectly. You also speak it so very well, but you still have a slight accent," she said, teasing him with a chuckle.

"Giselle, working for the Associated Press—the AP—is great. It is a serious promotion from Agence France-Presse. I would do anything to help you out, but, unfortunately, I must first check with New York. How about if I call you as soon as I hear from them?"

Giselle thought Rasheed was making an excuse for not helping her. Ten days later, the answer from New York came back positive but with guidelines. Rasheed's help could not last more than one year, and it must have nothing to do with content. He had to stick to guiding her in proper English, journalistic methods, style, and form.

When he told her what came back from New York, she was surprised at his sincerity and realized that her suspicions were wrong. After some reflections, she thought the new circumstances gave her a chance to check on his state of attachment to Natalia's memory.

During those five years of not having talked to or run into Rasheed, Giselle had gone through a bad experience of her own. She had given in to an arranged engagement to a fourth cousin, Habib, one of the more successful young men in her village. She came from a very educated but not necessarily very rich family.

Habib learned early on that Giselle's *dote*, the assets the bride brought into the marriage, was a meager fifty thousand dollars. Habib dissolved the engagement with Giselle's full blessings. With the engagement behind her, she felt free to contact Rasheed for his journalistic help and with a strong whiff of personal admiration.

After agreeing to Rasheed's proposal that he would teach her by example and try to help her edit her own AP articles, she asked about Omar. "Did I tell you how much I missed him over the last five years?" she said. "I always thought that if I were to have children, I would want them to be just like Omar. His sense of humor at the age of six was so endearing. He was a delight to be with. I am sure he has lost none of it."

"It took him nine months to stop asking about you," Rasheed said, "and I think he stopped only because in the end he got mad at you."

Giselle sounded regretful. "Oh my God, I feel so guilty. Listen, Rasheed, the first thing I want to do is see Omar, even before you start helping me. Will you arrange it? I mean it. I feel so guilty."

Shortly thereafter Omar, Rasheed, and Giselle got together over lunch. To both Rasheed's and Giselle's surprise, Omar was cool and distant. He did not engage in conversation unless asked. On the way out, Rasheed whispered in Giselle's ear to stay behind and wait for him at the restaurant. Rasheed went back after he dropped Omar off at the house.

When Rasheed returned, they planned how to soothe Omar's feelings. Rasheed suggested that the best way was to use reverse psychology and not give him a chance to get angrier. During the following week, he mentioned Giselle's name but avoided using sentiments or words of adoration. He gave Omar the impression that he was tutoring Giselle at the request of the Foreign Press Club.

On one occasion, as Omar was stuck on a French word, Rasheed pretended that he was not sure about its meaning. He then reminded Omar that Giselle was a graduate of a French university and that she probably knew the meaning of the word. Omar, in a lukewarm fashion, agreed to have Rasheed call Giselle.

Rasheed went to his bedroom and advised Giselle to have a lengthy conversation with Omar, all about that French word, its meaning, and its uses. As Rasheed went back into the living room, he called Giselle again, in the presence of Omar. After Rasheed asked about the word, pretending that the subject was brought up for the first time, he contrived a setup for Giselle to discuss the different uses of the word.

After Giselle gave Omar examples of the uses of that word, she then asked Omar if he minded her buying copies of his two French textbooks so she could follow along with him. Omar did not object. Little by little as Omar needed help with his French, Giselle got to help him over the phone.

Rasheed again invited Giselle for lunch and brought Omar along. Before too long, the relationship between Giselle and Omar warmed up considerably.

At the same time, the relationship between Rasheed and Giselle also warmed up. Not only did Rasheed help Giselle with her stories, but on one occasion he violated his own promise to *Time* and corrected her facts. The story involved a new type of fighter plane that the Soviet Union provided for Egypt, which was superior to anything the Israelis had at the time. Giselle mentioned in her story that the Soviet Union provided Egypt with twenty-four planes. Instead Rasheed reminded her that eighteen of those planes were returned to the Soviet Union as a result of a compromise agreement with the United States.

For two years the relationship between them continued to get closer. Omar started to contact Giselle directly, and the relationship soon resembled that of a tightknit family of three. Both Giselle and Rasheed harbored reservations—he in keeping Natalia's memory mildly alive and she in being afraid that emotionally she would end up being a second to his missing lover's memory.

CHAPTER 21

One early morning a handsome man in his late thirties entered *Time* magazine's bureau office. Rasheed came out of his office to greet him.

"You don't recognize me, do you?" the man said. "Nineteen years have changed my looks much more than yours. I am Taha."

Rasheed thought for a while before he recognized him. Taha had been his best friend in his senior year of high school. Rasheed apologized after the two hugged and kissed. They proceeded to the St. Georges Hotel bar, two blocks away, to reminisce. But that was not why Taha was there.

"I will be honest with you, I flew over from Europe with you in mind," Taha said. "I would like you to introduce me to the American ambassador to Lebanon."

Rasheed was slightly surprised. "I know the American ambassador well," he said. "We respect each other; he wants me to be on his team. But I am on *Time* magazine's team and nobody else's team. If I ask for a favor, they will want to be paid back, and that would be costly in my profession."

Taha asked Rasheed if he would mind having dinner with him and two friends the next day. Rasheed accepted but reminded Taha that his position was firm.

The dinner gathering was full of arguments and pleadings. Rasheed agreed to arrange the delivery of a sealed letter to the American ambassador. He told the three that he did not want to know anything about the content of such letter. They, in turn, said that they did not want him to know its contents either.

The letter was delivered, and contacts were established between the three Jordanian officers and the ambassador.

The ambassador and the three men agreed to meet, incognito, with their identities concealed from each other. They planned to sit twenty feet apart in a totally darkened room. The subject of their meeting was the corruption that was taking place in Jordan. The three strongly believed that such corruption was the cause of Jordan's continued poverty.

In a roundabout way, the ambassador was to understand that they were willing to overthrow the regime in a military coup. They promised him that the new regime would be totally aligned with the United States. Little did they know that they were talking to the CIA chief disguised as the ambassador. This was the same CIA chief who had orchestrated sabotage activities against the Syrian regime. Initially, the chief liked what he heard, especially that the Jordanian government had screwed up the anti-Syrian sabotage effort, specifically due to their corruption.

But before the CIA chief could do anything about it, the Jordanian government asked for payback for sharing some vital information about Saudi Arabia. In the give-and-take of the espionage world, it ended up that the United States decided to share the news of the potential coup with the Jordanian government.

In no time, Rasheed was visited by the head of Jordanian intelligence, General Radi. The general was courteous and smooth. He did not ask to know the names of any of the conspirators. He only asked to be provided with further details. Rasheed assured Radi that he did not know any details.

During another visit to see Rasheed, Radi asked for the name of the one conspirator that Rasheed may have known. Rasheed felt that he was cornered and gave Radi the name of a Moroccan liaison who was supposed to have helped the three conspirators in only a very marginal way.

He was totally convinced that the Jordanians would not dare harm that person, since he was a strong ally of the Moroccan regime. Furthermore, the liaison resided in Morocco, far away from the sphere of influence of Jordan.

Two weeks after Rasheed gave out his name, the liaison was found dead. To Rasheed's surprise and disappointment, they had even gotten to him in his own house in Casablanca. Rasheed felt very guilty at the whole sequence of events, causing him many sleepless nights.

The Moroccan government, having identified the Jordanian intelligence service as the culprit in the liaison man's assassination, made the Jordanian government account for their misdeeds. The Moroccan government first proved to them that the liaison was in Morocco at the time of the meeting, having left Beirut a day earlier. They then forced the Jordanians to compensate the family of the liaison man a million dollars, a sum much too hefty for the government of Jordan at the time.

Having assassinated the wrong man, General Radi then visited Rasheed to tell him that his first cousin, Kamal, was in custody for treason and that he would not be let out until Rasheed told them the true story.

At that point, Rasheed had no choice. He called Henry Luce and told him what had happened. Luce did not think that Rasheed had done anything wrong other than endangering himself with an authoritarian ally of the United States. Luce picked up the phone and called US Secretary of State John Foster Dulles. Dulles put his brother Allen, the director of Central Intelligence, on a three-way conference call. The two promised that they would pressure the Jordanians to stay away from Luce's key man. The Jordanians did so and informed Rasheed that he was off the hook.

But just as they were about to release Rasheed's totally innocent cousin, Egyptian intelligence got hold of the story. The Jordanians were afraid of a scandal and decided not to release Kamal. Rasheed couldn't do much, but he supported Kamal's family financially and paid for all their needs, including room and board for their four children at two different universities.

During that confusion, Rasheed needed and received Giselle's support and empathy. She tried as much as she could to soothe his feelings and ease his mind. One evening, after Omar and his nanny had gone to sleep, Rasheed complained to Giselle that he was not feeling well. She took him to his bedroom, where she took off his shoes and jacket and laid him on the bed. She lay next to him. At around six the following morning, Giselle woke up and got concerned because Rasheed was still asleep, and they both had gone to bed at nine the night before.

As she felt his face to see if he was all right, he woke up. "You scared me," she said. "I didn't think you usually slept that long."

"I am still kind of tired. I don't know why, but at least my headache is gone," Rasheed answered.

"Lie on your stomach. I think the best thing now that your headache is gone is a massage. It will help wake up your body."

Rasheed turned over, and Giselle asked him to take off his slacks and shirt. As the massage got into Rasheed's crotch, he turned around, grabbed Giselle, and started kissing her. She responded, and before long they were making love.

It had taken six years for Rasheed and Giselle to get intimate. They both knew it was the memory of Natalia that had been in the way. Rasheed did not want to downplay his feelings for Giselle. He was convinced that if it had not developed into a strong, loving relationship, he would not have gotten intimate with her.

Giselle loved Rasheed and saw him as her prince charming: very tall, very handsome, and debonair, but with an unassuming, quiet demeanor. She loved to help him with his tie and coat and took great pleasure in looking at him, a smartly dressed and very attractive man. She also respected his vast general knowledge and journalistic style. He wrote with confidence. She always hoped that she could get close to her news subjects, just as he did, without compromising her independence or clouding her neutral perspective.

They became a couple, and neither pushed the other to get married: for Giselle it was fear of her ultra-right-wing, devout Maronite Catholic younger brother; for Rasheed it was a lack of determination, though not any lack of care and genuine love. Natalia's memory faded, except for some special occasions indelible in his memory.

Rasheed became enamored with Giselle's feminine touch and caring attitude. He had the housekeeper prepare dinner for Omar, but he would wait for Giselle to come home to share a glass of wine and dine together. Although he was a hardworking journalist, he always worried about the additional hours Giselle put into her work.

From time to time, he would choose the dress of the day for her. Sometimes he asked Omar about one dress choice or another, and they would occasionally go out to the fashionable dress shops to buy dresses for Giselle. He could not think of anyone else more noble and more beautiful, other than Natalia.

CHAPTER 22

Although Giselle had her own house, she spent most of her time at Rasheed's. She loved to take care of his domestic needs, but above all she cherished taking care of Omar. She attended PTA meetings, and she accompanied Omar when he started seventh grade. Without consciously doing so, she acted like she was his mother.

Her presence revived Rasheed's confidence in himself. He stopped drinking hard liquor altogether and joined Giselle in the evening for a glass of wine. He maintained his mild personality but revived an assertive attitude, the same one he started to assume at the age of nineteen, before he graduated from high school. Giselle was much like Rasheeda, and they both accepted his clarity of mind, firm opinions, and gentle expressions.

Omar was tall and growing fast. He had tall grandparents in Kareem and Amina, and tall parents in Rasheed and Natalia. His father was fair, but Omar had an even fairer complexion. His hair was straighter than his father's, after his Polish mother. He was not as quiet as his father but just as expressive as Rasheed when he needed to be. His blue eyes were shiny and distinct, similar to his mother's. He carried himself gracefully and showed signs of being as handsome as his father but with a more European look. His father's influence was clear in Omar's choice of fashionable but understated clothing.

Omar got close to Giselle with time, although he remained very close to his father. Giselle made it a point to be open with the boy, as much as she could with a twelve-year-old.

He was rather mature for his age and let Giselle know his likes and dislikes. She used to be deferential in that regard, knowing when not to press the issue. On many occasions after getting nudged by Omar to discontinue a discussion, she would drop the subject and not reopen it again until she got Omar's nod to do so.

Omar enriched himself emotionally as he spent playful but serious time with Giselle and had rather short but poignant discussions with his father. The combination was to everyone's liking.

Omar's teenage years were somewhat challenging for Giselle, though he went through them reasonably well. As they lived by the sea, Omar grew up as a first-class swimmer and a very accomplished athlete. He ran the four-hundred-meter dash, played basketball almost every day, jogged, and biked. He turned out to be a top student, with emphasis on math and physics. He was also very good at languages, English and French particularly. After graduation from high school and passing his baccalaureate exam, Omar entered the American University of Beirut to study engineering.

Three years of university flew by. As he matured, he grew even closer to Giselle, who considered him and treated him as if he were her biological son. Omar, on the other hand, looked at Giselle as his older and wiser sister. Her admiration for him was almost bound-less. His respect for her was limitless. They would tease each other whenever they could.

One evening, as Omar was finishing studying for a test, Rasheed and Giselle decided to go to dinner and give him some space. Omar took the opportunity to call Zeina, an engineering student at the university.

Giselle and Rasheed found a sign at the Armenian restaurant saying that there had been a death in the family, and as such the restaurant was closed for a week. They decided to go back home and have cheese and wine for dinner.

Upon entering the house, they could hear Omar and Zeina arguing. "What is this, the grand prix of sex?" Zeina said. "The faster the better?"

Zeina barged out of the room and ended up face-to-face with Rasheed and Giselle. She could tell that they had overheard the argu-ment between her and Omar. In her anger, she said nothing to them on her way out. Omar stood in the doorway of his room wearing only his underwear.

Omar and Giselle said nothing and went into their room. Giselle then whispered in Rasheed's ear, "Don't say anything until he finishes his finals, after tomorrow."

The next afternoon, Giselle was waiting for him when Omar returned from the university. She told him that she was not going to ask him any questions but that she had a story to tell him. She told him about Father Federico and how his ideas about sex and faith had changed Rasheed and, consequently, Giselle. She told Omar that her doubts about such a sexual approach were pretty much eliminated in short order.

"After six years of mostly my courting your father, our encounters started and continue to be memorable," she said. "I have never questioned your dad about lovemaking since. He is not only my love and my life, as well as yours, Omar. He is a true lover, slow and deliberate—I hope I am not embarrassing you. I feel I have no way of making my points except by discussing them in an open fashion."

She continued. "Do me a big favor. Listen to your father and then decide for yourself. Otherwise, judging by your encounter with Zeina, you will become known as a very handsome and intelligent young man and a lousy lover, just like your father once was way back in Beit Azar."

Omar, after a long pause, with a grudging voice and complete surprise at the content of Giselle's story, said that he would listen to his dad.

Giselle informed Rasheed, who in turn tutored Omar in lovemaking according to Mohammad's principles and Federico's applications. Rasheed did not ask Omar to prove himself as Federico had insisted upon. He advised Omar to try to please Zeina, as he himself had to learn to do with Leila. "I want to record my words: your satisfaction is multiplied many times if you please your partner to the degree you please yourself. You will recognize it when it happens."

CHAPTER 23

1967
Beirut, Lebanon

A few weeks later Giselle took the initiative and invited Zeina for a foursome lunch. At first Zeina said no, but she accepted in the end, as she wanted to apologize for abruptly barging out without saying anything to either Rasheed or Giselle. Rasheed and Giselle left Omar and Zeina walking by the seashore. Omar apologized profusely to Zeina. He told her repeatedly that he had been most inconsiderate in the past. Zeina then accused him of saying such things because he was in the mood to have sex.

"No, that is not it. Let us just be friends again, and whenever you want to have sex, we can have sex one time. After which you will decide."

Zeina was surprised at the whole tone of Omar's conversation and what sounded like halfway sincere regrets. She kissed him and called it an evening.

Two weeks later, Zeina went to watch Omar play basketball

against a top Alexandria University basketball team. While Omar performed admirably, the American University of Beirut team lost the game. Zeina asked Omar if he wanted to have dinner together. She took him to her parents' house since they were staying with her aunt in the mountains.

The evening felt odd, as Omar did not persist in being sexual as he had before. In the end, Zeina looked him in the eye and said, "Are you going to show me the new Omar or not?"

"I did not have any plans, but I would love to."

Rasheed's tutoring worked like a charm. Zeina enjoyed the slow and gentle removal of each article of her clothing. While Omar worked his way to sexually warming her up, Zeina reached two climaxes before he penetrated her and then reached two more for his two after he penetrated her.

Zeina hugged Omar tightly and laid her left cheek on his left shoulder. She whispered in his ear, "What happened to you? You are totally a new man. You have changed from seeking pleasure for yourself to seeking more pleasure for your partner."

"Call it proper parenting, but don't ask for details," said Omar.

Zeina was not the romantic, marrying type. She wanted to go for a doctorate in engineering and marry in her midthirties. On the other hand, she enjoyed having sex with Omar. He wasn't sure if she was having sex with anybody else.

———

As Rasheed became the lead correspondent for *Time* magazine and Giselle became the deputy bureau chief for the Associated Press, they could not help but cooperate on many news stories. They got to be known as the two aces among the press corps.

In 1967 the Lebanese political system was rocked with another sex scandal. Three parliament members were caught running a young-girl prostitution ring. The chief of correspondents of *Time* decided that it was time to do a comprehensive report about not only prostitution in Lebanon but about sex in the Arab world.

Among the list of subjects to be interviewed, Rasheed chose the madam of a high-end prostitution ring who was only thirty years of age. He also wanted to interview the second queen mother of Jordan, who was known to have been sexually abused by her late husband.

To interview the thirty-year-old madam, Rasheed asked Giselle if she could accompany him, as he heard that the madam was still handling high-end prostitution clientele. Her current practice was even more perverse than before: She lured high-society young girls who were in financial trouble to engage in their first sexual experience. They were required to be virgins and were offered to oil-rich, older Arab businessmen. The price was reported to be twenty-five thousand dollars for deflowering and a relationship of three months.

Giselle was stunned at the madam's youth and great looks. She recognized the fragrance of the madam's perfume as one that cost four hundred dollars for ten grams, and she was wearing haute couture French clothing. Somehow the madam rubbed Giselle the wrong way. Her body language felt spiteful and beguiling toward Rasheed. Giselle instantly felt jealous.

The madam complimented Rasheed several times, mostly on his looks. Rasheed chose to ignore her expressions. He didn't even say thank you. It took him an hour to interview the madam. Any more, and Giselle would not have been able to stand it.

Three days later, *Time* sent Rasheed some follow-up questions. He asked Giselle to accompany him again, but she decided not to for fear she might lose her cool. The madam was pleased that Rasheed showed up solo.

As the madam intentionally avoided answering his questions, she also tried to lure him by massaging his neck. Rasheed briskly resisted but not before the madam rubbed her breasts against him a couple of times. She then stood behind his back and gave him a kiss on his neck, leaving a mark on his collar, an imprint of her lipstick. It must have been one of the tricks of the trade.

To Rasheed's surprise, when he went back to his office, he found the second queen mother waiting for him there. He took the queen mother into a next-door apartment he used to house temporary correspondents and rotating photographers. He wanted to have room to ask her rather intimate questions about her reputed treatment by her late husband.

He tried to be very circumspect in introducing his line of questions. He wanted to question the queen mother about her late husband making love to her for four to five hours at a time and then threatening to whip her as he went into a verbal tirade.

Instead of concentrating on giving Rasheed her answers, the queen mother showed clear interest in him. She seemed to like the lipstick mark on his collar, as though it revealed his womanizing nature. She was approaching sixty, while Rasheed was in his midforties.

He did not respond to her advances. She settled down and asked him if she could be of any help. He was anxious to switch from the series of approaches that were being forced upon him. He thought it was an opportune time to mention his cousin, Kamal, who was still in prison.

The queen told him that she would try to help him and then made a final attempt to seduce him. She grabbed him by the crotch, but Rasheed reminded her that she was related to the prophet and that he was a commoner.

"We, the Jordanian royal family, are very close to the people," she replied.

By the time she left, she was steaming about his rejection and felt spurned. Rasheed was surprised by her reaction and called Giselle and told her he had something embarrassing he'd like to share with her.

When he arrived home, Giselle came into the living room and immediately smelled the fragrance the madam had worn. She then saw the lipstick imprint and erroneously concluded that Rasheed had succumbed to the advances of the madam. In her mind, the whole thing was confirmed by Rasheed's phone call.

Without a word, Giselle barged out of the house, ran toward her car, and took off to her house. Rasheed did not know what was happening. She would not stop despite his repeated loud hollering. He was about to get into his car and follow her but decided to call her brother instead, just in case he knew something Rasheed did not.

He looked into the mirror before he attempted to make the phone call, and he saw the lipstick on his collar and, in the process, smelled the perfume on his shirt. He decided not to call Antoine, Giselle's older brother.

Giselle sent Rasheed a note by messenger that said, "I gave you my youth, abandoned my family and my religion, and in one split second you betrayed my trust and my love. I do not want to ever see you again."

Once she had confirmation that Rasheed had received the letter, Giselle left that Friday to go to Antoine's home. Antoine was a handsome, tolerant, and balanced full colonel in the Lebanese

Army. Both he and his wife sensed that something must have gone wrong between Giselle and Rasheed, but they could not persuade her to share her thoughts with them.

Rasheed, meanwhile, was hoping that Giselle would come back to her senses and return home on her own. After three days, he started to worry. He sent Nouri, his friend and a retired detective, to observe whether Giselle was making it to work. Nouri saw Giselle later, when she arrived to work on the fifth day.

Rasheed felt relieved that her irresponsible driving had not caused an accident. That afternoon, he got a call from Baher Abu-Nader, the head of the leading freight airliner, requesting to meet with him as soon as possible. Baher showed him large tin cans. One of them had busted and spilled its contents: British gold coins. When the airline company weighed the other 109 cans, they found them to be of the same weight as the one that had busted open.

Lo and behold, the shipper was none other than the second queen mother herself. Rasheed was thankful for the scoop. The fact that the shipment was taking place was not as important as the fact that it was so large. It followed rumors that the royal family was concerned about a military coup, to be orchestrated by Nasser of Egypt. Rasheed filed his report that evening but was not exactly surprised when he learned later that the report was intercepted and sold to Jordanian intelligence.

The theme of Rasheed's report incensed the Jordanian intelligence service, because he had written that the royal family was preparing to leave in case things got worse in Jordan. The royal family decided to do something against him. In revenge for Rasheed rejecting her advances, the second queen mother intervened and alerted them to the fact that Rasheed's cousin was still in prison with a death sentence for treason. She pushed and persisted to force the intelligence service to agree to put Kamal to death.

Within two days, the sentence of the fake conviction was carried out. Kamal was put to death by hanging. Rasheed and the journalism community were in shock, including Luce's successors and all the foreign correspondents of *Time* magazine. He felt especially unprotected since his mentor, Henry Luce, had died a year earlier. He strongly believed that if Henry Luce had been alive, the Jordanians would not have dared to carry out the execution.

Rasheed gradually went into a cascading shock. He developed a severe headache and could not think straight. He blamed himself for Kamal's execution. He went home and told Omar about Kamal and Giselle's misunderstanding of what happened between him and the madam and the queen mother. As he lay in bed, he slowly went into a psychological shock coma.

When Omar realized his father would not awaken, he checked him into the hospital. Omar then ventured into Giselle's office unannounced and steaming mad. He stood by the door and did not approach her or hug her as he always did. She came to him and lifted her arms for a hug, but he moved away.

She could appreciate his reaction, but she told him that her own reaction and follow-up absence was justified, for she felt betrayed by her own and only love. Above all, she felt insulted to the core.

In a stern voice and admonishing tone, Omar told Giselle, "This time you are wrong. Very wrong. What you smelled on my father had not come from the madam but from the second queen mother. The queen also used the same brand perfume, and the lipstick on my father's shirt collar was put there to embarrass him for resisting the madam's advances."

He further explained that his father was in a coma as a result of hearing about the execution of his cousin, and that his father believed that the second queen mother instigated the execution of Kamal since she felt spurned by him.

As Omar was finishing telling Giselle what had happened, her brother Antoine stormed into the room, agitated. "You have lived and loved Rasheed for over thirteen years, and in a split second you chose to act as a teenager," he said. "I just came from internal security, and they confirmed to me that Kamal was executed, and here you are accusing that noble creature of having betrayed you. You are not acting like the Giselle I know. How could you do this to him?"

Giselle broke down sobbing, bending forward and placing her head between her legs. She understood where her brother was coming from and equally where she went wrong. She pulled herself together and rushed toward Omar and hugged and kissed him.

"I ask you to forgive me. I don't know what happened," she said. "I think she got to me, that madam."

They all went to see Rasheed in the emergency room of the American University Hospital. Giselle asked to first see him by herself. She tried to talk to him, but he was unresponsive.

The neurologist dropped in to check on Rasheed. He advised Giselle that this kind of shock coma could be personal in nature: "It is usually a level of stress or an incident that impacts people differently. Sometimes routine or familiar things tend to bring the patient back in touch with reality."

The neurologist asked Giselle if she understood what he was talking about. She answered that she did completely. The neurologist asked her to talk to Rasheed as if he could hear her. He added that hearing is the last faculty to be lost.

The following evening, as Giselle was sleeping on the chair and having a nightmare, Rasheed grabbed her arm and murmured something. Giselle awoke but did not move, hoping he would talk more.

Suddenly, he said, "Giselle, move your arm away. I want to sleep," and he let go of her arm. She called Omar, though it was the middle of the night. "I think your dad is waking up. He just told me to move my arm."

After Rasheed woke up, the psychologist listened to his account of what happened. He then suggested that Rasheed may have been shocked not only by his cousin's execution but also by the fact that nobody was with him to lessen his pain.

The following day, Rasheed was released from the hospital, and within hours the house was full of visitors. Antoine and his wife were there, as was Basheer, Giselle's younger brother.

At least two dozen of his colleagues showed up. Two of them brought champagne to celebrate. *Time's* deputy chief of correspondents called and told Rasheed that they had canceled the plane they had chartered to bring him over to the United States for treatment.

———

When he felt one-hundred-percent better, Rasheed went with Giselle to stay at the family house in the mountains. Upon reaching the house, he asked her to sit down.

"I am disappointed not because of what you did but because you did it to me," he said, looking her in the eye. "You are my love and my life. I would never think of hurting you, and yet you cavalierly accused me of betraying you. If I were that kind of a man, how could you even consider being my woman and having me as your man?

Omar and I deserve more and deserve your love unconditionally, surely without the havoc of disruptions and emotional convulsions. Promise me that this is the last time."

Giselle looked at Rasheed while biting her lower lip and quietly crying. "I have nothing to say to you, as I am guilt-ridden and so ashamed of my actions. I want you to forgive me, and I promise it will not happen again." She stood up and slowly walked into the master bedroom, curled up on the bed, and continued to cry.

On the way back to Beirut the following day, Giselle and Rasheed stopped at a special bakery. As they waited for the pies, he put his hand on her hand and said, "You and Omar are what I care for most, and whenever I am mad at one of you, I develop a haunting emptiness. There are three of us, and whenever one is unhappy, the other two may end up being more unhappy than the one who started it all. Please remember this. Don't jump to conclusions, and do not get mad so cavalierly. Such episodes diminish the quality of our lives. Even when it is all over, it leaves a feeling of wistfulness."

CHAPTER 24

1968
Beirut, Lebanon

That Sunday Omar went for a jog along the seashore. He'd almost reached two miles when he landed on a rock. He stopped to clear it out of the way and noticed two joggers behind him who were slowing as they approached him. He could hear them speaking with a Jordanian dialect. He resumed jogging and glanced back and saw that they had matched his pace. He then sped up, but they could not maintain his speed, and he was soon able to distance himself from them. As he was concerned the two would catch up with him and knowing that his swimming abilities were superior to most, he chose to take a thirty-foot dive into the Mediterranean Sea, to first swim underwater and later to surface and head home. He let go of his jogging shoes.

In the safety of the house, he called his father and relayed the incident to him. Within the hour, Rasheed and Giselle were there. Giselle hugged him tightly and said, "I cannot have anything happen to you. It would kill me and your father if anything happened to you. You are our life and our future. You know that we have decided not to have any children. You are it. Are you listening to me?"

Omar nodded.

Rasheed asked him not to leave the house while he called Nouri, a Lebanese ex-detective who concealed his private-eye work by driving a cab. Nouri was very close to Rasheed and knew Giselle and Omar well. He brought three handguns with him, keeping one on himself and placing the other two at strategic points in the house.

That evening Rasheed called his sister, who had kept close ties with their Spanish friend Ibrahim over the years, and asked her about him. Rasheeda reminded him that Ibrahim and his daughter, Christina, averaged three trips to London a year, and that they stayed with her and David most of the time. Rasheed told her about the incident on the promenade with Omar. He wanted to consult with her whether she thought it was a good idea for Omar to move to Spain to finish his last two years of engineering.

Rasheeda said that she thought that it would be a great idea, and that such a move would give Omar a chance to see Christina in person.

At first, Rasheed did not understand what she was talking about. Then she explained that Omar had been corresponding with Christina for two years, and that the two had exchanged many letters and pictures and even movies of themselves.

All of that was news to Rasheed. When he inquired further about Christina, Rasheeda described her as the sweetest beauty queen she had ever met. "You mean you did not know?" she said. "Christina has called Omar a dozen times out of our house alone. They must have spoken to each other between Beirut and Madrid more than fifty times."

That evening, Rasheed and Giselle pleasantly and amusingly

confronted Omar. He told them that he would have mentioned it earlier, but he was secretly taking Spanish lessons to surprise everyone, especially Christina. He added that he did not want to rush things since Christina was seventeen when they started corresponding. "Now she is nineteen and in her sophomore year in college," he added.

When Rasheed asked him if he wanted to finish his education in Spain, Omar surprised them by saying that one of his visiting professors had invited him to attend Rice in Houston, where he regularly taught. He also told them that the same professor, upon listening to Omar tell about his endangered life, told Omar that he could arrange for him to register under an assumed name, and that he was aware of another student from Mexico who had to conceal his identity.

One afternoon, two weeks before the end of the school year, Omar and Nouri, the detective, observed the same two men who had chased Omar into the sea also following them for a short while.

That incident prompted Rasheed to call Ibrahim in Spain. He told Ibrahim that Omar was planning to go to the United States to finish his studies, but in order to camouflage his trip, would it be okay for Omar to first pass through Madrid?

Ibrahim said, "That would be great. Christina would love it." Again Rasheed felt he and Giselle were left in the dark about this long-distance relationship between Omar and Christina.

The following day, Ibrahim called Rasheed and told him that he, as the owner of twenty-two wineries, had a security staff numbering forty, and that he could send three of them to Beirut to take over from the local security team until Omar arrived in Madrid safely. Rasheed liked the idea and tentatively said yes.

Before long, Ibrahim called Rasheed again. "Christina heard

about Omar coming to Spain," he said. "I could not dissuade her from accompanying the three-man security team. Don't tell Omar. Javier, my head security man, will decide if she can see Omar while in Beirut."

As they waited for Omar to finish the school year, the plans for his trip were set in motion. Two days before leaving, Omar was moved to the Bristol Hotel, where the Spanish and local security men created a security cordon around him.

Christina, who was an accomplished flamenco dancer and a martial arts black belt, was looking forward to meeting Omar in person. To her disappointment, Javier decided against any get-togethers between the two long-distance admirers. But he acceded to Christina listening in on the security team's conversation with Omar and to watching Omar discreetly as he was being briefed and debriefed by the same Spanish security team.

After Christina moved into the hotel, they managed, as promised, to let her peek at Omar. She could barely contain herself as he interacted with the team. His athletic stature was impressive, and his smarts showed as he picked up the instructions easily and in short order. His mastering some of the defensive moves they taught him impressed her immensely. She had labored with some of the same moves when she was being coached a couple of years earlier.

For the first time, she felt she was sensing the real thing, and she liked what she saw and observed. On one occasion, she felt like instructing Omar on what to say, only to catch herself from getting carried away.

————

The team hired six cars, which they had to conceal several blocks from the hotel, all the same make and color. The cars were numbered on the right and left front wheels. The group was supposed to occupy cars three, four, and five. Cars one, two, and six were supposed to be used as decoys, for each to split off depending on the situation.

There were three Lebanese security personnel, two males and one female. The female was introduced to Christina as her bodyguard. The pictures of the men who had followed Omar were given to the Spanish team for careful study and potential recognition.

The whole team left the Bristol, hurrying on the sidewalk, with one security man in front, two behind Omar, and then Omar himself in between. The three other security men behind Omar had Christina in between them.

The same men who had followed Omar on the promenade were observed following him out of the hotel. In the meantime, Nouri had identified them as security personnel at the Jordanian embassy. Dressed in Muslim attire, the female security guard received a signal by the security men ahead of her. She broke ranks and went around the strange men. She then hit one on the head with her handgun, disabling him. His colleague abandoned their pursuit altogether.

At the airport, Omar boarded the plane ahead of other passengers, as arranged by airport security. The Lebanese security woman accompanied the Spanish team to London. The group exclusively occupied the first-class cabin. Per Javier's instructions, security on the flight was relaxed after the plane had left the air space of all Middle Eastern countries, which were in the habit of cooperating closely with one another. Over Greece, two bottles of champagne were uncorked to celebrate evading the men.

At that point, Christina signaled the Spanish security man who was sitting next to Omar to exchange seats. Omar was looking out the window and did not notice as she slowly and quietly sat in that aisle seat to his left.

He felt two fingers pressing gently on his lower left arm. When he looked to say something to the security man, he saw Christina. At first, he did not recognize her, but when he did, he did not know what to say.

He slowly exhibited an exhilarating smile followed by a slow-motion hug that got firmer as she placed her head on his shoulder. Once he eased her head off his shoulder, he silently looked at her. He took his right index finger and touched her nose ever so gently.

For a few seconds, she got confused and thought that Omar might not recognize her, although he had already held her in his arms.

"I am Christina," she said.

Omar looked at her, nodding. "I know! What a great surprise," he said. "I just don't know what to say. I was preparing my words to greet you in Madrid, and here you are next to me out of Beirut. Oh my God, how long have you been here?"

"I came with Javier, but they would not let me see you, for security reasons. What difference does it make? We are here together, and we will be in London and then Madrid by the end of the day."

"Oh no, I asked the Polish ambassador this morning to let my aunt know that I will try to pass through Warsaw to see her. Didn't Javier tell you? I am supposed to call him from London for confirmation."

"Do you mind if I go with you?" Christina asked. "I have never been to Warsaw."

"I would love you to go with me. That would be great."

"I will have to call my father first."

Throughout the rest of the flight, both Christina and Omar did not know how to behave. Their senses were challenged; it was hard to know how to shift from a long-distance relationship to sitting next to each other.

Were they regular boyfriend and girlfriend? Were they theoretical lovers who had never made love with each other? Were they infatuated with each other, waiting for further improvements in the relationship? It was obvious that neither knew the parameters and neither wanted to be presumptuous.

Their first impressions were identical; each in person looked better than expected. They knew that was a good start, but not enough.

Christina took the initiative by placing her right arm flat inside his left and hooking her fingers through his. Then with her left palm, she went down his right cheek, pulling his head toward her and kissing him gently on his left cheek.

Omar then summoned his courage and slowly placed his lips on hers, kissing her gently. All through the trip they caressed each other's arms, played with each other's hair, and kissed softly.

Upon arriving at London's Heathrow, Omar made a call. The Polish ambassador confirmed that Alicia, Omar's aunt, was waiting for him in Warsaw. Ibrahim acceded to Christina's insistence to accompany Omar to Warsaw. Ibrahim ordered Javier to accompany the two to Warsaw. The ambassador arranged the visa situation and informed Omar that they would be met by an official driver and a detective, both of whom spoke English reasonably well.

On the way to Warsaw, Christina slept on Omar's shoulder, and he took the opportunity to kiss her on her forehead.

They were met and cleared at the airport in no time and

proceeded to Alicia's house. They asked the detective to accompany them into the house just in case they needed a translator.

The front door of Alicia's house was open, presumably in expectation of their arrival. The detective stepped in after knocking on the door and then called for Alicia. Within seconds a very handsome and elegant middle-aged lady appeared with a blank look on her face.

She looked at Omar intently without a word. Tears began sliding down her cheeks. She took short, halting breaths, trying not to sob. She silently gazed at Omar despite the detective addressing her in Polish. After a while she looked at Christina and smiled.

Omar asked the detective to ask her not to cry and to tell her he was there to celebrate meeting his aunt for the first time. His aunt tried to talk to Omar, but she choked up and couldn't say anything. He took his handkerchief out and offered it to her. She took it and dabbed her eyes.

She then said in almost perfect English, "I am not your Aunt Alicia." She choked again. Omar had no idea what to think.

She collected herself after she wiped her tears and nose and said, "I am Natalia, your mother."

Omar opened his mouth and widened his eyes as he looked at her with disbelief. He then looked at Christina. She was also stunned by the news.

When Natalia witnessed the shock and bafflement on both Omar's and Christina's faces, she realized that she had to explain herself. She began sobbing again and said in a coarse, suppressed voice, "Oh my God. I had no choice. We had no food and very little milk to give you. You cried for four days, almost nonstop. Neither I nor your aunt slept much. We would wake up, boil water, and try to feed it to you. That worked the first day, but by the second day, it stopped working. We all were losing weight. By the fourth day, you had lost one kilogram. We either had to give you to an orphanage or send you to Kareem. The government had already contacted us to let us know that your father was doing well in Beirut. We turned them down at first, but as you got dangerously thin, we called them back and accepted that they ask your father if he would take you. You looked healthy when you got to Beirut, because the government provided us with adequate food. They did not want people coming out of Poland to look as if they were starving. We asked them to tell your father that I was still missing." She wiped her tears.

Suddenly Natalia almost lost her footing, and Christina rushed toward her and steadied her.

Natalia continued as Christina held on to her arm: "I thought I could hide and have you meet with your aunt, but the closer your visit got, the harder it was to keep my promise to myself. Alicia was supposed to come out, but instead I did. I just could not hold myself back. Please forgive me. I have not been fair to you or to your father, the only love I have ever known."

Without saying anything, Omar rushed toward his mother and hugged her with tears in his eyes and disbelief on his face.

Natalia hugged him back firmly and kissed him all over his face. "I want to kiss you like your father told me your great-aunt Hameeda used to kiss him, all over his face."

Christina joined them by first kissing Natalia on both cheeks and then hugging her and Omar.

Alicia suddenly appeared and said in a cheerful voice, "I am Alicia." The resemblance between her and Natalia was obvious. She was a couple of years older, a few pounds heavier, and one inch shorter. After everyone finished meeting each other, the detective excused himself, and the conversation started in earnest.

"Your mother forgot to tell you about me," Aunt Alicia said. "Shortly after Natalia arrived in Warsaw, I was raped by a Soviet soldier, a Mongolian. When we tried to report him, he and his friends threatened us. We thought one day they may come over and slit our throats, including yours. Their camp was down the street from our kibbutz. We had to find a safe place for you."

Natalia then told Omar and Christina that she gave birth to him in Warsaw and that he was a Polish citizen. The story about Albina saving the baby was made up to cover the fact that Natalia was alive but not well at the time.

She tried to explain to Omar why she decided to disappear. "I was raped twice by my captors, and as they tried to rape me the third time, two of them got into a fight, ending in one killing the other. The killer fled the scene and left the prison door open, and that is how I managed to escape."

She was in prison for seven months. They were not looking for her afterward, as the new Jewish state wanted to make room for the Arab prisoners. As a result of the rapes and the ensuing trauma, Natalia decided not to look for Rasheed. Albina helped Natalia reach Warsaw.

"I named you Omar because Rasheed had chosen it in advance," she said, "although he had no idea I was pregnant."

Natalia explained to Omar that she wanted to keep him, but their situation and the situation after the Soviets took over Poland was miserable. "If I had known your father was going to financially help Alicia, I would not have sent you back to Rasheed. That financial support started after you were delivered to your father."

Natalia asked about Christina. Omar said, "We fell in love while corresponding, talking to each other, and sharing movie clips of ourselves. This morning was the first time we met in person. She insisted on coming to Beirut, and I am happy about that."

Christina pointed at herself and said, "Me too."

After the three visited and shared their stories, Omar suggested that Natalia stay with them at the hotel so they could catch up and get more acquainted. She accepted with great joy. She had not been told about the danger Omar and his father were in until Omar told her the story that evening.

She then told Omar that she knew Rasheed had a new love in his life and that she was happy for him.

"Guess what?" Omar said. "My Aunt Rasheeda is married to David Alexander, and they have a sixteen-year-old daughter. I am told you introduced them to each other."

"I know my being alive was a shock to you, hopefully a pleasant shock," Natalia said. "It will also be a shock to your father. You need to think of a way to let Rasheed know. It is not fair to keep this from him."

Omar told her that he had already decided to let Ibrahim break the news to him. He then looked at Christina and said, "I will have Christina describe to Ibrahim how we all first met."

———

At eight the next morning the three met for breakfast. When Omar and Christina showed up, Natalia kissed both very warmly. The conversations continued. Omar explained to his mother that things were moving so quickly and that he would be in touch with her all the time. He asked her to visit him in Houston.

"Maybe you will come over with Christina. You two can meet

first in London or Paris and then fly together to Texas." Both Natalia and Christina liked the idea.

———————

The day before he left Warsaw, Omar left two thousand dollars for his mother, which was a huge amount in Poland at the time. When she initially turned down the money, Omar told her about the sale of the Mount Calvary land and about the fact that his father had become even richer by investing most of the money in firms recommended by the Vatican.

Out of nowhere, Omar asked if he could visit his grandmother's and grandfather's graves. Natalia told him that his grandfather had been exterminated at Auschwitz and that when they wanted to visit his grave site, they would go to Auschwitz. But his grandmother was buried nearby.

All four went to Natalia's mother's grave. Omar said, "Grandfather Jacob and Grandmother Adriana, I am Omar, your grandson. You cannot imagine how much I miss not having known you and not having you in my life. I would have met you here and would have wanted you to visit me in Beirut. Here in Warsaw, I would have enjoyed accompanying you to the Catholic church and to the synagogue. Somebody decided they were God and ended your precious lives. I am now with my mother, and she carries your legacy with pride but also with sadness. I will visit you in the future, as much as I can. I also have Christina with me, the greatest unexpected gift I have ever had. I will have three women in my life, and all are more precious than life itself. Rest in peace, until we meet again."

Natalia, Christina, and Alicia were crying at Omar's words.

———————

To Omar, finding his mother and then leaving her behind after a two-day visit was surreal. On the way to the airport, Christina told him that fate wanted them to get much closer to each other. "I feel so close to you, as if I have known you all my life," she said. "This is so unreal. It is even hard to tell our story to friends, but I do not care as long as it is real for you and me, and it *is* real for me." She kissed Omar on the cheek slowly and persistently with the hopes of relaying a sense of deep affection and appreciation.

CHAPTER 25

When Christina and Omar arrived in Madrid, Ibrahim was waiting for them. After kissing Christina, Ibrahim shook hands with Omar and took a close look at him. He noticed the poised demeanor and physical attributes of the man Christina chose to be close to.

Ibrahim told Omar that he was safe in Spain, but to ensure that he was risk-free, he would make available two of his security people to be close by twenty-four hours a day.

"I am so elated that finally you have found your mother. I am so happy that Christina shared with you such a precious moment. I cannot wait to let your father know. I have to be circumspect, and I will. I don't want to give your father a shock."

The following day, after Christina and Omar's arrival in Madrid, Ibrahim called Rasheed. After Ibrahim updated him on their children's trip, he said, "Please sit down, Rasheed. I mean it. You have to sit down first. I have good news."

"I am now sitting down," Rasheed said. "What is going on?"

"I have good news for you, and I hope you really are sitting down. Natalia is alive."

"Alive? Where?" Rasheed exclaimed. There was a long pause, and then Rasheed said, "Really?"

"Yes, for real. She lives in Warsaw. The Polish government knows where she lives." Ibrahim paused. "Please take a deep breath. Here are the facts: Omar and Christina saw her. Don't say anything. Just take another deep breath. They even spent two days together in Warsaw."

"You are not kidding?" Rasheed said. "You are serious?"

"I am dead serious. Omar did not know if he could handle telling you about it. She is alive and well. I will call you back in an hour and give you more information, after you inform Giselle. Natalia sends you and Giselle her love." With that, Ibrahim hung up.

Rasheed called Giselle and shared with her the strange news. He made sure to mention that Natalia sent *both* of them her love. After taking several deep breaths, she told Rasheed that she planned to talk to Omar. When she reached Omar by phone, Omar assured Giselle that his mother had known about her for a long while and that she had sent her love to both of them.

In a surprising way, things in Beirut were developing differently. After Giselle welcomed the news of Natalia, she could sense a certain confusion on Rasheed's part. She thought that Rasheed was confused as to who was his first love, under the circumstances. She once again reacted without probing or consulting anyone. She went to the house and left Rasheed a note:

> *My love—My only love,*
>   *What happened this week is overwhelming beyond belief.*

I am afraid I cannot help you here. You must decide for yourself. Now, you have two people who love you unconditionally. You need to decide and decide without my help.

Take your time, all the time you need, and let me know only when you have decided fully and with complete resignation.

Regardless of whom you choose, I will continue to love you unconditionally.

Your Giselle

She packed two suitcases and left.

––––––––––

After reading the note, Rasheed was shocked that Giselle had left it, especially because she had not shown any concern about the new developments. At first, he had every intention to call her and let her know that she was acting immaturely. But he then changed his mind, having reminded himself of Giselle's prior episode. He called Antoine instead and asked to meet. When Antoine arrived the following morning, he found Rasheed tense and in a bad mood.

Rasheed looked Antoine in the eyes and said, "God knows that I love Giselle and Omar more than anything. This is the second time Giselle has done this kind of thing. This time she has crossed the line without any justification. What does she expect, to not even deal with the issue of Natalia's resurfacing? I have not told Omar yet; he will be devastated when he hears of this charade. I am not

going to ask Giselle to come back home. She needs to make a decision on her own and come back on her own. I thought we resolved
all such suspicions last time. This is devastating, and I cannot go
through with this. Giselle is acting like a child. I am on my way to
see Omar, Christina, and Ibrahim in Spain. I just want to make sure
Omar does not become depressed over this. For all practical pur-
poses, Giselle is his mother, not Natalia."

"I agree with you," Antoine said, "but this development makes
even sane people act strangely. While I believe Giselle is wrong,
give her time to think things over and come to her senses. Rasheed,
you need to assure her that she is your one and only love. I can see
this; she is right in feeling the way she feels. She is emotionally
involved, not looking at things like me, from the outside in. She
has not gone back to work since yesterday afternoon."

"Neither Giselle nor I are indispensable to the AP or to *Time*
magazine," Rasheed said. "But Giselle cannot just skip work anytime
she gets mad at me. Go see her. Nouri and I will follow you shortly."

When Rasheed arrived at Antoine's house, Giselle was expecting
him to plead with her. Instead he told her, "I am not here to soothe
your feelings. I am here to drop you off at the AP office. Who do you
think you are? You and I are two of a hundred foreign correspondents in Beirut. In the final analysis, we are both dispensable."

Giselle was pleased with the attention. "I will have you drop me
off, after I change."

"No, Nouri will drop you off with his cab, and I will have
Antoine drop me off," Rasheed said, not wanting to appease
Giselle. "If you thought I was going to invite you back, you are
mistaken. This time you must decide on your own, and if you
decide to come back, you owe Omar and me a huge apology. I do
not know if an apology will do it. You did not bother to check on

how I feel about the whole thing. You think I would have hidden my feelings—my unwavering love for you? I am not going to stand for any of this teenage behavior anymore. You are thirty-nine years old, and you need to act your age. Or maybe you need to spend a year in a convent and humble yourself some."

Giselle was shocked at Rasheed's assertiveness and loud voice, but she proceeded to change her clothes and head with Nouri to her office.

Rasheed intentionally did not want to mention anything about his planned but secret trip to Spain. He wanted Giselle to find out about it and accept it on its innocent face value in his absence. He believed that while it was a minor thing, she would either start seeing the big picture or would miss it altogether.

———————

Omar was staying at one of Ibrahim's very plush inns, occupying a large suite. When Ibrahim dropped him off at the hotel, Christina left with her father to freshen up but promised Omar she would be back in no time to see him way before dinner.

When Christina arrived at the inn, she and Omar went to the bar to have a glass of wine. She then went to the room while Omar finished one more drink and, unbeknownst to her, practiced his Spanish with the barman. When he got to the room, Christina was in her slip, getting dressed rather quietly, with her panties in her hands. He had not expected her to have taken off her clothes in the first place.

Omar surprised Christina by gently taking her panties from her hands. He sat her down between his legs on the bed and pulled the panties onto her without saying a word.

Omar kissed Christina on her cheek and then whispered into her ear, "I want you to finish getting dressed and go out and knock on the door. Then we can do whatever you want to do. I am dying to start."

Christina slapped him on the face and snapped, "No." Omar put his palm to his cheek. Christina lifted his palm and replaced it with her own. She then kissed him softly on his cheek and just as softly on his lips.

"I don't want you to misunderstand me," Omar said. "More than anything, I would love making love to you, but this must be done properly. Again, I would like for you to get up and get out of the room first. Please don't get mad at me. What will come next will be much more enjoyable. Do you understand?"

She gave him a half-nasty look as she dragged her feet slowly and left the room. She waited a moment and then knocked on the door. Omar took Christina by the hand and gave her a big kiss on her frowning lips.

He pulled her in slowly and pinned her against the wall and started licking her neck upward to her earlobes, following his father's instructions, as devised by Federico, that were supposedly based on the guidelines of the prophet.

He undressed her and then undressed himself. He easily backed her into his crotch. He bent her gently over the bed and massaged her all over. She reached two orgasms in the process.

"Oh my God, this is the first time," she told him, looking into his eyes.

"It will be one of many, I hope," he said.

She pulled him onto the bed. He was cautious not to penetrate, but Christina suddenly flipped over him and helped him in. She thrust herself down forcefully, giving first a sound of pain and then a sigh of relief. She had just lost her virginity, and Omar had done it.

Christina not only made sure that Omar was the one who deflowered her but also that he was fully aware of her desire to have it done that moment, during their first interlude. Their lovemaking continued with intense passion for three full hours.

Later, after a lengthy discussion of Father Federico and his influence on Omar's family and their approach to sex, Christina told Omar that she did not care how it all started, but that she was very happy with the results. In fact, Christina was paying more attention than she let on.

The following day, through Ibrahim's contacts, Christina managed to call a professor of Islamic studies at the University of Madrid. She was not reticent to ask her, in a roundabout way, about Mohammad's foreplay admonitions. Her interest was in two specific aspects. She first wanted to know whether Mohammad recommended foreplay between men and women. Secondly, she wanted to know if the responsibility of foreplay was assigned to the man only or if it could be shared with the female partner.

Without pressing Christina to be specific, the professor knew what Christina wanted an answer for. According to the professor's interpretation, the objective was to reach a possible pleasure parity, which meant that both the man and the woman could lead such action.

"Are you sure?"

"Not only am I sure," the professor said, "it is a guideline prudent men and women try to follow." Surprised as she was at his answer, Christina was convinced she heard the facts from a credible authority.

———

Rasheed arrived at Ibrahim's mansion shortly after two in the afternoon the following day. Ibrahim wanted to surprise Omar and Christina at the cocktail party. He was now giving the party in both Omar's and Rasheed's honor.

Around the same time, Christina called the inn at the winery and ordered Omar's belongings be moved to the largest suite, a two-thousand-square-foot suite, with eighteen feet of hardwood space in front of the extra-large bed. She also ordered a tape player and enough speakers to place throughout the suite.

She was supposed to pick up Omar at seven that evening, an hour before the cocktail party. Instead, she arrived late afternoon. Expecting his room service male valet to bring him a cup of coffee, Omar was in a tee shirt and briefs and was holding a towel with which he tried to cover his briefs.

Christina approached Omar with playful and determined confidence. She pulled the towel from his hand, threw it on the chair, and studied his crotch.

She then looked him in the eye and said, "I haven't noticed this before, but you have matching gray briefs and tee shirt. My, my—very French. I am not going to be mean to you and ask you to get dressed, or to have you go out and knock on the door. I feel charitable this afternoon. You can stay in your briefs. I am going to do to you what you did to me last night. I am going to lead our foreplay to enjoy myself first, and for you to follow. I have found out that a woman is entitled to lead the action as much as a man."

"Where did you come up with this piece of news?" snapped Omar.

"From the head of the department of Islamic philosophy at the University of Madrid. I feel he knows more about Islam than you do. Come here. I want to hug you and tell you that I know that you are much stronger than I am. I cannot control your urges, except by agreement between us, through squeezing or pinching you, and if that won't work, I will have to bite you. All the while, you have to obey."

Omar did not hesitate. "I guess I have no choice. Go ahead."

Christina's intent was to dampen Omar's urges and excite hers and manage to reach one or more climaxes before Rasheed got totally excited. She turned on the tape player, which played soft flamenco music. As she danced and undulated to the music in her suede cloche skirt and cherry-embroidered Spanish blouse, she went through rubbing herself—including her arms, thighs, breasts, and genitalia—against Omar's half-naked body.

She took one deep breath after another to help her get aroused. She was slowly getting aroused, but so was Omar. Controlling Omar's excitement was much harder than elevating hers, she discovered.

Initially Omar dampened his excitement after she squeezed and pinched him. His responses got weaker and weaker as he got further excited, and before long he developed resistance to her squeezing and pinching. He found it difficult to control himself after getting bitten.

His erect penis became obvious, and to Christina's eyes it was an unacceptable physical protrusion and a potential impediment to her approach. She tried and tried to depress it by squeezing and pinching much harder. Some of her bites on his neck and shoulder produced drops of blood, but with no success. Omar nevertheless did not want to disappoint her, and he tried not to complain, even about the most hurtful bites, but he failed. "Oh my God, what are you doing, Christina? Are you trying to have sex or take revenge?"

Halfway into reaching her first climax, she said hesitantly, "Revenge for what? You are my love, my only love and one that I cannot live without. *Cariño*, you have not done anything wrong."

"Your biting seems like revenge for the eighth-century Arab invasion of Spain!" Omar said in Spanish.

Christina answered him sarcastically. "Honey, if I were taking revenge for the invasion of Spain, I would have bit your penis right off."

As Omar lost his erection and as Christina rubbed herself against his firm buttock, she reached her first climax. Suddenly she realized that Omar had spoken in Spanish. She interrupted her erotic movement and said, "*Cariño*, how come you have not told me you could speak Spanish? You have been lying to me by omission all this time."

"I was supposed to make it known this evening after being introduced by Ibrahim," he replied. "I did not count on you biting me."

"But you did not listen to me. I squeezed and pinched you so many times, *cariño*," Christina answered with a smile. "Let us finish what we started. Oh, look! You no longer have an erection. I was about to bite you right there—no need anymore," she said with a snicker.

Christina managed to reach another climax before she laid Omar on his back, in bed. With her hands, she slipped his briefs off. She mounted him and each reached climax. Then they were done. They cuddled in each other's arms with Christina jokingly asking to check on his figuratively injured penis. Omar would not let her check it out.

She then asked him when he'd started studying Spanish and learned that he had started two years earlier, only one month after they started corresponding with each other, right after she sent her picture.

"You are like most men. You go for looks and not for the brain; once you saw my picture, you made your decision. That is all right. I will forgive you. I know now that you loved me from the start."

They laughed, and then Omar took over. They stayed in bed until early evening, intermittently making love.

Christina confided in Omar that she, too, had been taking advanced conversational English during the previous eighteen months. "I know you have not noticed it, since we have been talking three to four times a week. I had an American tutor and an English tutor. One taught me conversational English, and another conversational American English, three times a week. Now we can go back and forth speaking in English and in Spanish."

After Christina went home and changed her clothes, Ibrahim took her by the hand to the living room, where Omar was waiting. Christina ran toward him and hugged him, to her father's delight.

───────

There were more than three hundred guests at the cocktail party that evening, including many business partners and associates, several government officials, and members of the diplomatic corps. Ibrahim noticed several bites on Omar's neck. Before he started as master of ceremonies, he asked Omar about the bites. In a tongue-in-cheek response, Omar said that he and Christina had an argument about the Arab invasion of Spain, and that Christina gave him a few love bites because she did not accept his narrative of history.

"It must have been a heated argument, as those are serious bites," Ibrahim said.

Before he introduced him to individual guests, Ibrahim explained why Omar was so important to him and his family. He recounted his meeting Rasheed and how Rasheed had saved him from bankruptcy.

"And now, it is my pleasure to introduce my dearest friend and the man who saved me from bankruptcy, Rasheed Dinar, the father of the man whom Christina is madly in love with."

Omar and Christina looked at each other with pleasant amazement.

As Rasheed came into the party room, Christina ran toward him to give him a very warm hug. "It is so nice to meet you finally. I have been looking forward to this great occasion. I am happy you are here, and I'm happy that Omar and I are together."

Omar walked slowly toward his father and hugged him. "Where is Giselle?" he asked.

"It is a long story," Rasheed said. "She is mad and confused about Natalia."

Christina looked at Rasheed with disappointment. "But why?" she said. "Natalia knows about you and Giselle, and she knows that she is the past and Giselle is the present. This is disappointing. I would have liked to see her. What a shame."

"I agree, but Giselle is like that," Rasheed said. "She sometimes acts immaturely." He then told them that after the party he wanted to hear about their meeting with Natalia.

Ibrahim told the crowd how Christina and Omar got to know each other through correspondence and through exchanging their pictures and film clips of themselves. He told the guests how apprehensive he was about Christina going to Beirut to meet Omar, because he thought both—or at least one of them—would be disappointed with the other.

"It is my great pleasure that I am tonight announcing that Omar, the son of my dearest friend, and my lovely Christina are in love. Not only that, but Christina will be joining Omar in Houston after she finishes her second year at the University of Madrid."

Omar had not been told the news. He was elated. He kissed Christina on both cheeks and then gave her a soft kiss on her lips and a big hug, holding her for a long while. She hugged him tightly back and rested her cheek on his chest.

They drank and danced all night. The crowd was very impressed with Omar and Rasheed, particularly with their looks, attitude, and in the case of Omar, relative command of the Spanish language. One young, beautiful daughter of an Arab ambassador had her eyes on him and made her moves. Christina made sure to tell her that Omar learned Spanish specifically because they were deeply in love.

After she stopped the ambassador's daughter's advances, Christina told Omar that he needed to sleep by himself that evening to give everyone the impression that they had not slept together. Omar, in agreement, made sure that many guests saw Christina kiss him goodbye for the evening as he left to go back to the inn.

As Christina kissed him goodbye, she whispered in his ear, "We still can do it in the morning. I want you to take it easy tonight."

During their brief visit to Warsaw and the two days in Madrid, Omar detected characteristics in Christina that had not gotten through to him during the two years of long-distance communication. He had learned that Christina was not only feisty but also strong-willed, playful, and sarcastic.

———

The following morning, Christina arrived at Omar's palatial suite at eight, six hours after Omar had left the party. She used a master key to get in, took off her shoes, and tiptoed toward the bed. She then took off her clothes and slipped under the covers and cuddled Omar.

Omar didn't realize Christina had crawled into bed with him until his hand accidentally touched her firm breast. They rubbed against each other with so much warmth, and both showed clear signs of being enamored with the other.

———

For four short days, Christina showed Omar around Madrid and the eight wineries Ibrahim owned that were within a one-day return trip from the city.

Similarly, Ibrahim showed Rasheed around town. But before he left, Rasheed asked that Christina show him around too. He considered her both an adopted daughter and a prospective daughter-in-law and loved spending the day with her. Christina described to him her experience in Warsaw.

Three days later, when Rasheed arrived in Beirut, he immediately headed to his office. There, he found a message from Giselle. He first hesitated to call her back, but when he did, the conversation was formal and specific. She asked if she could borrow his files on prostitution in Lebanon. Rasheed was firm. He told her that he would have nothing to do with her unless she genuinely apologized and showed real remorse.

"Don't be mad at me," Giselle said. "Haven't you heard? They caught two more parliament members engaged in the prostitution of young girls."

Rasheed had not heard the news. Since Giselle was the one who brought up the subject, he promised that he would lend her the files after he finished with them, subject to *Time*'s approval. He told her he would let her know and thought that New York may not mind since the files were not very recent.

Giselle went to Rasheed's office, hugged him, and gave him a kiss. "You still owe me a sincere apology," he said.

"Don't embarrass me in front of your colleagues," she said.

"I do not care. Just do it and mean it!" he said. "I cannot go through this ever again."

That night, Giselle bought a bottle of eighty-year-old single malt scotch. It cost a quarter of her monthly salary. After she and Rasheed kissed and made up, she told him that Antoine was on his way to share a scotch drink with them.

"There is no other man I would like to spend time with than Antoine," Rasheed said. "He is a gentleman's gentleman. I wish you were as balanced as he is! Such will save me all this heartbreak." He gave her a kiss.

He then looked her in the eye and said, "The reason I went to Madrid was because I wanted to make sure that Natalia knew well who you are and what you mean to me. According to Omar and Christina, she does, and she is sanguine about it. She knows that I will love her all my life, but she is no longer my woman. You are."

Giselle felt good about the whole affair and became more aware of her own rash behavior. Rasheed and Giselle's relationship was back on an even keel.

———

Javier, the head of security, drove Christina and Omar to the airport. Ibrahim was scheduled to meet them after they had visited with the deputy airport director. He needed to take care of a last-minute issue.

Christina had started tearing up on her way to the airport. Omar tried to soothe her feelings by reminding her that they were going to be together in less than five months, but to no avail. When she heard that Ibrahim was not going to make it, she started sobbing. She had expected her father to console her. She was desperately in love and very emotional about it. The same applied to Omar, though he seemed able to contain his emotions somewhat.

The farewell was an overwrought situation for Christina. Javier reluctantly tried to calm her. He was frustrated seeing this intelligent, gorgeous young woman in so much emotional pain and not being able to do anything to help her.

Yet to Christina, it felt as if her senses were floating in the air, without any solid foundation to anchor herself to. She felt as if she were separated from herself.

In the end, Omar intervened by publicly kissing her all over her face and wiping her tears with his kisses. He held her in his arms tightly and felt her tears fall over his shoulders.

Before Omar let go of her, he said, "You know I love you more than anything, more than the air I am breathing. Without you in my life, I would have a difficult time breathing this same air. I want you to be strong, not only for yourself but also for me."

He then let go of her and handed her to Javier, who was hesitant to hug her but did so when Omar winked at him.

———

Omar could not sleep on either flight. He tried to make himself busy, but to no avail. As he retraced their every move and action over the previous few days, he set his head back and tried to sleep, but that continued to elude him.

When Omar got to Houston, the first thing he did was call Christina, although it was two in the morning in Madrid. When he told her that he hoped he was not waking her up, she said, "Are you crazy? I could not sleep without hearing that you got there safely. Talk to me. I need to be able to sleep, but now talk to me. I want to hear your voice. I've cried since you left."

During the hour they talked, Christina relaxed considerably and even began to get drowsy. Omar asked her to hang up and call him after she woke up.

The routine of calling each other at least once a day was never skipped. They would go into full details of what they had done that day, including describing their lectures, their state of mind, and what they ate. On several occasions, Omar told Christina how much he missed her flamenco dancing.

She told him how much she missed holding him in her arms. "I want to feel you, hug you, and lay my head on your shoulder," she told him.

Their daily conversations continued up until the day before Christina's scheduled departure to Houston. She was so excited. Omar had told her repeatedly to bring very little to Houston, because they would go shopping together.

Finally the day of departure came. Christina checked things over and over. She opened and closed her three suitcases three times an hour. Javier told her not to worry, that her father would send her anything she left behind, and then he said that it was time to go. In an ethereal and giddy mood, Christina got into the car next to him. She was finally on her way to the airport. Javier was pleasantly smiling to himself. He had not seen so much love and longing as that exuded by Christina.

Once again, Ibrahim promised to meet Christina at the deputy airport manager's office, and once again he was running late. He'd had an important meeting and ended up getting into the car thirty-five minutes later than he had planned.

After the driver stopped to fill up with gas, Ibrahim ordered him to speed it up. Halfway to the airport, Ibrahim had the driver further increase his speed to try to beat a traffic light. The light had already changed when the car shot through the intersection. A large truck hit Ibrahim's car smack in the spot where he was sitting. The car flipped over, and Ibrahim was thrown out. He landed on the curb and was taken to the hospital. His driver was barely hurt.

The driver called Ibrahim's secretary, and she called the deputy director of the airport and told him what had happened. The director told Javier, and Javier broke the news to Christina.

Upon hearing the news, Christina became confused. One minute she was on top of the world. The next, she felt that somebody had pulled the rug out from under her. As a result, she fell into an emotional abyss.

For a few minutes she did not know what to do. As she partially collected her emotions, she told Javier to immediately take her to the hospital, where her father was being cared for.

At the hospital, it took four hours for one of the orthopedic surgeons to come out and let Christina know that her father had four broken ribs, a broken pelvis, a broken leg, and a serious concussion.

After eleven hours of procedures performed by five surgeons, Ibrahim was rolled out of the operating room into intensive care.

Two hours later, Christina was allowed in to see him. One half of Ibrahim's body was in a cast. He couldn't open his mouth to speak or eat and had to be fed intravenously. He wasn't in a coma, but he might as well have been. His eyes were still shut, and the physicians were waiting for the slightest movement.

Christina deferred some of the decisions to her father's personal physician and to his secretary. The three of them decided to send a private plane to bring back the top neurosurgeon from vacation. They were concerned that there might be permanent brain damage.

The results came through, indicating a minor brain hemorrhage. They were pleased with the decision to have the neurosurgeon interrupt his vacation. By the time the neurosurgeon arrived, Ibrahim's brain hemorrhage had stopped. The neurosurgeon decided not to operate. After being at the hospital for sixteen hours, Christina and Javier were exhausted. She decided to check in at the hotel next door, where she managed to sleep for four hours.

With all that was going on, and with the demands on her to make decisions related to Ibrahim's life and death, she was unable to connect with Omar. Meanwhile in Houston, Omar had checked into an airport hotel, where he and Christina were supposed to stay and celebrate before moving to his apartment.

———

At the airport in Houston, Omar waited for an hour after the passengers on Christina's flight to Houston had disembarked. He then checked with Air France. After the airport staff checked with Paris, they informed him that Christina had canceled her trip fifteen minutes before she was supposed to board in Madrid. He returned home and called Ibrahim's house. Nobody from the staff could tell him anything.

Omar was getting nervous about the lack of news, especially about the reason Christina canceled her trip. He was seriously considering buying a ticket to Madrid when she called him—thirty-six hours later—to let him know what had happened. She told him then that she could not go to Houston until her father recovered.

Ibrahim's accident impacted Omar deeply and caused him to think of his father and mother. He wanted to buttress his relationship with his mother, Natalia. He phoned her and asked her to meet him in Madrid. He thought spending time with her now could compensate partially for all the time they'd lost over the years.

Natalia got there first and was met by one of Ibrahim's security men. She was taken to the hospital, where she was greeted warmly by Christina. Although the two had not spent much time together in Warsaw, Christina was happy to see a mother figure come into her life. Her own mother had died in a car accident when she was one year old.

Christina could not contemplate the possibility that she could also lose her father in a car accident. It was too much for her to handle. Natalia's presence, while comforting, was a reminder of the lack of a motherly presence in her life. She was willing to do anything that would help her father recover.

Omar arrived a day later and went to the hospital directly. Christina gave him a warm hug, but when Omar tried to give her a kiss on the lips, she turned her face to have him kiss her on the cheek. Omar could sense that something had changed.

Christina had been going to a church next to the hospital. She had gone to confession for the first time in a long while. She confessed to the priest that she was in a premarital sexual relationship with Omar. She told the priest that Omar was the only one ever in her life.

The priest was rather disturbed by what Christina told him, especially that Omar was a Muslim. He was not forgiving. He advised her that in this case, her true forgiveness would come from her devotion to her father and from abstaining from sex. He said Christina had slipped into a daze and was very vulnerable.

But Omar knew nothing of this interaction with the priest. Instead, his conclusion was that she would soon recover from the trauma of her father's accident and return to acting normally. Natalia also thought that Christina was confused and would put things in order after she got over the shock, but she did notice how Christina reacted when Omar got close to her and how Christina interacted with Natalia much more than she did with Omar.

———

For the fourth night, Omar arranged to have dinner with his mother alone. For the first time in his life, he sought her advice. "Do you sense that there is a change in Christina's attitude toward me since you saw her in Warsaw, Mama?"

The word "Mama" was music to her ears. She gently placed her palm on Omar's cheek and said, "Christina is confused after her father's accident. Whether or not the effect of the accident will have a permanent impact is too early to tell. Give her time and don't pressure her. I can empathize with her, based on my own experience."

"The thought of my losing her is unbearable," Omar said, "but the thought of Christina losing herself is even more unbearable."

"I am sure you are losing her temporarily, but even if it's permanent, you are losing her for reasons beyond your control or hers. Don't torment yourself."

He then asked his mother if she could stay with Christina for a couple of weeks longer after he returned to Houston for university. Natalia welcomed the opportunity, and Omar was relieved.

The redirection of Christina's attention—from Omar and toward Natalia—became increasingly visible to both Omar and Natalia. Still unaware of the influence of the priest next door, Omar wanted Christina to come out of the trauma whole, but emotionally he was thinking of how not to lose her.

CHAPTER 26

Omar went back to Houston two days later. Natalia saw him off at the airport while Christina stayed at the hospital. The thoughts that swirled in his head became negative and emotionally disturbing, because he could not figure out the rationale or explain the psychological trauma behind Christina's upended behavior. Under the circumstances, he thought that she would lean on him, and together they would do their utmost to help the situation.

But that was not what she chose to do. She did not want Omar to sacrifice his own future due to Ibrahim's situation. She wanted him to be happy, even at the expense of losing him—a rather simple thought. She thought that in time he would get over losing her and eventually be happy without her.

It was a sort of misguided but selfless move, devoid of any consideration of the fact that she was influenced by a priest she barely knew, who, like most clerics, possessed a dogmatic and tunnel-visioned outlook. She was totally oblivious to the potential for her actions to cause deep unhappiness to others.

———————

Three months later, Omar and Natalia were back in Madrid. Natalia had gone back a second time in between. All through the three months, Omar called Christina often, but not once did she call him. Now in Madrid, he asked if Christina could have dinner with him alone while Natalia watched over Ibrahim.

At dinner, Omar held Christina's hands and said, "I need you to be honest with me all the way, just as you have been ever since we started corresponding. I need you to tell me how you feel about us."

"If you had asked me this question before the accident," she said, "I would have said without the slightest hesitation that I could not imagine life without you. My love for you has not diminished, but this accident has put it on hold. I wish I could say more."

Christina kept holding on to Omar's hands and started sobbing silently, her tears falling on both their hands.

Omar kissed her on the forehead and said, "I want you to come back to me, and I will wait for you no matter what."

"Omar, please let us go back to the hospital," she replied. "I cannot take any more of this."

Omar left to go back to Houston while Natalia stayed behind. Natalia started to insist that Christina, from time to time, go back home and rest while she took care of Ibrahim. Natalia, at Christina's request, had already moved in with her.

Almost every time Natalia sent her home, Christina would stop by the church. She averaged going to confession once every week. Somehow things developed spiritually between her and the priest. She gradually accepted the thought that what had befallen Ibrahim had probably been caused by her sins, particularly her having premarital sex with Omar, who was not a Catholic.

One evening, Catholic Christina confided in Catholic Natalia that she believed that her father's accident had been caused by her sinning.

Natalia tried to dissuade Christina away from such thoughts, but it was to no avail. Natalia shared with Christina that she had had premarital sex with Rasheed, Omar's father, but that she did not feel she had sinned. "Christina, we will always be sinners. Only the sacrifice of our Lord will erase our sins. Our sins are endless."

None of Natalia's words or efforts made a dent in Christina's psyche. On the contrary, she told Natalia, "I vow that if my father recovers fully, I will join a Catholic order and become a nun."

Upon hearing such a vow, Natalia was dumbfounded. All she could say was "You are not serious." Natalia confirmed that she was entirely serious and that she had already told her priest the same.

While shocked at Christina's vows and the potential for a more permanent separation between her son and the woman he loved, she kept the news to herself, hoping Christina would have a change of heart before Omar returned to Madrid.

But nothing changed before he returned, and Natalia had no choice but to relay the whole story to Omar.

"If she is going to become a nun after Ibrahim recovers," he said, "and she is now so distant from me, where does this leave me?"

Natalia again put her palm on Omar's cheek and said, "You are now my only love. You must wait and see. Things could change, but for the immediate future I think what you see is what you get. I couldn't have chosen a more lovely girl for you. She is adorable, but none of us is perfect. She has a strong streak of stubbornness and a touch of off-center behavior."

As Omar watched his mother in the hospital room, he noticed the special care she was providing for Ibrahim. It was more than the care for a young friend's father. He could sense a closer emotional attachment. He noticed that Ibrahim, while unable to talk, looked at Natalia intently and that Natalia in response was taking care of him as if he were her man.

Omar wanted to be sure before he jumped to the wrong conclusion. He knew that Christina might have noticed something more concrete, since she and Natalia kept each other company almost all the time.

He met with Christina as his mother went home to rest. He mentioned his satisfaction with his mother living with her and caring for Ibrahim. He emphasized that he was there for his mother.

"Your mother is the best thing that ever happened to me," Christina said, "and although I have not expressed my gratitude to Natalia, I am most grateful for her help and for her sacrifices."

"You are missing the point. I am here to ask about Natalia's emotions and state of mind," he said. "Am I imagining things, or do I sense that my mother has developed more than a mere liking for your father?"

"I did not want to volunteer my opinion," Christina said, "but you are right. I think she has grown to love him, either as a brother or as the man she has been missing in her life. I think it is the latter." She then asked Omar to wait and see—as she was doing—and time would tell, when hopefully Ibrahim was able to talk.

Six months after Ibrahim's accident, one early morning after Omar had gone back to Houston and Christina was at church, Natalia thought she saw Ibrahim's left hand move. She zeroed in on his hands and arms and found out she was not imagining things: his left hand moved again.

Natalia rushed to call the nurse but ran into Christina. She told her what was happening, and Christina rushed to the room and discovered that Ibrahim had opened his eyes fully. He could barely open them before.

She was about to hug her father, but Natalia stopped her and asked her to consult with the physicians first. They called the nurse, and before the physician showed up, Ibrahim managed to point to the cast around his mouth. He wanted it removed or reduced.

Another physician was summoned and managed to cut out some of the cast. Ibrahim started stammering: "What happened? How come I am in the hospital?"

He opened his arms, ushering Christina to give him a hug. Christina did. She took Natalia's hand, put it on Ibrahim's arm, and said, "This is Natalia, Omar's mother. Do you recall? We talked about her before your accident. I met her in Warsaw."

"What accident?" Ibrahim exclaimed.

By the time Christina finished explaining to her father how much Natalia was of help to her and how much she sacrificed to take care of him, he'd opened his eyes further and was rubbing Natalia's lower arm, expressing his gratitude.

When the attending physician arrived, Ibrahim's face was slowly getting over some of the visible effects of his accident. His sedation, having been considerably reduced, ceased to slow his interactions.

Natalia intentionally did not want to engage in lengthy conversations with Ibrahim, lest they stress him out. Within hours, Christina and Natalia had told him what had happened and how it came about that Natalia was there.

He then asked about Omar. Christina told him the bright side of things: "Omar has been flying to Madrid every three months."

She did not mention her change of feelings, and Ibrahim did not notice her omissions. It took him a couple of days to absorb what had happened to him and what had transpired during his ordeal.

Finally, Christina looked her father in the eye and told him of her vow. "Dad, I am sure you will recover fully, and I will keep my vow. As soon as that happens, I will become a nun."

Ibrahim was shocked at what he heard. "Is this a joke? What about Omar?" he asked.

"I have already told him, and he understands the situation."

"I have thought of Omar as a son, and now you are telling me I am not going to have him in my life. At the same time, you are also leaving my normal life. This means I will never have grandchildren. I wish you could reconsider. I don't think it is too late!"

Natalia was convinced that the faintest hope had evaporated when Christina challenged Ibrahim's wishes. Later that evening she relayed the situation to Omar. But he nevertheless flew to Madrid to see Ibrahim and to visit with his mother.

Ibrahim could sense Omar's frustrations, sadness, and wistfulness. He encouraged Omar not to give up and told him that this time Ibrahim wanted him to stay at his mansion. Omar refused.

Omar had not planned to meet with Christina by herself, but then he ended up asking her to have dinner with him alone, prefacing his request with the explanation that the dinner was for the purpose of discussing something else.

During an awkwardly silent moment at dinner, he said, "Now I am sure. Both my mother and your father have feelings for each other." He continued jokingly: "I guess we should not feel bad about our separation, since Natalia and Ibrahim's love will make up for that."

Christina looked at Omar pensively and held back her tears.

Omar, for the first time, shook Christina's hand and refrained from trying to kiss her, not even on the cheek.

"I think I will love you the rest of my life, nun or no nun."

"I will love you too," she replied, "nun or no nun, but I vowed to marry the Lord, and I know you don't want me to break a vow of this kind." They both teared up. Omar could not help hugging her, and he wished her good luck.

Ibrahim recovered fully, and Christina quickened her preparations to become a nun. Within several months, she was accepted as a Benedictine novice. Everyone was disappointed, but in the end none more than Rasheeda, who had groomed Christina's relationship with her nephew. Both Ibrahim and Natalia were disheartened not to have Christina in their lives. Ibrahim asked Natalia to keep visiting them.

Rasheed, on the other hand, was convinced that Christina was serious about her vows, and that only she on her own, remote as it may be, would change her course. He and Giselle specifically flew to Madrid to address this issue with all concerned. He suggested Natalia be there, but she intentionally did not make it.

In the presence of Giselle, Omar, and Ibrahim, Rasheed asked everyone to drop all efforts to convince Christina to act against her vows. "Please resign yourself to the fact that it is all in Christina's hands," he said. "Any effort to change her mind, now or in the future, may end up being more harmful than helpful."

Ibrahim responded first. He agreed with Rasheed completely. Giselle also agreed.

Looking at the floor, Omar said, "I will refrain from trying. Let things take their course." He then turned around, not wanting to look any of them in the face.

Ibrahim called Natalia in Warsaw that evening and told her about Rasheed's wisdom and message to them. Natalia could not agree more. Ibrahim told her that it would have been an opportune occasion for her to be there, as the subject was most serious and of keen interest to everyone.

"I know you are right, Ibrahim, but I was not able to put it all together," she said. "I blinked at the last moment."

Natalia followed with further visits to Madrid but came less often. She continued to stay at Ibrahim's mansion in one of the three guesthouses. In the evenings, she and Ibrahim would go out for dinner. Ibrahim made it a point not to draw Natalia in all the way. He was all the time considering and weighing Rasheed's potential reaction.

Within two months, he decided to invite Rasheed and Giselle over, which he did. Omar was also invited, and the four of them relaxed together. On the fourth day, Ibrahim asked Rasheed if the two of them could have dinner by themselves.

"I have something that relates to you and me, Rasheed, and I would like to discuss it exclusively between the two of us," he said.

Rasheed had no idea what Ibrahim was referring to.

Before dinner, as they were having port, Ibrahim said, "Look, I wish I had the style of others, but I don't. So I will get to the point directly. First I need to say that what I am going to tell you has not been shared with anyone else."

Ibrahim paused for a long while and then said, "This is about Natalia. I have become fond of her, and I think she has become fond of me. At my age, I do not want to be coy, but before I take the next step, I strongly feel I need not only your understanding but your approval as well. Shall I go forward or not?"

Rasheed looked at Ibrahim intently and said nothing for a minute, trying to absorb the news. He then replied, "This is a big surprise simply because I had never expected it. I have never given it any thought. Who am I to control Natalia's life, especially since she has no control of mine?"

Rasheed leaned back against his chair and said, "I will never stop loving Natalia. She is the mother of my prize in life, Omar. She will always have a place in my heart. But my real love is Giselle. Natalia is entitled to move on. If I had planned it this way, I would not have been able to do it any better. You are the brother that I never had; you have my blessing, my love, and my good wishes. Oh God, this is great!"

Ibrahim stood up and hugged Rasheed with great affection. Rasheed then told Ibrahim that he needed to tell Giselle and Omar upon their return from dinner. Rasheed asked to see Giselle first. He started by telling her that what he was about to share with her met with his full approval and blessings.

Afterward, he was surprised to learn that Omar had already confided in Giselle, letting her know that Ibrahim and Natalia had feelings for each other. At that time, Giselle told Omar that she could not relay any of that information to Rasheed, as she was an interested party and any move on her part could have been easily misconstrued.

Rasheed and Giselle together met with Omar. Rasheed started the conversation in the same manner he started it with Giselle. He told Omar that what he was about to tell him met with his own approval all the way.

Omar stopped his father and asked, "Is this about my mother?" When Rasheed said yes, Omar again asked, "Is this about Ibrahim?" When Rasheed said yes again, Omar said, "You don't need to say anything else. Ibrahim must have told you; they are in love."

Rasheed nodded quietly.

Giselle was particularly happy, as she had waited for almost fifteen years just to see Rasheed being unburdened by Natalia's tragic experiences. She had not an iota of doubt about Rasheed's love and devotion toward her, but she was still relieved that the news would further unburden him.

The following day, Rasheed took the initiative and visited Christina in the convent. He told her that he was there to convey happy news. "Omar has already told me that you know that Ibrahim has feelings for Natalia."

Christina expressed her full satisfaction and joy with the news and then said, "I hope Omar is as happy with this news as I am."

Rasheed told her to rest assured that Omar was most happy.

Later Omar went to see Christina. He was in a relaxed and playful mood. He told Christina that he was all for his mother and her father to love and care for each other. He expressed to Christina his satisfaction that somehow he and she would have a relationship after all. "A brotherly relationship," he said with a sarcastic chuckle.

She said that she already, as a nun, had heard so many strange stories.

Omar told her teasingly, "I bet you did not think of this aspect: if Ibrahim and Natalia were to marry and have any children, they would be both your siblings and mine."

"Omar, you always tend to think of strange things," Christina said. "You are right. I never thought of it that way. I guess this way we will be related forever." Although a nun, Christina gave Omar a hug.

Omar got resigned to Christina being a nun as he pursued his engineering studies, but his love for her never diminished. A year later, he graduated summa cum laude. He applied to several medical schools and got accepted by most, including the Baylor College of Medicine.

At Rice's commencement, Omar attempted to have his father and mother attend and be together for the first time in many years. He hoped they would try to forget the past and open a new chapter. Rasheed, Giselle, and Natalia welcomed the idea. Omar later thought of Ibrahim, and he suggested that he accompany Natalia, a proposal that Ibrahim welcomed.

Having heard of Natalia's cancelation, Rasheeda and David decided to fly to Houston and join the rest of the family. It was a most pleasant reunion. Both Rasheeda and Giselle tried to soothe Omar's contemplative feelings.

He knew that just about everyone had tried to dissuade Christina without any positive results. He was wistful but understanding that it was all beyond his control. At the same time, he was mindful of Christina's state of mind, albeit strongly believing that her decision was based on raw feelings and wrong influences.

CHAPTER 27

1974
Houston, Texas

In late 1974, Omar was finishing his third year of medical school at Baylor. He was one of the top students in his class, and he spent most of his free time working on a mechanical heart. As an electrical and mechanical engineer, he thought he might be able to make a more advanced human heart than was available at the time.

His loss of Christina and his mechanical heart project sidelined him from paying much attention to any of the female medical students, although two had shown keen interest in him.

He was aware of their interest but never gave it any importance. He was still forlorn about Christina to the degree that sometimes he thought it had been a mistake to make love to her before marriage. But in fact, it was just general remorse and a sense of loss that made him isolate himself from the opposite sex.

On occasion, although not actively seeking to socialize with his male colleagues, he would accept their invitations to the neighborhood bars, and sometimes to their homes to celebrate one holiday or another.

One of the female students, Janice, caught Omar's eye. She was stunningly beautiful. She had not approached Omar until two months from their medical school graduation, when she pretended Omar might have better insight into a problem she contrived, since he was an electrical engineer. She asked if he could spare fifteen minutes to go over the question. When she told him that she was a mechanical engineer, he became suspicious about her seeking his advice in the matter. Janice did not know that Omar was also a mechanical engineer and understood that her contrived question could have been easily answered by any engineer.

Omar played along, but he didn't approach her afterward, and she didn't approach him. At the commencement, Janice was with her parents, her sister, and her brother-in-law. She observed Omar taking pictures with his father, Rasheeda, David, and Giselle. They looked very handsome. Both Giselle and Rasheeda were dressed smartly and very elegantly.

As Omar was greeting some of his other classmates, Janice took the opportunity to compliment Giselle on her dress. Janice then introduced herself. She learned where they were staying in town, at the elegant Warwick Hotel, only blocks from Baylor.

Janice tried to find where Omar was heading for his residency, but none of his family members knew. He had been accepted by half a dozen medical training programs and had not shared his choice with them.

The following day Janice called the Warwick to ask for Hanibake, Omar's assumed last name. The hotel told her that there was nobody with such a name at the hotel, and as she prodded the reservation staff, they told her that there had not been anybody with such name in the last month. She grew incensed, thinking that Omar's parents did not want her to know where they were staying.

She doubted the hotel's story. She and Linda, a classmate and close friend, decided to have a drink at the bar of the hotel to see if they could spot someone from Omar's family. In no time, Omar walked in, and within fifteen minutes he walked out with the rest of the family. Janice did not know what to think of it except that she was convinced that Omar's family was not lying about where they were staying.

Her visit to the hotel was not without some success. On her way to the bathroom, Linda overheard Omar talking to his aunt, Rasheeda, telling her that he had decided to be an internal medicine resident at Baylor. Janice, who had also been offered the same position by Baylor, decided to join the same program.

Several weeks later, Omar and Janice recognized each other and exchanged greetings minutes before the residency orientation began. Janice took the initiative and invited Omar for barbecue on the Fourth of July. Omar, in his usual form, accepted the invitation, as he had done with so many of his classmates if he had nothing better to do.

Janice picked him up and took him to a barbecue ranch, thirty miles from Houston. They got along well. Although she was a stunning beauty, Omar treated her as a friendly classmate rather than as a date. To him, she was a forbidden fruit, considering his languishing feelings for Christina. In less than two weeks, Janice invited Omar again, and he accepted on the condition that he would choose the restaurant. He took her to his favorite Chinese restaurant. It was a hit with her too. He recognized that Janice was interested in him, but to what extent he could not tell.

He decided that in fairness to her, he would tell her about Christina. "I do not want to drown you in my grief, a grief I carry with me all the time. In short, the love of my life, Christina, is now a nun. I cannot stop thinking about her. You are smart enough to figure out the rest."

It was most disappointing news to Janice. She admitted to Omar that she had liked him a lot since their third year in medical school, and she told him that she would like to keep his friendship, not necessarily as a possible boyfriend but as a good friend and classmate. She asked if such a casual arrangement would suit him; otherwise, she told him, she would not bother him.

"I think you are great," Omar replied, "in every respect, and I appreciate your being so understanding. I would be overjoyed to have you as a friend. What more can I ask for under the circumstances?"

Janice and Omar kept in touch and had many dinners together. Neither displayed any romantic feelings for the other, although Janice harbored such feelings. Omar was always on her mind. Not only was she attracted to him, but he was the fruit she could not have.

As a result, she became slightly reserved. She knew that Omar was not dating anybody. She was observed, by more than one friend, quietly moving around from one place to another, almost aimlessly, thinking and daydreaming without paying attention to what was happening around her.

Her mother noticed the same and questioned her. She asked about Janice's refusal to date one interested professional football player and another man who had just started as a cardiologist. Janice had not told anybody about Omar, but she decided to share her thoughts with her mother, Rose.

"What is wrong with you?" Rose said when Janice told her about her crush. "Can you not tell that you are a fabulous-looking young woman *and* a physician? You are wasting your time waiting for some damaged man to respond to your advances. Wake up, Janice. Your sister decided not to have any children, and you are going to end up with none, shedding tears over some Don Juan foreign doctor."

"Mother, I cannot even explain it to myself. I just fell in love without even having talked to Omar."

"You mean he is Mexican?" Rose said.

"No, he is an Arab."

"They are heathens, worse than the Catholics," her father, Malcolm, said.

"Dad, stop saying ugly things about other races and religions. The Catholics are not bad people. Many of my friends are Catholic, and Omar is a very nice and considerate guy."

Janice and her father got into it again, for the twentieth time. Her born-again Christian evangelist father liked to insult the Catholics every time he had an opportunity. In the end, Janice told her parents that she was not after Omar romantically anymore since he continued to be stuck on Christina.

"That is what you get when you get mixed up in the affairs of Muslims and Catholics—a crazy situation," Malcolm said.

A month later, Janice heard Omar telling a friend that he'd be happy to go to lunch with him in Galveston, but that he didn't have a ride.

Janice went to Omar and said, "Listen, I overheard you canceling going to Galveston. You and I can go in my car, have lunch, and drive back to Houston."

Omar accepted the offer. He told her he hoped she did not mind walking for at least ninety minutes by the sea, something he did in Beirut and Galveston.

She readily said, "Not at all." Then she asked him why he didn't have a car. Omar told her that at first he didn't want to put his parents under financial pressure, but now he was used to it. She followed that by asking him what his father did. Omar lied and told her that his father was a plumber in Lebanon.

Omar's name, Hanibake, was fabricated to conceal his identity. Since his arrival in Texas, he had played the role of the son of an economically challenged Palestinian-Lebanese plumber who was hard-pressed to send a son to expensive schools in the United States.

In Galveston, Janice tried to kiss Omar on his cheek. He instead took her hand and they walked hand in hand. The relationship advanced very slowly, until one day Omar had a change of heart, having heard that Christina was moving to a remote convent in the Basque country of Spain. The move convinced him that Christina was gone for good, with no planned return route. Janice, as usual, tried her soft approach, but this time Omar responded by kissing her. She did not know what to make of it. She hesitated at first but engaged Omar with more kisses and caressing.

On the following trip to Galveston, after a heavy session of passionate play, Janice told Omar that she had reserved a suite at one of the plushest hotels in town and asked if he was interested in joining her.

"I'm interested, but I do not know whether you want to engage me in such activity," he said.

Janice did not know what to say after hearing such contradictory statements.

When they got into the suite, Omar advised Janice to follow his instructions. He then performed as his father had taught him. He undressed Janice piece by piece while massaging her and bringing her to two climaxes before he penetrated her.

After three hours of sex, Janice thought it had all been worth the wait. And her attitude seemed to change after her successful interlude with Omar. Her mother noticed a change in her and immediately asked her about Omar, to which Janice answered lightheartedly that he was doing just fine.

Janice's mother, Rose, did not need to read the tea leaves. She got the message. She was curious about Omar, and so she invited him to a Texas home-prepared barbecue.

When he arrived, Rose could tell right away why he'd won Janice's heart. He was a tall, handsome, and athletic-looking young man who spoke four languages and carried himself elegantly, with great confidence and style. The mother was willing to overlook Omar being a foreigner and a Muslim. She thought that despite her daughter's exceptional beauty and professional accomplishments, Omar was a professional equal to her daughter and a real catch.

It was not the same with her father. He thought dating or marrying a foreigner was more sinful than marrying a Catholic.

Dinner went well except for a couple of racial slurs by Malcolm. Janice helped her mother clean after the meal, and then Rose excused herself to accompany Malcolm to his sister's for the night, seventy miles north of Houston.

Janice took the opportunity to take Omar to her bedroom. Without saying a word, she closed the blinds and started taking off her clothes. "Undress and lie in bed," she told Omar as she finished taking off her blouse.

As she looked at Omar lying in bed fully clothed, she stopped removing her clothing and began to take Omar's clothes off, piece by piece, as he watched. She then stripped down until she was totally naked except for her alligator-skin boots.

As she walked toward the bed, Omar said, "You still have your boots on!"

"And my special spurs," she said.

She turned her back to him and stretched her right leg toward him, placing her boots and spurs at the edge of the mattress.

Aroused, Omar asked, "What are the spurs for?"

"I dig the spurs into the bed to push and pull much better, and if you don't perform well, I can then use them up you-know-where."

Janice led the lovemaking session and, as promised, knew when to push and when to pull. She did not have to use the spurs except for occasional anchoring. Although the score ended up two to two, it was still a fruitful engagement, with less preparation and less hassle, as far as Janice was concerned.

The following week she went to the hospital coffee shop, hoping to catch Omar. Instead, she was approached by another Arab internal medicine resident, Sami Sandook. When Sami told Janice that he was from Lebanon, she asked if he knew Omar Hanibake.

"Hanibake," Sami laughed, exhibiting his usual dismissive attitude. "This is not his real name; his real name is Omar Dinar. Hanibake is his mother's old maiden name, two generations back."

When she asked Sami why one would use a different name, he could not say, but he volunteered that he and Omar had been high school classmates back in Lebanon, and that the Dinar family was one of the richest families in the country.

"They are very humble and do not like to flaunt their wealth or let anybody know that they are filthy rich." Sami added in pure jest, "Especially female contenders. Maybe that is why he uses the false name."

Janice did not know what to think. She thought Sami must have been mistaken, but when he insisted that Omar came from the rich Dinar family, she was beside herself. If what Sami Sandook told her was true, then surely Omar had fabricated the story about Christina and about his father being a plumber, since he did not want her to be after his family's money.

She asked Sami about Omar's father's profession. "He is a very famous journalist. You can look for him in *Time* magazine. He is listed under special correspondents."

As soon as she finished with Sami, Janice went to the library and looked up Rasheed Dinar's name. She then called the Warwick Hotel and managed to confirm that a Rasheed Dinar was a hotel guest at the time of the commencement. Upon looking further, she could see the strong resemblance between Omar and Rasheed Dinar's picture in *Time*.

That did it. She was convinced that Omar had fabricated the story about Christina and being the son of a plumber so that he could date girls without being pressured to marry them for fear they may be after his money.

For a week she stopped going to the hospital coffee shop and avoided seeing Omar altogether while she steamed inside and tried to think what to do next. Omar did not seek her out either. When she saw Sami again, he told her that he and Omar were going to Galveston that day to eat at Gaido's.

She became convinced that Omar managed to use reverse psychology to lure her, and now, after his success in seducing her, he was neglecting her altogether. She asked Sami when they were having lunch, and Sami said one o'clock.

That Saturday Janice drove to Galveston and hid behind an electric pole. Sami was waiting for Omar to catch up with him, after he stopped to listen to a sidewalk musician. As Omar approached Sami, Janice came from behind the pole, hurrying toward him, totally agitated and unsettled. She hesitated for a second and then slapped Omar on the face, as hard as she could.

She looked at him with piercing eyes and said, "You thought I was after your damned money, you bastard. Fuck you and fuck your money. I thought you had feelings for me. But all you have is contempt for other people, just because you know you are so rich. Fuck you."

Deeply hurt, Omar stared back at her, totally silent and shocked. Sami grabbed her by the arm and said, "You bitch, I thought I was telling you all of this in confidence. Instead, you acted in a trashy way. If Omar does nothing, I promise you I will get you, just wait."

Janice was totally surprised at Sami's response. She was confused, as she thought he would be much more understanding since he was the one who told her that Omar was hiding his riches from suspected gold diggers. She never considered that Sami may have been kidding about that.

Omar, on the other hand, asked Sami to let go of Janice's arm and said, "What is done is done, and this is the end of the road for a relationship that should not have started in the first place. I take full responsibility for my mistake. It has been mine all along, and I deserve what I got. I screwed up by going out with the wrong person. It is all over. Let go of her."

Sami reluctantly let go of Janice as he looked at her with total disdain. She instead looked baffled as she zeroed in, staring back at Sami. She was even more surprised at Omar's response. She had thought he might slap her back or apologize to her for faking his identity. She never expected him to act without any degree of guilt or, alternatively, without an angry reaction for having been physically attacked.

CHAPTER 28

Monday morning, Sami spoke to Dr. Small, the chief of medicine at Baylor. He accused Janice of stalking and attacking Omar. Sami argued in writing that Janice should not be allowed into the program and that she was not fit to be a practicing physician.

Dr. Small summoned Dr. Kishkain, head of neurology and an Arab American, who knew Omar's background and the reasons behind Omar changing his identity. Thoroughly briefed, he asked Dr. Kishkain to handle the matter and then to report to him. Afterward, Dr. Small would present it to the disciplinary board.

The following day, Janice was summoned to Dr. Kishkain's office. He also happened to be one of her residency professors. She was completely surprised. She never thought that her actions would reach the administration.

Dr. Kishkain first asked her whether she knew what she had done. Surprised at being questioned by the head of neurology about a sour love affair, she described it as a quarrel between two close friends because one of them was a cheat and an imposter.

Dr. Kishkain then told her that he knew Omar's father and that he knew that he was a journalist. "A very famous one," he added.

Dr. Kishkain looked her straight in the eye and then explained to her that Dr. Hanibake was not trying to deceive her or anybody else.

"The school knew that Hanibake was not his real family name, that it was Dinar," he said. "We knew all of that. You decided that you, Dr. Young, knew why Dr. Dinar changed his name to Hanibake and acted upon your own notions, without making a single inquiry. I need to tell you plainly that his name, status, and identity were changed because his life and the life of his father were and still are in danger. Otherwise we would not have accepted a change of his identity.

"Now, thanks to you, his life is in danger once again. You need to understand that Omar, by pretending his father is a plumber, had to live projecting himself to be of limited wealth instead of living comfortably. If you want to stay at Baylor, please think of the names of individuals you need to apologize to and come and see me tomorrow. Otherwise, the board will seriously entertain Dr. Sandook's request for your dismissal from Baylor based on your very immature behavior."

Janice was stunned and disturbed at how mistaken she had been, and she was concerned about being investigated by the medical school. She turned pale and kept silent for a couple of minutes.

After she collected herself and her thoughts, she managed to address Dr. Kishkain. "I am so deeply sorry. I am the first to admit, after hearing what I heard from you, that I acted immaturely and improperly. I know that I owe Dr. Hanibake and Dr. Sandook heartfelt apologies. I also owe all my professors and the board the same. I acted unprofessionally and, yes, cavalierly. I insulted Drs.

Hanibake and Sandook, and on top of my apology, I will ask for their forgiveness. I also promise not to bother Dr. Hanibake ever again. I hope that you would consider this episode an aberration. I am confident it will continue to be an aberration in the future." She then promised to prepare a full list of all the names of persons she intended to apologize to.

Janice looked for Omar outside the lecture halls, but he managed to avoid her altogether. Omar heard about Sami's complaint against Janice, and that prompted him to go see Dr. Kishkain. He asked Dr. Kishkain if he could dismiss the complaint. Dr. Kishkain explained to him that he could not, but if he would give a written statement describing Dr. Young's action in milder terms, it would serve to almost dismiss the case, after proper consideration.

Omar did that and dropped a copy in the mail to Janice. Dr. Kishkain then met with Janice and discussed Omar's letter with her, letting her know that he and Dr. Small believed that the case against her was much mitigated, to the degree of being relegated to a mere nuisance, but that he, Dr. Kishkain, had to keep it open until he could convince Dr. Sandook to drop his complaint.

Dr. Kishkain met with Dr. Sandook and told him that he was partly to blame, having disclosed Dr. Hanibake's real identity to Janice. Dr. Sandook, under the circumstances, felt he had to drop his complaint.

Two weeks later, Janice managed to face Omar. He let her know that he wrote the letter and that he did not hold a grudge against her. He then proceeded to leave.

"Let us meet somewhere quiet," Janice said. "I just want to apologize to you properly, not like this in public. Just give me a chance to do nothing more than to apologize sincerely and properly."

Omar tried to convince her that her apology had already been accepted. Yet she insisted on meeting in private, promising to show her sincere apologies, once and for all, and then each of them could go their own way.

Omar finally agreed to meet with her in the gym the following day. Janice asked that he listen to her without interruption. She told him that she would not take more than ten minutes. Omar answered that the floor was all hers.

"I don't know where to start, because there are ten places from which I can start. My mistakes were that varied. I was foolish, stupid, and arrogant. I was arrogant in pretending to know what I did not know, and I was stupid in acting on notions, not on facts. I abandoned everything I learned about the scientific process and acted immaturely. Although I am a woman who is twenty-eight years old, I gave the care and love we had for each other no consideration, and I acted in a self-centered way. Blinded by my desire to take revenge, I neglected any need to learn the truth. In the end, I caused so much harm to you and to your family, but psychologically, I caused myself greater harm. And for my act I feel diminished and small. One day in the future, I would like to know I caused you no permanent harm and that you have forgiven me for all the mindlessness of my behavior. I thank you, and I look forward to hearing your voice years from now, letting me know that you forgive me in earnest."

Omar had great admiration for her apology and humility and even more for her eloquence. He suspected then that she said what she said not to save her hide but because she was sincerely sorry.

"I don't have to wait years to forgive you; I have already forgiven you. In my religion, which I sometimes follow, even prophets make mistakes. Janice, you are neither a prophet nor a saint. You are just like me, a hard-driving physician who made a human-size mistake. It would be arrogant of us to think we don't make such mistakes."

Omar then approached Janice and kissed her on the forehead. "I don't want to kiss you on your lips, for fear of taking advantage of the situation. You were beautiful before you met me, and you never stopped being a gorgeous and hopefully sincere lady. I will be seeing you."

They waved goodbye to each other and left quietly.

The balance of the third year of residency progressed smoothly, but it did leave its marks on both Omar and Janice. In the meantime, when the former lovers ran into each other, they exchanged cursory greetings in a polite and reserved way.

As they got to the middle of the fourth and final year, there was an article in the college paper that made big news. A mechanical heart designed by Omar had gotten FDA approval for human testing. Janice had not known about it, but she recalled Omar asking her a couple of mechanical-engineering questions that may have been related to his design of the heart.

There was plenty of praise for Omar, especially that he had designed such a heart before finishing his residency program. Omar's fellow residents congratulated him on the accomplishment.

Janice felt that she needed to congratulate Omar too. It had been a year since their separation. She called him. "I didn't want you to feel that I am not proud of you," she said. "Everyone is. I felt it was only proper to congratulate you on your mechanical heart.

Have you celebrated this achievement yet? Tomorrow I understand the *Houston Chronicle* is going to feature your work!"

"I have not had time to celebrate," Omar told her. "I have done three different local TV interviews, and I am scheduled to do a national interview next week."

"How about if I take you out to celebrate this great occasion, for old times' sake? I assure you it will not be a date."

Omar agreed, and Janice told him to let her know when he'd like to go, and she would take care of the rest. Two days later, Omar called and let her know that he was free that evening. She picked him up and asked him if he didn't mind stopping by her house, as her mother wanted to congratulate him on his new mechanical heart design.

Rose said, "I guess the girls now will be after you even more than before!"

"Mother, this is not why we are here," Janice said. "Omar and I are just friends and colleagues. We just want to celebrate together. What Omar achieved is special."

"I just read one of your father's articles," Rose said. "For a plumber, he writes very well." Janice then took Omar's hand and proceeded to leave while looking at her mother sideways.

As they were having dinner on the patio of the restaurant, Janice said, "You know, I think I fell in love with you the first time I saw you, and I have not stopped loving you since, but my sense of disappointment in myself has overwhelmed my emotions and subdued my desire for men, including my desire for you."

"Disappointment for what?" Omar asked.

"Disappointment for having insulted you publicly, like a fool," she replied.

"If you and I are going to see each other in any capacity," Omar said, "I will insist that you forget this subject. It does not do you any good, and it does not do me any good. I don't want you to feel indignant about yourself." He looked at her sternly.

"I will try, and I think I will be able to forget about it someday," she said.

———

A couple of weeks later, Janice invited Omar for dinner. She wanted her mother to hear from Omar directly about how he had to change his name and fake a new identity because of the threats on his life and not because he was trying to avoid sharing his wealth with possible female prospects.

Omar reluctantly accommodated Janice and told Rose his story, in detail. In the process, he mentioned that his father had been caught up in political maneuvering between Jordan, Iraq, and the American CIA, and had angered all sides.

Malcolm, in the next room, did not like what he heard, and defended the CIA as one of the finest organizations the free world had ever known. He added even before Omar had stepped outside, "Don't believe those heathens. Just because he is a doctor, it does not mean he changed his stripes."

Realizing that Omar had heard all of that, Janice just about lost it and gave it to her father. She was on the verge of attacking him physically before Omar stopped her.

While restrained by Omar, she looked at her father and said, "You know, you are nothing but a prejudiced asshole. You hate everybody. Fuck you." She gave him the finger.

Janice's anger and her almost possessed look overshadowed Malcolm's racist statements, but above all, it scared Omar. He left in a hurry, forgetting a slip of paper he had taken out of his wallet, on which he kept his father's secret home phone number.

To dampen the situation, Rose repeated everything Omar told her. Malcolm then found the slip of paper with Rasheed's number. He immediately called the CIA and naïvely asked them to refute what Omar was accusing them of. At the same time, he gave them Rasheed's phone number, which they passed on to the Jordanians.

With those details, the Jordanians revived the investigation into the old attempt to overthrow the government years before. They first called Rasheed using his secret phone number. They followed it up by dispatching two agents to visit him, to try to squeeze more information out of him.

The agents, at first, had initially mistaken the neighbor's house for Rasheed's. The neighbor got his shotgun out and tried to chase the agents off. In the process, one of the agents shot him, wounding him badly.

Rasheed, hearing the shots, ran to his neighbor's aid, followed by Giselle. Rasheed punched one of the agents, and the agent's partner shot him. Giselle went into a rage, trying to help Rasheed. The two agents fled. The ambulance carried Rasheed and his next-door neighbor to the hospital.

The doctors operated on Rasheed and his neighbor. The neighbor did not make it. Giselle called *Time*'s office and told them what happened and asked them to call Omar, before he heard about it on the news, and tell him that his father was okay.

Omar and Janice got together in the college coffee shop. Janice expected to find Omar mad at the situation and possibly mad at her.

At first, he did not want to tell her anything, but later he told her the whole story. He told her that his father's insiders in the Jordanian ministry of defense had told Rasheed that his number had been given to the CIA by a source in Houston.

"It was your father, Janice," he said.

Janice was shocked and livid. She was at a loss for words. She excused herself and headed home, where she found her parents.

Without even asking one question, she said to her father, "You have ruined my life step by step, first by alienating me from my Catholic friends and now by separating me from the man I love. You managed to kill Rasheed's neighbor, and Rasheed is in intensive care, all as a result of your sharing information about them with the CIA. If Rasheed Dinar dies, you will never be my father again. You are causing so much grief and heartache, I don't know why I even have you in my life. You have ruined my life, piece by piece, with your asinine beliefs about other religions and other cultures. I no longer like you. You are a monster, yet you cannot see it. I think I need to leave this house and maybe this town to be away from you. Go to hell!"

Janice sobbed and went to her room. Rose looked at Malcolm and said, "If my daughter decides to leave, I am going to have you leave this house. You'll leave this house, and for the first time we will live in peace, which you have not given us for many years."

The following days were very difficult for both Omar and Janice. Rose stopped talking to Malcolm. The American media picked up the story, and some of the residents and professors heard the news. *Time* knew about Malcolm Young's involvement and wanted to interview him. Dr. Small, chief of medicine, called Omar to let him know that Baylor was ready to help in any way they could.

Only then did the other residents realize who Omar's father was and that Omar was not the average financially challenged foreign student but someone who was extremely rich yet humble in his attitude and demeanor. Some started wondering if Janice knew from the start that Omar came from money and whether that factor played a part in her being attracted to him.

Omar contacted *Time*'s Beirut bureau twice a day, hungry for every bit of news. One afternoon, as he was talking to the bureau, he overheard someone in the background say, "Yeah, he died," and although he had no idea who the person was talking about, Omar thought he was talking about his own father. In his mind, he became sure of it. He went numb.

Before his thought process almost stopped, he called Natalia and made one short statement before he hung up: "Father is dead. He was assassinated." He then dragged himself to bed. Slowly he took a fetal position. He covered his upper torso unevenly. In short order, he went into a comalike condition, just as his father had after hearing about the hanging of his cousin, Kamal. It must have been a family trait.

Natalia tried to call Omar back, but there was no answer. She then called Janice, crying, and told her that Omar had called her to tell her that his father was assassinated by the Jordanians.

Janice could not control herself. She hugged her mother while crying. "Rasheed is dead," she told her. Rose was unsuccessfully trying to console Janice. Janice called Dr. Small to let him know. He in turn told Dr. Kishkain. The news got around the student body. Malcolm's involvement became known. Janice could barely make it to class without some of her fellow residents staring angrily at her.

Above all, nobody had seen Omar. Sami and his other friends went looking for him to keep him company and ended up at his apartment. They called the manager, who in turn opened the unit and found that Omar was totally out. The ambulance took him to the emergency room.

In short order, Ibrahim called Beirut's *Time* bureau and was surprised that Rasheed was alive and recovering. Before he asked any more questions, he called Natalia to let her know that Rasheed was alive and recovering and that Omar may have mistaken the death of Rasheed's neighbor for Rasheed himself.

Natalia immediately called Janice and corrected the news about Rasheed. Janice followed by calling Small, Kishkain, and Sami. She asked Sami to spread the word around the college.

Kishkain was the attending physician, being the top neurologist at Baylor. Upon examining Omar and taking all kinds of images and measurements, he announced that Omar did not suffer from any physical ailments. It was all a reaction to the mistaken news that his father had died. "He is in a type of shock coma or acute stress disorder," he announced.

Kishkain engaged the services of a psychologist, Dr. Smith. Between the two of them, they concluded that Omar needed to come out of it as fast as possible. They were pleased his organs were functioning well, which Dr. Smith believed was a sign that his chances of recovery were very good.

As Omar was being attended to, Natalia was preparing to fly to Houston. Rasheed, from his hospital bed, was in constant contact with *Time* magazine, not knowing how to react under the circumstances. His mind was on Omar's condition while *Time* magazine was concentrating on the assassination attempt. Ibrahim was facilitating Natalia's trip to Houston. His office planned door-to-door service for Natalia.

By the time Natalia arrived in Houston, she was confused as to how to treat Janice. In the end, she decided to be as open and cordial with her as possible. She wanted to wait for Omar to come out of his comalike condition, to listen to him before she decided how really to treat Janice. She also had Sami's name and the names of two more of Omar's friends.

When she got to Omar's apartment, she called all three friends. Sami helped in getting himself and the other two to meet Natalia. Natalia had heard about what Kishkain had said about Omar benefiting from listening to familiar voices. She asked them if they could identify some of those who fit such a description.

Those were Sami, Robert (another resident), Janice, Rasheed, Giselle, and Christina. Unfortunately, Natalia herself did not meet the requirements, as she had never spent enough time with Omar. In the end, and after checking with Dr. Smith, it was decided that Janice should not interact with Omar lest he have a negative reaction.

Since Rasheed, Christina, and Giselle were not there, the whole thing fell on the shoulders of Sami and Robert. Kishkain told them that the school would be most accommodating about their training. Some of the professors volunteered to help make up Sami's and Robert's missed residency training while they attended to Omar.

Natalia met with Janice. Natalia was most open with Janice and told her that she did not know where she fit in the picture and that everything had to wait for Omar's recovery.

Janice told Natalia that she would make herself scarce but would be ready to respond anytime, anywhere. She asked Natalia to stay in touch, if for nothing else than to update her about Omar.

"You may not think so, Natalia," Janice said, "but he is still my love."

Natalia said nothing.

———————

Two weeks passed with Sami and Robert talking to Omar as if he were sharing a beer with them, yet there was not a sign that their words were helping. Drs. Smith and Kishkain kept encouraging Sami, Robert, and Natalia not to give up.

"It could happen anytime or it may take a whole year," Smith said. "His condition is not classical, and we are in the mode of trying anything noninvasive."

Within three weeks, Rasheed and Giselle arrived in Houston, despite the fact that Rasheed had not completely recovered from his wounds. They met with Natalia in a private hospital room. Rasheed rushed to Natalia and gave her a very warm hug and kissed her on both cheeks. Giselle followed suit.

"He is our son," Rasheed said to Natalia, "the only one we will ever have. It is nice to see you." They studied each other, trying to take in the other's older age and changed features.

Natalia looked Rasheed in the eye, touched his cheek, and said, "It is great to see you. It is my mistake that it has been such a long time. You look very good."

Natalia updated Rasheed and Giselle and then arranged for them to meet all the physicians attending to Omar. As Natalia and the attending physicians briefed Rasheed, he took over and started directing matters. He told Giselle to talk to Omar for the first three hours. He would take the next three hours. That routine went on for another three weeks, but without any signs that Omar was responding. Omar's physical condition had not deteriorated much, helped by the fact that he was constantly administered physical therapy exercises, and his mind was still active under the cloud of total silence.

Rasheed talked to Omar every day, as did Natalia. Although Natalia knew that Christina could potentially be the one whose voice or touches Omar would react to, she made it a point not to mention it, simply because she knew well Christina's convent restrictions.

As Omar's condition showed no signs of improving, Rasheed told Natalia that the situation was no longer a simple matter, and that Omar's physical condition could start deteriorating at any time. He directed her to ask Ibrahim to bring Christina. It was potentially a life and death issue, and nothing should stand in the way.

Ibrahim jumped at the idea and went to see Christina at the convent. He told her that Omar's condition might start deteriorating any day, but his pleas went nowhere. Ibrahim persisted. Over three weeks, he described Omar's condition and told Christina every detail about what Rasheed, Natalia, and Giselle were going through. Little by little, Christina became more emotionally involved.

After five weeks of Ibrahim's contact with Christina, Christina on her own went to the mother superior, Sister Isabella, and asked her if she could go to Houston to try to help Omar, who would die if he did not eventually wake up.

Sister Isabella was adamant: "You now belong to a different world, a world where you are married to the Lord, and you are not in any deep relationship with any man or woman outside this convent."

"But, Mother, Omar may die if I do not go," Christina answered by raising her voice.

"Shall I remind you, Sister Beatrice, that you are favoring your duties toward one man over your comprehensive duty toward humanity itself, for which our Lord gave his life?" Sister Isabella said. She added, "For that you need to scrub the floor of the chapel today before you go to sleep."

Christina accepted and bowed her head, asking if she could scrub the floor in the evening as she was helping another sister in the meantime. Sister Isabella agreed.

That evening, Christina started scrubbing the floor of the chapel at around eight, knowing that it would take her close to six hours to finish. She gave it her best. The sisters passing by all evening were certainly impressed. The task given to Christina was not totally unusual, but it was rare considering the infraction Christina was accused of, an infraction of thought rather than one of action.

Christina had a good reason for wanting to scrub the floor starting at eight. When the sisters had gone to bed, including the ones who prayed in the chapel at night, Christina acted. She slowly opened the gate of the convent and eased herself out. She headed to the taxi queue, and within forty-five minutes she was at her father's mansion.

The security man did not recognize her until she took off her caul. She hurried toward her father's room, but he met her halfway, having been awakened by the security guard.

"Father, I left the convent, and I left it for good. I cannot bear that Omar may die without me at least trying to save him. I want to go to Houston."

Christina and Ibrahim hugged warmly.

"Christina, you cannot know how much I have dreamed of this day," Ibrahim said, "how much I missed you not being part of this family. You are supposed to be the mistress of this house. Welcome home."

"They would not even consider my trying to save Omar's life. What then is the meaning of being a nun? They may not be bad or evil, but they are confused. They appreciate form over substance. I am done with them."

In the morning, Ibrahim called the archbishop and tried to explain to him what had happened. The archbishop expressed his disappointment and disapproval, perhaps hoping to get a contribution. He got it later in the day from Ibrahim, who sent an amount that was acceptable to His Eminence.

Ibrahim then worked diligently to renew Christina's passport and secure a US visa, which he managed to accomplish in a day. The two of them took the plane to London and then to Houston. As things were all arranged for their visit, Christina and Ibrahim were met by Natalia and Rasheed. Giselle was attending to Omar.

It was a meeting no different from any other of the kind, like a mother meeting her long-lost daughter. Rasheed, in the evening, briefed Christina about Omar and told her that both he and Giselle spent hours and hours trying to connect with his son, but to no avail. He also told her about Sami's and Robert's attempts. Christina said nothing and gave no indication of what she had planned to say or do.

In the morning, Ibrahim, Natalia, and Christina went to see Rasheed and Giselle. Giselle was beside herself. She could not take her eyes off Christina. She would touch Christina on the cheek and on the arms, as if she had been lost and now found.

Christina, who sat between Natalia and Giselle, stretched her arms and hugged the two of them at the same time. She told them she planned to stay with Omar twenty-four hours a day and that she hoped nobody objected to that. Rasheed was elated to have Christina talk that way.

Rasheed called Dr. Kishkain and informed him that Christina, Omar's ex-girlfriend, was in town and planned to try to connect with Omar.

"I do not know exactly what her plans are, but she loved Omar deeply, and I think she still does. Above all, I have full trust in her and in her genuine care and love for my son."

Kishkain asked, "Is this the nun you told me about?"

"She is no longer a nun. She left the convent for good a few days ago, to come help Omar. This is why I think she still loves him and will do anything possible for him. I know he still loves her deeply."

They proceeded to the intensive care unit. Christina looked beautiful, energetic, and radiant. Her new outfit had been custom-made for her. As she entered the hospital, she turned heads. Christina, Natalia, Ibrahim, Giselle, and Rasheed arrived just as Kishkain arrived. The look on his face said it all: "This stunning beauty used to be a nun, less than a week ago!"

After meeting Christina and Ibrahim, Dr. Kishkain called some of the attending physicians and three attending nurses. Christina took off her jacket, rolled up her sleeves, and sat down on a stool after the bed was lowered at her request. She first made the sign of the cross, and several Catholics in the room followed suit, including Natalia and Giselle.

Everyone was expecting that Christina would start talking to Omar. Instead, she bent over, placed her right cheek against his right cheek, and then licked Omar up his cheek very slowly and deliberately until she got to his ear lobe. She then started sucking on his ear lobe while everyone looked on with stunned bewilderment.

Rasheed looked at Giselle and got concerned that Kishkain may object to the whole exercise. He was even afraid that Kishkain would suspect that Rasheed had known about Christina's method but intentionally did not want to share it with him in advance. The nurses looked at each other with astonished smiles. One of them left the intensive care unit to return with three more nurses and two more physicians.

Christina turned Omar's head and did the same to his left cheek. She then put her hands on his ears and massaged them and the areas behind them. Then she slid her index and middle fingers down Omar's neck, going all the way to his crotch. She then flipped her hands over and used the backs of her hands to massage all the way down to his thighs, just above his knees.

She slowly went up his thighs and to the side of his genitalia, where she was more deliberate. At that point, Omar suddenly jerked his legs open a little, his first voluntary movement since the onset of his condition.

Christina continued deeper on the side of Omar's genitalia. He moved some more. As she pressed the back of her hands firmly against the very upper part of the thighs, she leaned over Omar and whispered audibly, "*Walhan*, this is *walhana*. I am back."

Walhan meant a deeply in love, mesmerized male. Omar and Christina used to use these two terms to call each other. Omar picked up the terms from his own father, as Rasheed and Natalia used to use the same terms. "Can you hear me, *walhan*?" asked Christina.

Suddenly Omar's left eyelid moved. Christina asked, "*Walhan*, do you want to hear flamenco music?" Ever so slightly, Omar nodded his head agreeably. Christina took a tape player from a bag she was carrying and turned it on.

As the flamenco music started playing, Omar said to Christina, "This time you can only squeeze and pinch."

Christina could not help herself. She laughed with a wide smile. She started dancing to the music, gently and slowly undulating in harmony with the rhythms. Rasheed and the others, hearing the music and the noises, slipped back into the room.

Rasheed did not know what to say. Kishkain moved his head slowly sideways in disbelief. It had taken the ex-nun twenty minutes to accomplish what they couldn't in three months.

The music attracted more staff members. Two cleaning ladies joined in watching Christina dance. Ibrahim was more apprehensive and was concerned that Christina may be thought of as a nun trying to make up for lost time. Christina repeated the routine three different times. By then Omar was visibly awake, trying to recognize where he was.

One of the younger physicians went out and brought back a camera. He took pictures of Kishkain handing his stethoscope to Dr. Smith, gesturing that his medical knowledge was of no value.

Within two hours Omar recognized everyone related to him and then yelled, "Christina, where is your habit?"

"They did not allow me to dance flamenco, so I quit," she said, laughing.

Omar also laughed and held on to Christina's arms with great adoration. The pleasantly stunned staff could not believe what had transpired.

Kishkain was the first to speak: "My family has been Catholic on both sides—Italian and Palestinian—since the eighteenth century, but I doubt that any of us has witnessed this kind of healing on the part of any nun."

CHAPTER 29

1975

Houston, Texas

Within minutes the news was all over the hospital; it didn't take long to reach Janice. She could not understand all the details and did not know how Christina had managed to be there.

Natalia suddenly remembered that Omar had two lovers, now in the same hospital. She asked Kishkain if he could arrange a meeting with Janice. He contacted Janice, and within an hour Janice and Natalia were by themselves, in Kishkain's office.

Janice told Natalia that she had heard about the miracle worker.

"Everyone's emotions are raw, considering the trouble your father caused the Dinar family and their friends," Natalia said. "I would like you to keep your distance until Omar himself can address the matter." Janice accepted the arrangement without hesitation.

To what extent Christina contributed to Omar's coming out from his comalike condition was hard to assess. The physicians and his family saw what they saw, and they were willing to give Christina the benefit of the doubt. Privately, everyone thought that Christina's actions sped up Omar's coming out of his condition but did not necessarily cause the recovery.

At that point, nobody had talked to Christina to find out her thoughts about her relationship to Omar.

When it came to Omar, he had to wrap his head around his potential relationships to Christina and to Janice and also to consider his mother's relationship to Ibrahim.

What concerned Natalia particularly was the possibility of ending up with only losers, including herself. After all, she and Ibrahim had talked about the possibility of marriage, and yet the relationship between Ibrahim's daughter and her son was as murky and as risky as could be.

The Alvarez family and the Dinar family both were relieved watching Omar recover. Christina took the initiative in attending to Omar, and Natalia was her backup. Natalia could not tell whether Christina was continuing with where she left off before becoming a nun, or if she was simply being the caring friend.

A curious nurse came into the intensive care unit and approached Christina. She introduced herself and then asked, "Did you know that Dr. Hanibake was going out with Dr. Young?"

Although the questioner may have been a troublemaker, Christina answered her crisply. "He is no longer Dr. Hanibake; he is Dr. Dinar. And just as he is abandoning one temporary name in favor of his real permanent name, he is abandoning one temporary lover to return to his real lover. That is me."

Natalia, who was listening to the conversation, was pleasantly surprised at Christina's crisp answer.

"He had to do what he had to do since I became a nun," Christina said. "I loaned him to Dr. Young." The nurse managed to give a faint smile and left quietly.

Christina stayed at the hotel and spent her days at the hospital with Omar. Natalia was sure that no sex had taken place between them. As a matter of fact, Christina was not openly showing great affection for Omar, just showing great care. She nevertheless seemed very happy that they were together.

Natalia arranged to have lunch with Christina, and over their meal she asked Christina what she thought about her new situation.

"I am so happy for leaving the convent and happier for being with everyone—you, the Dinars, and my dad," Christina answered.

In a contrived, casual manner, Natalia then mentioned Janice by name, without identifying her, saying that Janice had not visited Omar.

Christina's answer continued to be nonspecific: "You know American girls, Natalia."

Natalia decided that she had to be more direct. "Do you know if Janice and Omar were going together, or were they just friends?"

"They may have been going together, but you know they were going out together American-style," Christina said. "Janice probably was going out with two other residents."

In order to elicit a clearer answer, Natalia told Christina that she admired her for going back to civilian life so fast and easily. "It must have been hard not having contact with men."

"Actually, it wasn't. I always knew that Omar would wait for me, just in case I changed my mind, and I was not interested in

any other man. It was either Omar or the convent. In the end it
was Omar."

That was one of the answers Natalia was hoping to hear. She
could not wait to finish lunch and go back to Omar's apartment
with the clear objective of trying to facilitate, as much as she could,
the resumption of the relationship between Christina and Omar.

———————

Natalia did not want to waste any time. She told Giselle what
Christina had told her. Giselle loved hearing such news. Natalia and
Giselle agreed to work toward full resumption of affairs between
Omar and Christina.

They arranged for a lunch with Christina, during which time
Janice could visit Omar per Natalia's promise to Janice. They both
believed that if Omar and Christina were to renew their bonds,
Omar needed to sever his relationship with Janice.

Natalia told Janice not to discuss any controversial matters with
Omar and added, "You are a doctor; I don't need to coach you
about that."

Janice was very quiet, knowing what had transpired at her house
before Omar went into shock. Omar was also reserved. He told
Janice that he wanted to discuss with her a few private matters after
full recovery. Natalia then excused herself and told them that she
would return after an hour.

Janice again apologized to Omar about her father's indiscretion in releasing the name of General Zayyad and Rasheed's secret
phone number. She then told him that she knew that Christina had
left the convent and returned to civilian life.

"This should not have any bearing on our love for each other or the relationship we intend to keep between us," she added. "You and Christina have been apart more than six years."

When Janice left Omar's apartment, she went to see her best friend, Linda, who initially encouraged Janice to defy her parents and go after Omar. Linda herself thought that Omar was a catch, a handsome, smart doctor with a sense of humor. Linda was Janice's confidante and closest friend. Janice respected Linda's opinions, as she did not agree with Janice on numerous occasions and was right most of the time.

Janice then went home to talk with her mother.

After Janice expressed some concern regarding Omar's intentions, Rose said, "If I had not met Omar and had not gotten to know him some, I would have opposed your marrying a foreigner. I want you to know that Omar is a great match for you, and you should go after him. Just do what you did as a cheerleader—go and compete. Do you hear me? Go do your best!"

That short speech on top of Linda's assessment of Omar bolstered Janice's attitude. In her mind, she decided to fight for Omar and not accept playing second fiddle in the competition.

Without having met Christina, Janice was under the impression that she was promoting her own interest, with her magic healing act as an example of the level she would go to to revive her relationship with Omar.

Giselle confided in Natalia that their choices were limited and that they needed to be resolute in supporting Christina over Janice.

Among their contributions, they managed to reduce the number of helpers servicing Omar's recovery. They wanted Christina to be there and act as if she were his wife.

Left alone, Christina made a few mild romantic approaches toward Omar, but they were not serious attempts. Natalia sensed as much when she returned to see Omar.

Giselle and Natalia started having doubts about Christina. They asked themselves many questions, including if it could be that life as a nun had changed Christina into a celibate. Out of desperation, they asked Christina about her plans regarding Omar.

"My plan is that I am going to propose to Omar that we get married soon. We have lost six years during our separation," Christina said matter-of-factly.

What they heard was music to their ears, except that it was hard to hear real affection in Christina's words.

To test Christina's attitude toward sex, Natalia contrived a conversation about her niece, and about how her niece got pregnant at seventeen. Christina took the bait. "We all have weaknesses of the flesh, but we should try to resist," she said. "I will this time."

Giselle knew what she meant but pretended that she did not. "What do you mean, Christina? You have never been married."

"You know that I have never been married. I was referring to Omar. He has to wait this time," Christina said.

Natalia commented, "You are both adults. Omar is twenty-nine. You two can decide for yourselves."

Giselle and Natalia were satisfied that they had gotten their answer. They realized that Christina's hesitation was not a result of a lack of warmth toward Omar, but it was one of Christina's typical, stubborn fixations. This time she was intent not to have sex, and maybe not foreplay, until she married Omar.

When Giselle was alone with Omar, she was open with him. She told him that while everybody was so pleased that Christina was back in their lives, and that she looked the same, there were things that had changed in her, and other things that looked as if they had changed but actually were very much the same.

"Christina told me and Natalia that she no longer believes in premarital sex," she said. "The only sex she believes in is sex between a husband and wife."

"This does not bother me," Omar said. "I know I still love her, and she still loves me, and I will do anything reasonable to accommodate her wishes."

"This is great, but what do you plan to do with Janice?" Giselle asked.

"I loved Janice and may still love her, but my love for Janice came about as a result of having believed that I had lost Christina for good. This did not turn out to be the case. I plan to tell Janice that it's over."

Giselle told him that it would not be easy, since Janice may be in love with him.

"I am confronted with a black-and-white situation. I must choose one of the two," he said.

Giselle told Omar that she believed it was true that Janice was still deeply in love with him. She also told him that Janice may not give up too easily, first because of her love for him and second because Janice now had a rival, and rivalry tends to exacerbate matters rather than mitigate them.

"Honey, Omar, I want you to be careful and kind. This is not a good situation. I don't want Janice to feel like she is a spurned woman. I don't want her to get to the point she got to when she went all the way to Galveston to slap you in the face. Your mother and I have been worried about a possible nasty confrontation. I know she is a physician, but affairs of the heart overwhelm our better senses. Your mother or I could tell her this, but it would not be right. This is something you have to take care of yourself."

Omar told Giselle that regardless, it would be less than ethical to have anybody relay to Janice the sour news. "I must be able to appeal to her better senses. I just have to do it," he said.

———

While Giselle was discussing the situation with Omar, Janice, Linda, and Rose were also planning and scheming. They were determined not to lose, realizing that Christina's reappearance had raised the level of the challenge at hand.

The plan Rose and Linda concocted concentrated on Janice's attitude and behavior. All three agreed that they would try not to give Omar any room to ignore Janice. Janice was supposed to pretend that Christina did not exist, just like Christina pretended that Janice did not exist.

As their residency program resumed, Janice witnessed Omar being congratulated by his colleagues. She hurried toward him and gave him a kiss on the lips, which was totally out of place. The act aroused some suspicions among the other residents as Janice had given the impression to many in the class that she and Omar were kind of alienated from each other. It was not her best performance.

By agreement between the two, Sami and Robert sat Omar down and opened the subject directly and without ambiguity. They told Omar that the whole scene with Janice was awkward and that they were afraid that if it were repeated, it would look weird and unseemly.

After they exchanged ideas for a while, Omar suggested a sit-down meeting, which would include Omar, Sami, and Robert on one side and Janice, Linda, and Rose on the other side. He explained to them that Janice had told him that Linda was her confidante and that Rose was on her side when it came to her father. Sami chuckled, as he was familiar with such tradition, which no longer existed in urban areas of Lebanon.

The following day Omar invited Janice, Rose, and Linda out for dinner. Sami and Robert joined them. Omar explained their presence by saying that his mother insisted that he be accompanied by a friend or two all the time until his medical condition improved fully.

Rose could not help herself. She had to probe further, although both Janice and Linda had advised her not to do so. "I understand now that your father was never a plumber and that he is a rich man, just like his Spanish friend, the wine man!"

Janice and Linda tried to get her to stop, but Rose continued. "I understand that Ibrahim has one daughter and no other children, and that she will be inheriting all the twenty-two wineries."

Omar got mad at Rose's insinuations, implying that his interest in Christina was financial. He upped the ante: "Actually, according to Spanish customs, she should receive a portion of the estate upon getting married. They call it *dote* in Spanish," he answered. "She does not need to wait until her father passes away."

Sami and Robert smiled at Omar challenging Rose, but Linda and Janice were hardly amused. Rose suddenly stopped, since she heard something new from Omar, not only that Christina was the sole potential beneficiary of her father's estate but that she would be receiving part of the estate upon getting married.

Linda had never heard of such an arrangement. The news subdued her inclination to act as an interrogator.

The dinner finished with cordial pleasantries but lacked much warmth between the two sides. After dinner, Omar disagreed with Sami and Robert that the other side must have gotten the message. Omar said that they did not want to take no for an answer, and that they certainly would not take a weak no. He described them as persistent and dedicated to the cause. But Omar believed that their behavior had given him an opening that made it easier to meet with Janice directly and confront the subject at hand.

CHAPTER 30

Janice and Linda could not help but discuss the matter further, and their determination dominated their better senses. They decided Janice should invite Omar for lunch, in Galveston, and Linda would join them, unannounced. Omar accepted Janice's invitation but insisted on driving himself to Galveston. As he was about to set out on the drive, Janice called to let him know that Linda would be accompanying her.

Omar in turn invited Sami to join, who grudgingly did, only to balance Linda's presence. Omar had decided to tell Janice that he could not continue with two close relationships, and that he had decided to romantically reconnect with Christina.

Before Janice and Linda left for Galveston, Janice called Natalia, pretending it was a courtesy call, to let her know that she intended to spend the afternoon with Omar, in Galveston. The call was really intended to aggravate Christina and possibly cause a rupture between her and Omar. Natalia was mad at Janice's attempt.

Wanting to defy Janice, Natalia lied and told her that Christina and Omar had decided to get married. Janice was completely beside herself and almost out of her skin. She could barely reply.

When the phone conversation ended, Natalia knew she may have seriously complicated things for Omar. She immediately called Christina, and the two were chauffeured to Galveston in Ibrahim's leased limousine.

When Janice first saw Sami accompanying Omar, she got mad. She'd wanted to have a dominant presence—she and Linda together facing Omar, alone.

Linda managed to ease Janice's mind. "Let us make the best of it," she said.

———

In front of Gaido's restaurant, Omar approached Janice with a reserved posture. After they said hello to each other without any hugs or kisses, Omar right away asked if he could read a poem by the eighth-century poet Rabi'a al-'Adawiyya. Even Sami was surprised. Omar said that the poem was his absolute favorite about love.

The insertion of the word "love" into the conversation confused just about everyone. It took around two minutes for Omar to commence reading the poem, since Sami kept interrupting to filibuster the whole process. He was confused and thought that Omar may inadvertently create a puzzle rather than end a relationship.

Omar took a deep breath. He sighed and finally managed to start reading:

One day Rabi'a was asked how she saw love.

Between the lover and the beloved, she said

There is no distance.

There are words only through the power of desire.

Description only through taste.

He who has tasted has come to know.

And he who has described has not described himself.

In truth, how can you describe something when in its

presence, you are absent, in its existence, you are dissolved.

In its contemplation, you are undone.

In its purity, you are intoxicated.

In your surrender, you are fulfilled.

In your joy, you are parted from yourself.

—Rabi'a al Adawiyya (717–801)

None of the three could tell in what direction Omar was going. Linda thought for a moment that Omar was romancing Janice, with a most descriptive and romantic poem, yet she was not sure. Sami and Janice were confused by the poem, since it seemed to contradict what Natalia had said about Omar's relationship with Christina.

Then Omar started speaking in a firm and confident voice. "You see, Janice, this poem describes our relationship with the exception of one aspect. It is described in the first line that there is no distance between a lover and the beloved; well, you know that there is a wide gap between us, as I cannot accept your father as my father-in-law, and you should not and cannot abandon your father for my sake. As such, the distance that Rabi'a described in the poem still exists between us. I came here to thank you for the year we spent together and to say wholeheartedly goodbye and good luck."

The shock was most visible on Linda's face, as she was leaning toward an interpretation of the poem as being an expression of love. At that moment, Natalia and Christina arrived and approached from behind Linda and Janice. They stopped some distance away.

As Janice absorbed the shock of hearing a confirmation of the end of the relationship, she looked at Omar with her eyes bulging and her veins throbbing and said, "You thought you could rationalize your duplicity by reciting a poem? Go fuck yourself."

She then tried to slap Omar, but Linda grabbed her arm. Janice then managed to slip loose from Linda's grip and slapped Omar as hard as she could.

Christina saw Omar's cut lip bleeding, and she ran toward Janice with her right arm widely swinging. Omar took two fast and long steps toward Christina to grab her around the waist, preventing her from slapping Janice seconds before she could reach her. Linda and Natalia were looking at Janice with unbelievable shock and surprise. Sami had seen the same behavior once before.

They were shocked to see how badly Janice lost it, almost instantly reversing position, from preserving a love relationship to taking revenge on a lover. The language used was vile and abrasive and escalated to physical force.

After holding back Christina, Omar composed himself before handing Christina to Sami. He looked at Janice with resignation and some satisfaction: her resorting to violence had given him a clear and justifiable way out.

"You have said your piece," Omar said. "Please go and never get close to me again, as long as you live."

Christina slowly but grudgingly simmered down while giving Janice a menacing look. Natalia took over from Sami, restraining Christina, who slowly and gently removed Natalia's arms from around her waist and walked toward Omar. She wiped his cut lip clean and kissed him. Natalia hugged Omar and Christina at the same time.

Linda was shocked into silence for a long while.

"She apologized to Omar after she slapped him the first time," Sami said. "If he accepts her apology ever again in the future, I will never talk to him. She is unstable; her true self comes out when she is challenged."

"I am sorry I was involved," Linda said to Omar. "I never thought she would do such a thing."

"The occasion calls for a celebration," Sami said.

He, Omar, Natalia, and Christina had champagne afterward at Gaido's. With Sami's help and sense of humor, everyone managed to enjoy the alcohol and lunch. Christina was all over Omar, kissing him and caressing his arms and face.

She took the opportunity and called her father to ask him if he could free himself for dinner and if he could arrange for Rasheed and Giselle to join in. She also invited Sami and Robert.

As the group got together to celebrate, they ordered more champagne and premium wines. Christina took the floor and announced, without first checking with Omar, that she and Omar were getting married soon.

Ibrahim and Rasheed looked at her with surprise. Tipsy as she was, she said, "I made a mistake and became a nun, abandoning my one and only love. Omar had fun with stupid Janice in the meantime. But he forgives me for becoming a nun, and I forgive him for associating with Janice. From now on, he cannot make love to anybody other than me."

Everyone knew that Christina had too much to drink, and they did not dwell much on what she said, especially about sex. Natalia hugged and kissed her and then rested Christina's head on her shoulder.

————

Upon reflection, Janice managed to recognize her transgression and aggressiveness against Omar. She recalled that Omar had forewarned her regarding his undying love for Christina. He had told her he did not believe he could love anybody else as much as he loved Christina. She felt remorseful and decided to write him.

Dear Omar,

Upon reflection I have found my actions to be unjustified, immature, and unreasonable. I apologize to you, Christina, Natalia, Linda, and Sami from the deepest bottom of my heart. Last time I apologized, it was for us to get back together; this time I am apologizing to wish you and Christina a very happy and fruitful life. I think she is an outstanding human being, a most beautiful and charming female, who will make you a perfect companion. I have already transferred to the University of Texas program next door, but most

*probably you and I will not come face-to-face ever
again. I sincerely ask for forgiveness, hoping that you
will be kind enough to relay my sentiments to everyone.*

Good luck.

With love,
Janice

Omar gave Christina, Sami, and Linda a copy of the letter, and
each expressed their tepid satisfaction and wished Janice happiness
while also expressing their hope that they would never see her again.
Copies were later given to Rasheed, Natalia, and Giselle. They were
all convinced that Janice was erratic and unpredictable.

————

During the following days, Christina ran the show. Unexpectedly,
she was approached by Rasheed. He told her that he could read her
mind, just like he had faith in her reviving Omar.

"I know that you want to have your father marry Natalia. How
about if they get married at the same time you and Omar are getting
married?" he asked.

Christina pretended to be surprised and said that she liked the
idea a lot. She hugged Rasheed and asked him if he could talk
about that with her father.

"Better than that," Rasheed continued. "How about if Giselle
and I join the activities and get married at the same time?"

"Don't say another word, Rasheed," Christina said. "Give me an
hour, and I will get back to you."

She went to see Giselle and Natalia. "Girls, we have it wrapped up. We are going to have a three-way wedding. Rasheed made the suggestion, as if he could read my mind. He is supposed to talk to my father and let me know. I am sure my father will say yes."

But Christina could not wait after hearing the good news and went to see Ibrahim. "Dad, if you really want to make me happy, you will do what I am going to ask you. It is very simple: I want you to marry Natalia very soon."

"I hope to marry Natalia, but why so soon?" Ibrahim said, in a coy mood, pretending that he and Rasheed had not talked it over.

Christina answered with a smile, "Because I want to marry Omar very soon too, and you should get married at the same time."

Ibrahim hugged Christina and held on to her for a long time. "I will do whatever you want, provided Natalia says yes."

"Don't worry, Dad. She said yes already."

Christina then went to Rasheed and hugged him. "It is a done deal," she said. Rasheed asked her to explain herself. She told him then that her father and Natalia said yes, and he and Giselle said yes.

"You mean you have already checked with Giselle?" Rasheed asked.

"I checked with her before you even suggested it," she replied.

Rasheed hugged Christina and jokingly said, "Not only would I have been mad at Omar if he had not decided to marry you, I would have disowned him. You are the daughter that I have always dreamed of having."

"Don't get too excited, Rasheed," Christina said. "You and Giselle are young enough to have your own daughter."

"No, nobody can compete with you, Christina. It is going to be you and you alone. Giselle already has a son. His name is Omar. She and I will be expecting a grandson," he said.

Rasheed then asked for all three couples to get together. He told them that Omar was not part of the scheme but that he and Ibrahim had already agreed that there would be three weddings, even before Christina had said a word.

"You girls were playing a game, and we were playing the same game, in the same direction, and now we are all on the same wavelength. We are the winners, thanks to Christina." Rasheed winked at Christina.

Christina in turn got two champagne bottles and started celebrating. Natalia and Giselle could not control themselves in their admiration of her.

Christina told the two, "I want to share with you a couple of things. First, I will have two mothers-in-law at the same time. Also, when my father and Natalia have children, they will be my siblings and Omar's siblings."

Natalia and Giselle had to think for a few moments before they burst out laughing.

Rasheed called Kishkain and asked him if he could arrange for him to meet briefly with Janice. Janice was there at Kishkain's office the following day. Rasheed approached Janice and stood about ten feet away. Rasheed gave a short speech:

"You are a most beautiful and very intelligent girl. Omar was lucky to have dated you. It was not meant to be. What happened here was not as bad as what happened to me, losing my first love for over twenty years. Look at us now. I am happy knowing she is marrying Ibrahim, and she is happy attending my and Giselle's wedding. One day, I hope that Omar will look at your happiness with care and kindness, and you will look at his happiness with the same care and kindness. I know you may not think this way today, but when Omar starts thinking in the terms I am describing and when you do the same toward him, I hope he or you will have the courage to find one another and express such feelings to each other. I wish you the best and my best to your parents. They should be as proud of you as I know they are, as any parent could be of their special son or daughter. You have my best wishes, and I am sure Omar's as well. Good luck and farewell."

Janice gave Rasheed a kiss on his cheek and then smiled at Kishkain. Without saying a word, she left.

Rasheed started walking out after he shook hands with Kishkain, who said in a low voice, "Thank you. You are a true gentleman."

Christina invited all the residents in the program with Omar, including some men who had crushes on Janice. Christina particularly wanted Sami and Linda.

The residents gave Omar a boisterous bachelor party. Sami hired three belly dancers and three flamenco dancers for the occasion. Four of Omar's professors accepted the invitation to attend the wedding in Madrid.

Unknown to the invitees, Ibrahim leased a plane to fly 152 people from Houston. They stayed free at Ibrahim's inns. They were wined and dined for three days ahead of the wedding.

There Christina danced the flamenco to everyone's delight. She told everyone that she was going to dance the same way she danced for Omar the first week she met him. She teased the residents, almost one by one. They found her very beautiful and charming. She then made a public announcement, mainly directed at the residents: "First, I want to thank my dear aunt, Rasheeda, who not only engineered my relationship with Omar from the very start but also gave me the idea that three related couples in deep love deserve to get married at the same time."

Rasheeda smiled broadly and glowingly and waved at the guests, holding David's hand with her right hand and holding her daughter's hand with her left. She then pressed her right hand on her lips and gave Christina a passionate and warm air kiss, whispering to her, "Thank you, my most precious niece."

"There is another thing none of you know about us in full," Christina said. "You know the American part of the story, but you do not know the Spanish or the Arab segments of the story. You all have heard that I was a nun for six years, which meant I was celibate for six years. I can assure you that I was not playing house with any of the priests."

Everyone burst out laughing.

"During the same time, Omar was having fun, with you-know-who." They laughed again.

Rasheed then spoke and reminded the guests that Omar and Christina were having one wedding and that everybody was talking about that wedding and not about his and Giselle's or Ibrahim and Natalia's weddings.

"As a result, instead of celebrating, we are developing a complex," he added. "Not in my wildest dreams would I have imagined sharing weddings with my only son and my best friend, weddings that include three of the most outstanding women. We are blessed they want to share their futures with the three of us. This is a dream in every sense, a dream that has come true for all six of us. Thank you for sharing this celebration with us.

"On a more serious note, what is happening tonight is something that cannot be planned and cannot even be contemplated. It is the subject of dreams with a rare bonus that says it is a dream graced by being shared among three loving couples with their most precious relatives and friends. All three couples are celebrating what they had hoped for separately but also for what they ended up with, to rejoice together for themselves and for each other. Friends and colleagues join us in this dream by celebrating to your heart's desire."

The wedding was described as the merriest and most glorious that had taken place in Madrid. There were twelve hundred guests, mostly from Spain, but many from Lebanon and the United States. Over a hundred of Rasheed's classmates and colleagues from Rice and Baylor attended.

Ibrahim chartered a second plane and flew most of Natalia's relatives from Poland. Eleven of Giselle's office staff attended. Her brothers, Antoine and Basheer, were there. Ibrahim gave Christina four of his wineries as a *dote,* against Omar's and Rasheed's protestations. Rasheeda and David observed the celebrations joyfully but quietly.

Rasheed said, "I don't think there is anyone happier than us, the three couples, except for Rasheeda. To her heart's delight she is witnessing the continuation of happiness and bliss between Omar and Christina, Giselle and myself, Natalia and Ibrahim. She is too euphoric to say anything this evening since she knows that we are all joining ours with her own and David's bliss. She waited a long time, but she will savor this celebration for many years to come."

The wedding was covered by three of Madrid's papers and by several radio stations. Christina danced flamenco all night long.

At the very end, Rasheed pulled two people from among the guests. "This is Federico and Aisha," he said. "Federico is our great guru, and Aisha is the love of his life. Without him, life would have been much different."

Many of Rasheed's colleagues and Omar's resident physicians had heard the story about Federico. They laughed and were most pleased to meet him.

Rasheed and Giselle had arranged for five *Time* magazine and AP photographers to take pictures all night. Finally, all five took several grand memorable photos, with the three couples up front; visible behind them were Federico, Aisha, Rasheeda, and David. And behind them were all twelve hundred guests. Several of those pictures were published in two Madrid papers and one was published in the *Houston Chronicle*.

ACKNOWLEDGMENTS

As a person who has written extensively throughout my professional and personal experiences, I am fully aware of the challenges that an aspiring novelist faces when he or she is transitioning into a new genre. With this in mind, I was intently eager to test my transformation tendencies privately, before I would test them with the public at large.

As such, I needed confirmation of my ability to add a new platform to others that were long established. Nothing could have helped in this effort more than the ten readers I engaged, mostly made of creative friends, to give me their open and honest opinion as to my new endeavor. I owe any potential success to their indulgence and candor.

I appreciate every one's contribution and encouragement, but I would like to mention two in particular, Kalpa Munier and Jesse Taylor. While all ten read my manuscript and offered opinions, these two went to the trouble of detailed criticism, which resulted in many improvements that would not have happened without their contribution.

With my trust in myself having been buttressed by their contribution, as readers, I would also like to refer to the few whom I approached to provide endorsements. My advice to them was that they should provide such endorsements only if and when they were abundantly comfortable with the many subject matters and the quality of the manuscript.

With my set perimeters, writing a religiously, socially, and politically controversial novel limits the potential number of endorsers. I am thankful to those who have contributed endorsements of this novel and thankful to even those, for justifiable reasons, who chose not to. In the end, I chose not to add endorsements in order to free this novel for the reader to judge it on its own merits. They have their beliefs and I have mine. I respect theirs as I know they respect mine, and in the process such civilized differences are still items worthy of mutual respect.

Above all, I want to thank my late father for training me intensively in journalistic and other styles of writing, not the least of which is the Timese style, which enabled me to be properly descriptive and stylistically creative.

ABOUT THE AUTHOR

 WAGIH ABU-RISH is a Palestinian-American author and activist. He spent much of his career as a businessman, specializing in acquisitions. During a long and varied professional career, he was a foreign journalist in Beirut, Lebanon, and an ad executive on Madison Avenue in New York.

He has been active in promoting progressive causes such as democratic practices and equal rights. Among those causes, he feels strongly about the need for the liberation of women in the Middle East, which he considers to be the most overlooked and abridged human right of all.

It is his hope that this book highlights the themes he believes in. The most salient of such themes is the fact that most adherents are ignorant of the essence of their own religions. This applies equally to the adherents of Islam and to all other religions.

His second and mostly implied theme is the difficulty people have in humanizing others, whether that means another gender, ethnicity, or nationality. Such humanization is the starting point for resolving difficulties and conflicts between competing individuals, parties, and countries.

Mr. Abu-Rish earned bachelor's and master's degrees in journalism from the University of Houston and the University of Oregon. This is his first novel.